# CRUEL
## *deception*

KOZLOV EMPIRE BOOK TWO

# MONICA KAYNE

ISBN 978-1-778270-42-0

Book Cover by Opulent Swag and Design

Interior by AJ Wolf Graphics

Editing by Krista Dapkey

First edition, 2023

I have to not harden my heart, because I want to stay open to feel things. So when I hurt, I hurt all over. And when I cry, I cry real hard. And when I'm mad, I'm mad all over. I'm just a person; I like to experience whatever the feeling is and whatever I'm going through.

— DOLLY PARTON

## AUTHOR NOTE

Cruel Deception is a dark mafia romance with mature themes and profanity. Please reference the FAQ section of my website for trigger and content warnings.
https://monicakayne.com/faq

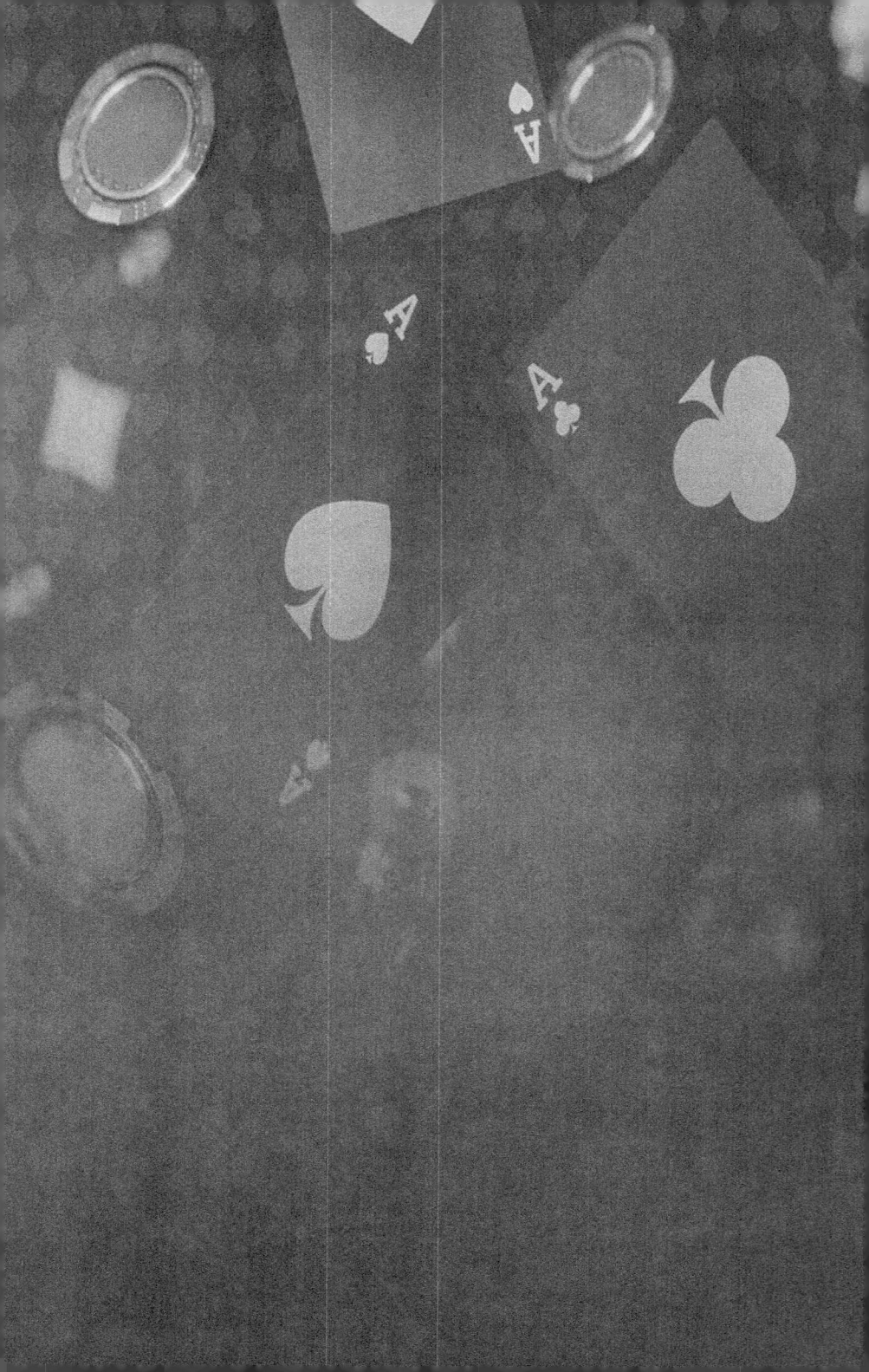

# CHAPTER ONE

## DANIIL

I STAND with two hands pressed against the railing of the second-floor balcony and survey my kingdom below. The casino floor of the Bellair Grand—the newest addition to my family's empire.

There's something inherently extravagant about a place where huge sums of money are exchanged, but we've taken all the expected glitz and glamor and turned the dial up to eleven, because the Bellair is only for those with serious money to burn ... or money to clean.

Tonight, every table buzzes with action under glittering lights and crystal chandeliers, a mix of socialites, famous faces, and the biggest players in New York's organized crime world. The beautiful and ruthless mingle while dressed to the nines, sipping free champagne, and happily feeding their money into our pockets.

My younger brother, Leo, joins me at the railing, pressing a tumbler of whisky into my hand before his eyes dip to the action below.

"I'd say opening night is a success. Congrats, *brat*." He

pounds me on the back, and I have to tighten the hold on my drink. Sometimes I'm not sure what gene pool Leo sprang from. He reminds me of a Russian Jason Momoa, hulking in stature with dark eyes and hair always pulled back in a ponytail. A contrast to our older brother Andrei and I, who inherited our mother's lighter coloring.

"I'm not complaining," I acknowledge. But now the hard work begins, and that hard work falls on my shoulders. The Bellair is my vision—a high-stakes, members-only casino—that I sold Andrei on, and I'll be responsible for the day-to-day operations. He's not only my older brother but also the Kozlov Bratva *pakhan*. Our leader.

But the real draw? The casino is a veritable laundromat for illegal cash. Bring it in dirty and pump it out squeaky clean. Every mob boss from here to Moscow will be knocking down our door for the chance to rinse their bills. Or at least that's the plan.

"We might have your first customer right there." Leaning his forearms casually on the railing, Leo gestures below to where Andrei stands by the circular glass bar in the center of the room. His wife, Georgia, is tucked into his side as they converse with a striking, sharply dressed couple. The man has slicked-back hair, bronzed skin, and a crooked smile—a smile I'm familiar with. He's known as Jorge "The Madman" Días. Top lieutenant to the notoriously reclusive Emilio Morales, head of the Zega Cartel.

I'm not surprised to see him here, considering it's a who's who of organized crime. The Zegas are based in Colombia, but over the last five years, they've expanded to Miami, and I have no doubt they're looking to grow the base of their cocaine trafficking up through the East Coast. Which likely explains why Días is hanging on Andrei's every word. He's making nice with the pakhan. No one traffics in our territory without our nod of approval and a hefty cut.

The Madman's arm is snaked around a stunning woman with flowing chestnut hair, wide-set brown eyes, full red lips, and fuck … *that body* Curvy as hell with full breasts and a proper ass poured into black Dior.

She looks up, as if she feels me staring. Captivated, I grip the edge of the railing, unable to take my eyes off her. She holds my stare, and a sliver of electricity passes between us before she turns to rejoin the conversation. There's no ease in her posture, but she's breathtaking all the same.

Something twists in my chest. Who is she? And what's she doing with a man that has all the charm of a poisonous snake?

"What's The Madman doing here?" I ask Leo, my voice sharper than I intended. "I don't remember including the Zegas on the invite list "

Leo shrugs, running a thumb over his bottom lip. "Andrei must have invited them. With the DEA all over the Mexican border, it's time to cozy up to the Colombian cartels."

I swallow a mouthful of whisky. It slides down my throat and warms my chest but does little to shake the flicker of unease. "There's something about that guy I don't like."

We've never done business with the Zegas so there's no specific reason he rubs me the wrong way. It's just a gut feeling, and my gut is never wrong.

Leo's chuckle is low and dark. "Well, he is called The Madman for a reason. I heard he skinned an entire family alive because they were late on one of his protection payments for their little family-run restaurant."

"*Khuy*," I sneer, proof that I called it right. Only the lowest of the low would hurt a woman and children. Dragging a knuckle over my jaw, I lower my gaze to watch Días laughing too hard at whatever Andrei just said, his bleached-white teeth are practically blinding, even from this distance. His arm remains shackled around the gorgeous woman beside him, his hand tightly clamped on her hip. I don't miss the way she flinches at his touch. I make a mental note to find out who she is to Días before the night is over.

A statuesque brunette saunters in, fashionably late, and heads over to greet our sister, Kira, who is deep into a game of craps. I count down from ten in my head, and just as I get to zero, Leo straightens, placing his empty glass on the bar behind us with a soft thud. Checking his cuff links, he announces, "Time to mingle."

"You mean, mingle with a certain unattainable bombshell?"

Leo's mouth tightens, but he doesn't respond. Instead, his eyes track Alyona's graceful form as she takes her place at the craps table.

Alyona is the younger sister of Yulian Nikitin, head of security for the Kozlov Bratva, and our oldest friend. Their father was the right hand to our papa before he was killed in a shootout. Like his father, Yulian grew up to be a *vor*, a made man in the Russian mafia, but Alyona has always refused to have anything to do with bratva life, spending the last few years in Paris working in fashion.

Leo and Alyona have been circling each other for years—since we were teens, really—but have never moved forward. Every time she comes home for a visit, Leo is in fucking knots. Even if he refuses to acknowledge it.

Like right now.

He huffs out a breath, flips me the bird, then prowls away, probably to go hit on some unsuspecting woman in hopes of making Alyona jealous.

I turn around and motion to the bartender for another whisky. I'll need it to get through the rest of the night. Mixing and mingling with polite society is not my thing. I'd much prefer to be balls deep in some hot blonde or two. My idea of a good night is one where no-strings-attached sex is all that's on the menu. But alas, duty calls. I might be the spare to Andrei's heir, but tonight is my night.

The alcohol has the intended effect. Feeling looser, I head downstairs to work the room, chatting up various guests ranging from a famous actress to a notorious Chinese triad boss. After an hour, my face hurts from smiling, and I need a moment to hear myself think.

The outdoor terrace overlooking the Hudson is mercifully empty, probably because of the cool September evening. I settle into a lounge chair, lighting a Cohiba cigar as I bask in the stillness. This might be the last moment of calm I'm afforded for a long time. Because running New York's most exclusive casino is a huge undertaking, but it's a challenge I'm ready for.

My father's assassination two years ago turned my life upside down. I could no longer be the idle party prince of the Kozlov family, spending months traveling, living the high life, bouncing from yachts to private islands. Like my brothers, I was forced to step up virtually overnight to run the Kozlov Bratva. Under Andrei's leadership, our brotherhood is now more powerful than ever and our business is expanding, so with that, my responsibilities have grown as well.

But I'm restless for something more, I just don't know what that is. At thirty-one, I'm too young to be having a midlife crisis, aren't I?

Laughter from the party filters towards me, and a glance in the direction of the terrace's double doors confirms I'm no longer alone out here. I remain bathed in the shadows, my Cohiba long snuffed out. The Madman and his date step out onto the stone terrace. Before I can make my presence known, I'm startled by the sound of a vicious slap.

My head whips up to see the young woman holding her cheek, tears filling her eyes as the asshole advances on her. "You fucking bitch. You know how important tonight is to me. Why couldn't you keep your mouth shut? Of all people, you insult the fucking mayor."

She releases a heaving breath. Dropping her hand from her face, a red mark blooms on her cheek from where he struck her. It takes all my willpower not to plow into him, give him the chance to pick on someone his own size. I don't tolerate violence against women. Ever. But if I get involved right now, it might only make it worse for her. So I wait to see how this will play out.

Her jaw clamps down so hard it looks as though her teeth might break. "He pinched my ass. I asked him nicely to keep his hands to himself. How is that insulting him?"

Días grabs her arm, his hand gripping like a vice. His hold is meant to inflict pain. "Wrong answer. When a man like the mayor wants to pinch your ass, you allow him."

"Let go of me," she grits, attempting to rip her arm from his grasp, but he doesn't release her. She juts her chin out stubbornly, and I admire her bravery in the face of his violence. This fucker really is a madman.

"I'll never let you go, *bonita*." He pulls her body against his. "You're mine ... forever."

Her eyes spark with fury, but she manages to flatten her expression a moment later. Her bowed head and downcast eyes are met with Días's approval.

Tenderly, he cups her chin, tipping her head up to examine her face. The Madman has retreated, but in his place is something far worse. A wolf in sheep's clothing.

"I'll take you to the bathroom to clean up." He brushes a hand down her cheek, and she tenses, her eyes squeezing shut. He releases her, and she takes a moment to compose herself, smoothing her hair down and straightening her silky black dress. "Vámonos," he beckons, a possessive hand on her lower back. Her delicate chin rises and for a moment I think she'll tell him to go to hell. But she doesn't. Shoulders slumped, she allows him to lead her inside.

My fingers curl into fists, ice threading through my veins. Maybe I should have intervened, but there was something about her quiet strength and composure in the face of Días's abuse that made me stand back. For now. Because I have no intention of ignoring the shit I just witnessed.

Entering the casino, I notice the crowd has thinned as the night winds down. Only the most hard-core of gamblers remain, or at least those too drunk to realize polite company has left. Those with cash to burn and a daring streak relish this time of night, when the highest of high-stakes gambling takes place. And if I know anything about Días, he'll be the first mobster seated at the after-hours poker table. Just as I'm approaching the stairs to take me to the VIP room, Andrei steps into my path.

"There you are," he remarks, clasping me on the shoulder. "Where have you been hiding?"

"Working the room as instructed," I rib. Andrei made it clear I couldn't just slink in the shadows all night. I'd have to shake hands and kiss babies on behalf of the Kozlov family. And I had ... most of the night.

"Tonight went well." He gives me a dad-like approving nod. Even though he's only two years older than me, as head of the family, he's technically the boss. "Now let's see how you manage running the day-to-day operations."

"Have some faith, brat. I've got this." Andrei takes great pleasure in busting my balls, but he wouldn't have put me in charge of casino operations if he wasn't confident in my skills. Like Andrei, I have a sharp business sense, honed on the streets of Brooklyn. We grew up in the bratva—always listening, learning, and observing the high-ranking *avtoritet*. I studied my father during his prime, saw how he conducted business, the deals he made to grow the Kozlov Bratva to the most powerful brotherhood on US soil.

Andrei's eyes roll upwards. "Handsome *and* modest."

"Rich too," I say, tossing a coin from my pocket in the air, but his attention has already wandered toward Georgia, his wife of over a year, sitting and chatting with Kira, Alyona, and Rowan, Yulian's wife. When Georgia catches us looking over, she gives me a friendly smile and wave. But the look she gives Andrei communicates something else entirely.

"Eager to get your woman home?" I tease.

"Always," he says, returning his wife's hungry stare. Damn, these two never stop.

"I'm going to stay for a while. Maybe even play a few hands." And deal with The Madman. But I don't mention that.

My brother regards me with narrowed eyes. "Should I bother telling you to stay out of trouble?"

I shrug, a playful smile on my lips. "You could, but I make no guarantees."

Especially not tonight.

## CHAPTER TWO

### BIANCA

I SET my palms on either side of the bathroom mirror and stare into my reflection. The makeup has done its job. The red bloom on my cheek brought on by Jorge's slap is still sore to the touch, but at least it's well concealed. A shiver runs down my spine and settles in a seed of repulsion. How long can this go on for? How long can I keep pretending?

He's been rough with me before, but never like this. Still, I always knew what he was capable of, what his brutal nickname suggests. Men like him can only lock up their violence for so long before it explodes like a geyser under pressure. And tonight the stakes are high. Jorge is acting as my uncle's emissary, a chance for him to wheel and deal with the crème de la crème of East Coast crime families.

I run my finger along my reflection in the mirror. The night is far from over, which means playing the role of perfect, submissive girlfriend is far from over. With a deep breath, I steel my spine and step back out into the lobby of the casino, where Jorge and his henchmen lean against the wall, waiting for me. His gaze lifts at my arrival, his piercing gray eyes assessing every inch of me, ensuring that like Humpty Dumpty, I'm put back together again.

I must meet his approval because he pulls me towards him, and whispers in my ear, "You're so goddamn beautiful."

Acid burns the back of my throat, and I fight the urge to shake off his touch as he leads me around the casino floor, parading me around like a show dog, which I suppose I am. The niece of Emilio Morales, head of the Zega Cartel. A valuable prize, considering I am his only heir. Jorge was already my uncle's right hand when he set his sights on me a few months ago, but with my hand in marriage comes the keys to the kingdom. A far more powerful position.

Of course, I'll never let it get that far. He is but a means to an end—and the end is in sight.

The evening continues—a blur of faces, elegant jazz music, and the buzz of a casino's grand opening. But as the main event winds down and the crowd thins, we end up in a private poker room on the second floor. Despite Jorge's earlier outburst, he's now in good spirits as he sits down at the circular table where both booze and conversation flow. The other men here are all mafia, cartel, and other crime magnets. This is where the real gambling happens. Everything until now has been for show. A friendly game of blackjack or craps.

I sip my soda, grateful his attention will be diverted for the next few hours. The knot in my chest loosens, and I can breathe a little easier, tucked away at the discreetly appointed bar in the far corner of the room. If we can get through this night without further incident, I'll feel a lot better. Jorge's whisky dick coupled with my well-guarded virginity means he won't touch me tonight. But the clock is ticking. I have no doubt he'll propose soon and push for a quick wedding. Which means I need to make every second count.

Lost in my own head, I don't realize someone has taken the seat on my left until a deep male voice rumbles beside me, "Penny for your thoughts?"

I look up to see a stranger. The man from the second-floor balcony that I'd noticed earlier. He'd been staring at me, which might be why he'd caught my attention. Once again, his gaze locks on mine, making it was impossible to look away.

He cringes. "Jesus, that was cliché."

I can't help but laugh at his reaction to the corny line. I'm struck by deep-hazel eyes and tousled light-brown hair with natural gold highlights most women would kill for. Cut cheekbones. A strong jaw with a little indent in the center of his chin. A roguish smile. He's even more handsome up close; it's nearly blinding. Even through his tux, I can make out a solid chest and broad shoulders, tattoos peeking out from his collar. I don't know who he is, but damn. In another life, I would take the time to get to know him.

Just not in this life.

I offer him a small smile. "No thoughts, just enjoying the poker game," I lie, even though my back is literally towards the action.

He smirks and flicks his gaze behind me. "I bet. Fascinating stuff watching half-drunk mobsters play shitty poker. You don't want in on the game?"

I sneak a glance at Jorge, knowing he would not react well if he saw me talking with another man, especially one as handsome as this guy. Thankfully, Jorge's back is to me, and he's absorbed in the game.

"Only the men play. The WAGs just watch and cheer," I say, motioning my chin towards the other women in the room.

"WAGs?" he asks, lifting an eyebrow.

"Wives and girlfriends." Though they're probably strippers and prostitutes.

"Right." He releases a bark of laughter. Then he holds out his hand. "I'm Daniil Kozlov by the way."

I stare at his hand, knowing the shitstorm it'll cause if I touch another man. After a beat, Daniil seems to take the hint. He drops his hand and clears his throat.

"Ah, the infamous Kozlov brothers," I say to lighten the sting. "You own the place, right? I met your brother Andrei tonight."

"Yes, our fearless leader. I'm the forgotten middle child who never got enough attention."

I take a sip of my soda, a reluctant smile tugs at my lips. "I'm Bianca Harper," I say, but I don't give him any more details. Like my family connections. "Congratulations are in order. This casino is very impressive."

"Well, thank you. I'm glad that you could join us tonight." His voice is low and smooth like syrup, nearly a purr. Goose bumps erupt down my arms. He's not flirting with me, but there's that crackle and pop of attraction between us. It's been so long it's almost a foreign sensation.

*My god, what is it about this guy?*

I force myself to ignore it, homing in on his tattooed knuckles instead. But staring at his strong hands does nothing to calm my staccato heartbeat.

He clears his throat and tilts his head towards the poker table. "You here with Jorge Días?"

By the way he spits Jorge's name, I take it there's no love lost between them. I wonder if they've done business before or if he knows Jorge by reputation. I don't want to explain my relationship, so I simply nod.

His lips pucker in distaste, but he doesn't comment further. "Where do you live?"

"Miami," I say vaguely, though the truth is we live between Miami and Colombia, depending on where my uncle's business takes us. Or his level of paranoia. "Are you a New Yorker?"

His lips twitch. "Brooklynite. Born and bred. Though I spent time in Russia growing up. Maybe that's why I don't have the typical accent. My father would have beat it out of me if so."

I wince at his comment, and his face falls like he didn't mean to say that. Like he knows ... but how could he?

"Sorry. That was in bad taste." He drags an agitated hand through his thick hair.

I reach up and touch the tender spot where Jorge hit me earlier, and Daniil's eyes glint black. Maybe I hadn't done a very good job with my makeup.

"If you need help ..." he starts to say quietly, and then the moment explodes when a rough hand wrenches me from my seat.

"What are you doing?" I gasp, but Jorge is too fast, too worked up. He's dragged me across the room and into a private area behind the bar before I realize what's happening. My body slams against the wall, pain exploding everywhere.

"Why were you talking to him?" he seethes, his red face inches from my own. "Do you know who he is? He's bratva. You shouldn't even be looking at him." Whisky wafts off Jorge's breath, and barely contained violence thrums under his skin. He's drunk and angry. Usually he's drunk and sloppy, but not tonight.

"I ... I didn't know." I hold my hands up in surrender. "He was only making small talk. I'm sorry."

All I feel is fury, but my fear pacifies him, and right now, that's the only thing that matters. I play the part to a T. Hugging myself, head bowed, a tear escapes down my cheek.

Finally, his erratic breathing calms, and he composes himself enough to glare at me in warning. "You will sit behind my chair and say nothing for the rest of the night. I don't even want you looking at anyone else. Eyes down or on me, understand?" He wrenches my hair back, and I clench my teeth to keep from reacting. I won't give him that.

"Of course, *cariño*, of course." The words burn like acid on my tongue.

"Good." He kisses me then. Hard, brutal, possessive. It's for no other reason than to remind me I am his property. His to do what he pleases with.

How wrong he is.

Jorge storms out from behind the bar, dragging me behind him, his hand locked around my wrist like a shackle. As we step out of the back, Daniil's eyes find mine, livid and wild. He must have seen it all, and from the looks of it, he does not approve. I give him a slight shake of my head, a warning. I don't need him getting involved. This is my war.

Jorge leads me to the poker table where a game is about to start.

"Buy-in is five hundred thousand," the dealer announces. No one bats an eye. Only the highest rollers are sitting down to play tonight.

The last seat at the table is about to be taken by a slick-looking man with his hair pulled back in a ponytail when an inked hand drops a highball of amber-colored liquid on the table in front of the spot.

"Sorry, brother, this seat is taken."

Daniil doesn't look sorry at all. Whoever ponytail guy is, he takes the hint and hightails it the other way. It's Daniil's casino, he's the alpha here.

I do as I'm told, sitting right behind Jorge with my eyes glued to the floor. I don't want trouble. I need to get through tonight unscathed. But somehow, I know Daniil is not going to make it easy.

The game starts much like they always do. Players ante up and bet. Liquor flows. The smell of cologne and cigarettes mingle noxiously in the air. It starts out as a raucous game with taunts and laughs passed back and forth, but as cards amass face-up in the center of the table, there's less talking and more concentrated stares.

Jorge isn't holding back, losing some hands, but winning many more. I hear little from Daniil—it's clear he's methodical and calculating in his play. All my senses are attuned to him, aware of his presence in the room. Every time I peek up, he catches my eye, his face intent, serious, and I am quick to avert my gaze. I know little about poker, but I do know they aren't playing five-card draw like my dad used to play. This is different.

HOURS LATER, my head throbs and my ass is numb from sitting in this chair, unmoving. It's well past three in the morning, and only three players remain in the game: Daniil, Jorge, and a 'Ndrangheta boss named Cosimo.

The dealer turns over an ace of hearts, ace of spades, and a queen of clubs, and the table goes still. Even though most of the players have folded, they're riveted by the action.

"Raise," Cosimo says, sliding half of his towering stack of chips towards the center of the table.

"All in," Daniil announces.

I glance up to see him push all his chips forward—there must be at least a million dollars there— not seeming the least bit concerned, his expression like ice. Unlike the others, he's turned down every offer of alcohol since joining the game, only sipping water. I don't understand everything that's happening here, but I understand the calmness in his voice when he speaks, the cunning intelligence as he surveys the table.

Jorge and Cosimo follow suit, pushing their chips to the center of the table like mini skyscrapers lined up in a row. Every chip on the table is in play, millions of dollars at stake. It's all or nothing now. My chest turns cold knowing Jorge will win this hand. He always does when the stakes ratchet up.

On the next round, the dealer turns over a jack of diamonds. Cosimo sighs heavily and lifts his hands in the air before announcing that he folds. But he doesn't move a muscle from the table. Like everyone else in the room, he wants to see two brutal mafia bosses face off.

It's between Daniil and Jorge now. The dealer turns over the last card, a seven of clubs, and Jorge flips over his cards with a whoop of victory. I sneak a quick look to see Daniil smiling, but his smile is sinister. A baring of teeth. If Jorge were sober, maybe he'd catch on sooner, but it's obvious to me—he's about to get knocked down hard.

"Well done," Daniil says, his voice a deep timbre. "Now what do you say we have some real fun tonight. Bet on something with a little more value." His gaze cuts from Jorge to me and back again.

From behind, I watch a muscle tic in Jorge's jaw. "What are you offering?"

Reaching into his pocket, Daniil produces a set of keys and lays them on the table. "Keys to my Brooklyn penthouse overlooking the New York Harbor. Worth twelve mil."

Jorge is quiet, considering. He's money hungry, always has been. "And in return?" Jorge asks.

"Bianca," Daniil says simply. "If you lose, she's mine."

What!? My heart lurches in my chest. A slow trickle of sweat makes its way down my back. What is he doing? Jorge roars in laughter and throws a sharp glare over his shoulder at me. "Really, you want my little jewel?" His voice is dark ice. "How sweet."

All eyes land on me. My mind spins out of control, rioting and evading my command, much like my heartbeat. Why would Daniil want me? Unless he knows who my uncle is. He hadn't seemed to earlier, but he's bratva. Despite his gentlemanly exterior, he's not to be trusted.

Jorge is considering it. I can tell from the way he swipes his thumb over his lips. And I know why.

Jorge is a cheater.

He fixed the game by colluding with the dealer at the table. The dealers are supposed to be neutral, but Jorge ensured one of them was in his pocket by offering a sizable percentage of his winnings. It's the oldest scam in the book, a method cheats have used for centuries.

I heard his men whispering about it, this is what Jorge does. He isn't reckless or flashy. He'll lose a few hands, so no one looks at him too closely, but he always makes sure to win when it counts. Like now. He wouldn't risk losing my hand in marriage unless it was a guaranteed win.

The men sitting around this table might be ruthless and corrupt, but they live by their own moral code. Not Jorge. He only cares about the final payout. And right now, he stands to risk nothing, all he knows is he'll line his pockets handsomely by the end of the night.

My throat constricts as I wait to see what will happen.

"Okay." Jorge's voice is light, taunting. "Let's play."

"Excellent." Daniil turns to the dealer. "Mario, you deserve a break, why don't you clock out for the night."

Mario hesitates. He looks at Jorge with panic in his eyes. "That's okay, I'm fine." He laughs nervously.

Daniil's jaw hardens. "That wasn't a suggestion." He tosses a ten-thousand-dollar chip his way. "Grigory will take your place."

Jorge tries to intervene. "Don't be silly, Kozlov, just play the hand. No point in changing dealers now."

Daniil doesn't throw around accusations, but he knows. He knows Jorge has been cheating all night, and he's tolerated it. Until now. He leans back in his seat, crossing his muscular arms casually across his broad chest. The tension in the room is palpable, and if weapons were allowed in here, I have no doubt everyone would be reaching for their piece.

Jorge knows better than to push the issue; that's as good as an admittance of guilt. Instead, he rolls his shoulders and tosses back the rest of his whisky as Mario leaves the table, head hung low, for another dealer to take his place. The first thing Grigory does is break out a fresh deck of cards.

Daniil smirks and rubs his hands. "Now where were we?"

The blood whooshes in my ears, drowning out the noise of the room. I can't focus, I can't do anything but grip the seat of my chair tightly and pray to the gambling gods that somehow Jorge wins. Without cheating, Jorge is a mediocre player at best, and I don't know what will happen if he loses this hand. What could Daniil possibly want with me? I was fooled by his friendly smile, his easy charm. He's as twisted as the rest of them. An amber-eyed wolf waiting to make me his dinner, and I'm powerless to object.

I can't bear to look at the play, so I keep my eyes on my lap, my hands fidgeting with the silky material of my dress, unable to be still. The absurdity of this moment isn't lost on me—my fate will be determined by two ruthless gangsters and a pack of playing cards.

Fuck me.

"Four of a kind." Daniil's sharp voice echoes off the walls of the now silent room.

My heart beats so wildly I think it may thump out of my chest. Even I know what that means. It's a winning hand; one that can only be beaten by a straight or royal flush. And judging by the look of absolute shock on Jorge's face, that's not what he possesses.

My eyes snap to the table. Four kings are laid out on the green felt, that damn poker chip still flipping between Daniil's thumb and forefinger. I follow the line of his forearm up to his bicep, then up to his shoulder, and up and up until he's staring back at me, his expression stoic, except for a little curl of his lips.

Dread, thick and heavy, floods my bloodstream.

I'm Kozlov property now. And there's not a thing I can do about it.

# CHAPTER THREE

## DANIIL

I KNEW Días was lowlife scum the moment he put his hands on Bianca, but I didn't realize he was also a cheat. But there's no doubt that he is one. I spotted it after the first twenty minutes of play. Wasn't hard to figure out what was going on. The drunker he got, the sloppier he got. The furtive glances to the guard behind me were no longer quick and stealthy. They were unfocused, obvious. Others may have noticed if they weren't half in the bag themselves.

I allowed Días to continue his crooked play until I was ready to go in for the kill.

And kill, I did.

Victory pumps through my veins, giving me a high like no other, when Días's face crumples in fury as I lay down the winning hand. I push back from the table and stand. As much as I want to savor this moment—Días's wrath and the shock on everyone's faces—there's no point stretching it out longer than necessary.

"Good game," I announce brightly, "but I must run. And I'm taking my prize."

My eyes cut to Bianca still sitting behind Jorge, eyes averted, quivering in ... fear? But when her deep-brown eyes finally meet my own, it's not fear I see but anger. Rage as blind and all-encompassing as The Madman's.

I don't know what I'd expected from her, but it wasn't that.

Straightening my suit jacket, I jerk my head in the direction of the door. Bianca rises slowly, her eyes darting between Jorge and myself. His hands grip the table, knuckles white, eyes so dark they're practically leaking poison.

Walking around the table, I approach Días. Dipping my head down so my lips are next to his ear, I say quietly, "Next time, grow a pair of fucking balls and pick a fight with someone your own size."

His fists thud on the table in front of him, and he shoots up from his chair, bristling in anger, but he doesn't take a swing at me. A beat of tense silence passes, my guards on alert. But I know he doesn't have the balls to take me on.

"That's what I thought," I sneer at him, before turning to Bianca, who still glares daggers my way. But there's no time for soothing words, we need to make our exit. With one hand on Bianca's elbow, I lead her to the back exit, then down a desolate hallway towards my office. She's practically vibrating beneath my hand, and I don't know what to make of it. But I'll find out soon enough.

I'm right. The moment my office door shuts behind us, she spins on me, hands on her hips.

"What in the hell do you think you're doing?" she hisses, piercing me with a scorching look. "Buying me in a card game, like I'm fucking property to be owned."

A pulse flickers in my jaw. "I saw what he did to you. Días doesn't deserve to be in your presence, much less touch you ever again. He's an abusive asshole. I bought you your freedom."

"Are you serious?" She throws her hands in the air and paces the room. "Freedom? This is the opposite of buying my freedom. You don't know what you've done."

Annoyance blooms hot in my chest. "What I've done is help you." I stop her pacing with a firm hand on her arm. "I'm not asking anything of you in return. Nothing. I have money, influence, I'll help you get set up on your own, far away from that scoundrel. You don't have to worry about him ever again."

As compelling as she is—with curves for miles and plush lips that I'd like to see wrapped around my cock—I didn't do this to get laid. Or to make her mine. I did it because I don't like to see bullies win.

"Are you serious?" A hysterical laugh bubbles up from her throat. "You have no idea who I am, do you?"

The hairs on the back of my neck stand on end. "No," I snap. "Should I?"

"Yes." Her intense brown eyes drill holes into me. "I'm the niece of Emilio Morales. Head of the Zega Cartel."

Shock blasts through me. I had no clue Emilio had a niece or any family for that matter. I assumed Bianca was Días's current flavor—like she'd said earlier, a WAG.

But this makes everything ... complicated. As the niece of Morales, she's a valuable prize, and my brazen act tonight won't go unpunished.

So this is messy.

Very messy.

Fuck me.

One look at my pinched face, and Bianca sighs heavily. Her delicate hands rise and rub at her temples. "You really didn't know, did you? Unless you want your life to get a hell of a lot more problematic, we need to walk back into that room. Return me to Jorge. Smooth it over with him. You can say it was the booze, or"—she waves her hands in the air—"all the excitement of the evening."

The muscles in my jaw throb as I grind my teeth. I should take her up on her suggestion. I should mind my own business and take a big step back from the fucking political minefield I've just stepped into, but I won't.

"He's your uncle's second-in-command. Emilio stands by while Días hurts you?"

"It's none of your business." She looks tired now, defeated. Drained of her earlier bravado. "I can handle myself."

"Too late," I state plainly. "I'm already involved." It's the truth. By morning, word will have gotten back to Morales. While I'm sure he'll be furious at Días for gambling away his niece, he'll be more furious with me. With the Kozlov Bratva.

"It's not." She grabs my arm, intent on holding my attention. "Jorge is humiliated, he'll do anything in his power to keep tonight under wraps. He's probably paying off every guy in the room right now to erase it from their mind. We part ways here. You leave, and I'll handle it. And Daniil ... maybe try to keep your hero complex in check next time."

My laughter ripples through the room. She's right. I could walk away now and wash my hands of her, of this mess. Días will definitely want to keep tonight quiet. And, let's be honest, it would be really fucking convenient for me if Morales never heard about this. She's giving me a solid out ... but I can't stomach the thought. Even now, picturing his hands on Bianca causes a vein in my temple to throb.

"Don't go back to him now. He's drunk and pissed off. I humiliated him. He'll take out his anger on you, and it'll be ugly." Looking at the dark bruise on her arm from where he'd grabbed her earlier sends my pulse careening. "I'll deliver you to him tomorrow. He'll still be furious, but at least he'll be sober."

She scrubs a hand over her face, considering my words. Finally, she huffs out a breath, her arms wrapping around her middle in defeat. "Fine. Just for tonight."

I nod. "I'll take the fall for it. I'll say you fought me, did everything you could to get away."

She just shakes her head sadly, her shoulders slumping in defeat. "There's no such thing."

I want to offer her words of comfort or reassurance, but I

can't. At least not truthfully. So for once in my life, I keep my mouth shut.

THREE HOURS LATER, I watch the sun crest over the horizon on my penthouse terrace. Bianca is sleeping in the spare bedroom and has been since the moment we arrived here. I'm on my fifth glass of Stoli, and the vodka is doing wonderful things for my nerves. I won't sleep, but at least the vicious thoughts knocking around in my brain have subsided. Now I feel numb. My emotions are muted, tamped down like a cigarette stubbed out underfoot. It's a good place to be.

A familiar place.

Because I'm not the guy who gets involved in other people's shit. I don't like complicated entanglements, especially with women. I learned early on you can't get hurt if your feelings don't run deep. It's a lesson that life taught me, and it's proved to be a great shield, especially living in this world.

Yes, I love my family, but that means I worry about them like fucking crazy. And I don't need to worry about one more goddamn thing in my life. So best to hand Bianca over to Jorge tomorrow and forget her. Even if her potent mix of vulnerability and strength has crawled under my skin. It doesn't have to mean anything.

I'm pouring myself the last shot in the bottle, watching the day bloom over the smooth water, when my cell rings. I don't have to look at my phone to know who's calling at this hour.

"Brat," I say, taking the call. My brother hates when I call him that. It's Russian for *brother*, but I'm always amused by its meaning in English. "Calling so early?"

"What did you do, Daniil?" His voice is laced with dark ice. Word traveled faster than I anticipated.

"What I had to. You don't have to concern yourself with

this ... *situation*. I have it under control." Blatant lie. I have nothing under control.

He releases a hiss on the other end of the line. My big brother. Always so serious. "You clearly don't, or I wouldn't even know about the *situation*. Also, you're too drunk to be clever right now, so shut it. I'm sending a driver for you. Drink a coffee, take a shower. I'll see you in an hour."

The line goes dead, and a laugh bubbles up from my throat. Sometimes I wonder how I'm related to such a pompous ass, but then I remember Papa was a pompous ass too, so it must run in the family. You don't rise to pakhan without big dick energy, and Andrei has that in spades. Though Georgia has smoothed out his hard edges. Mostly.

But none of this matters. Andrei wants to hear what happened, and I'll be more than happy to fill him in.

# CHAPTER FOUR

## DANIIL

BIANCA IS STILL SLEEPING as I head downstairs to meet the car Andrei sent. I know because I just went to check on her and watched her sleep—all golden limbs and silky hair fanned out on the pillowcase—for way longer than I meant to. She really is fucking gorgeous, and it's a shame I have to hand her over to that animal she calls a boyfriend.

A half hour later when my car pulls up behind our garment factory on the outskirts of Brighton Beach, my mood has soured. I enter through the back entrance, the *clickety-clack* of the industrial-size sewing and cutting machines creates a cacophony of white noise—enough to drown out the cries of men being tortured. Because it's on the third floor of this building that my brothers and I take care of our less than savory business.

Bratva business.

And that's why this place is a well-kept secret.

Andrei is already waiting for me when I enter the bare-bones office. Just a wooden desk, a few mismatched chairs, and a couch that looks like it came from some babushka's attic. It's nothing like the sleek, modern offices we keep at the family estate in East Hampton. This place is no frills, and for some reason, I like its utilitarian feel. We might wear Armani and get chauffeured around, but our roots are in the streets of Brooklyn.

My brother doesn't take his eyes off me until I'm seated across from him. He studies me carefully, probably checking to see if I've sobered up. Sadly, I have. The shower and drive chased the vodka from my veins. Now I'm left with a dull thump in my head and a reminder of everything that's gone to shit in my life.

"Alright, I'm here." I spread my arms wide and slump back in my seat, knowing it'll piss Andrei off. "What's so important it requires a face-to-face at seven in the goddamn morning?"

I'm laying it on thick. But I figure if he's going to give me shit anyway, I may as well have fun.

Andrei shakes his head, going all disappointed big brother on me. "Emilio Morales called me this morning, quite alarmed I might add. Something about you winning his niece in a card game." His voice is deceptively calm as his thumb brushes down the centerline of his lips. "Do you want to tell me what the fuck happened?"

I meet my brother's eyes without flinching. "I didn't know she was his niece when I bet on her. All I knew was The Madman was knocking around his girlfriend. I saw it happen not once but twice, that *mudak.* So when the opportunity presented itself to free her from that scum, I took it. He didn't have to accept the bet," I point out.

Andrei lets out a harsh breath. For all his diplomatic maneuvering, he's also not someone who would stand idly by while a woman was being hurt. "Where is she now?"

"At my penthouse. But before you get your panties in a knot, you should know she fucking lost it on me afterwards. She wants me to return her to Días today." Bitterness singes my throat. It must be fear that keeps her loyal to Días and her uncle. I don't understand what she's been through, but I understand that there are many reasons victims remain in an abusive relationship. As much as I hate it, I can't force her hand. "She was hoping to keep all of this from Emilio," I add. "Guess it's too late for that. How did he find out?"

"You know how mafia kings gossip." Andrei shrugs but remains stone-faced. "Any of those men in the room would rat Días out in a hot second to win favor with Emilio. He found out and called me ..." Andrei releases a tight breath. "Let me ask you, brother, what was your plan when you made that bet? To make her yours?"

I stand and pace in an attempt to outrun my twisting thoughts and the exhaustion weighing on me. A sinking feeling in my gut tells me I will not like the direction of this conversation. "I was going to buy her freedom and let her go. Set her up with an apartment, school if she needed it. Money."

Andrei's lip twists. "Admirable."

"You would have done the same," I scoff.

That vein in Andrei's temple throbs like a heartbeat, and an entire conversation takes place between us without saying a word. Our mother was the victim of powerful, corrupt men who used her as a pawn. We were kids then, we couldn't protect her, but like hell I'm going to sit by and watch as another innocent woman is strung up like a puppet.

Andrei is the first to look away. "Except I would have done my research and known who she was. Unlike you."

*Khuy.* I wouldn't hesitate to take a bullet for my brother—and I know the reverse is true—but let me be clear: He can be a real dick. "Point taken," I say between gritted teeth. "Now tell me why I'm really here."

Andrei stands. The bare bulb in the room casts a circle around him. He clears his throat. "Congratulations are in order." My breathing stills, and my gaze flicks towards Andrei. "You won Bianca fair and square, she's now yours. Emilio is insisting you marry her."

Unease rises to the surface of my skin. "What the fuck?" I spit out. "Marriage? I don't think so."

He cocks a brow. "I don't believe you have a choice in the matter."

"Jesus, Andrei," I bark. "Tell Emilio no fucking way. The Kozlov Bratva is more powerful than the Zegas, we don't have to give in to his demands." Eventually marriage will be my duty, but not now. I'm thirty-one. I'm owed at least another decade of freedom.

Andrei spins a pen between his fingers, his expression way too fucking smug. "Don't underestimate Emilio Morales, he's as savage as they come. He won't hesitate to declare war over this." My brother shoots me a withering look. "And he's not wrong. Word has already gotten out. If you don't put a ring on it, you compromise her honor. Maybe if you'd handled the situation a bit more discreetly, we wouldn't be here, but seeing as half of the city's gang bosses saw what went down, she's yours."

My blood roars in my ears as I feel the booze sweats come on, but I won't back down. I refuse to be bullied by my brother or Emilio. "It's not happening. You know I'd make a terrible husband anyhow. She deserves better."

"Like Días? Because if it's not you, that's who she'll marry. Emilio said as much."

My hands ball into tight fists. The thought of Bianca marrying The Madman sends a violent impulse through me. It's out of the fucking question. Except, that only leaves one alternative.

Andrei perches on the edge of his desk, crossing his arms over his chest. He knows he has me backed into a corner. "I didn't think I was the marrying type either ... turns out, I'm quite a fan."

"You chose Georgia. You fell in love with her. It wasn't some fucked-up mafia alliance that you were forced into."

"Bianca is a beautiful woman. You must have been taken with her to go to all this trouble." A flicker of sympathy passes over his features, but he's not backing down. He never backs down. "If it's any consolation, Emilio wants to use the casino to clean his money. This will be a very lucrative alliance."

Money. That's what it always comes down to in the end. "And you trust Emilio?" I shake my head bitterly. "She could be a spy."

Andrei barks out a laugh. "True, but he couldn't have predicted the events of the evening. For argument's sake, let's say she *is* spying for her uncle. What can she learn? Your pretty new wife is going to traipse around all day spending your money and lunching with her friends. No risk of her learning our deep dark secrets." I narrow my eyes at my brother, but as usual, he takes it all in stride, his lip curling as he adds, "More likely, Morales wants to cement an alliance with a powerful East Coast family. That's why Días attended last night in the first place. The Zegas want to bring their product to the streets of Brooklyn, and for that, they'll need our blessing."

I lower my head into my hands, my temples throbbing. Andrei may be my brother, but he's also my pakhan, and he's giving me an order. And as fucked-up as this all is, if I marry Bianca, she'll be free of Días.

When I lift my head from my hands, Andrei is still staring at me. He looks vaguely amused, taking pleasure in my misery.

I swallow the bitterness in my throat and straighten my spine. "When are we to get married?"

"Tomorrow."

And just like that, it feels like the walls are caving in on me again. "Why so soon? What's the rush?"

"It's what Morales wants. His people will handle everything. All you have to do is show up in Miami, tux in hand, ready to walk down the aisle."

Annoyance, prickly and hot, edges down the back of my collar.

A distant part of my brain chimes in, "What does it matter?" If we get married, today, tomorrow, in a week, in three years, I'm still promised to Bianca. Bound to her for the rest of my life.

Andrei stands to meet me and drops a hand on my shoulder. "I hate to say it, but you made your bed, now—"

"Do me a favor and fuck off," I say, brushing his hand off me as his gruff chuckle ripples through the room.

After Andrei leaves, I stay in the same spot, staring out the window for a very long time.

## CHAPTER FIVE

### BIANCA

W HEN I WAKE, it takes my sleepy brain a minute to remember where I am, and why I'm in a room I've never been in before. But within seconds, it all comes rushing back to me. I'm in the home of Daniil Kozlov. The man who won me last night.

Jeez.

A picture of his handsome face materializes in my mind. A jaw cut from granite, piercing hazel eyes, more jade green than brown—except when he's angry; then, they turn black like onyx. He is striking, no question. Like a shape-shifter, he can go from arrogant and flirty to protective and savage in one breath. And while he's strangely compelling, I need to get away from him as fast as I can.

Sitting up, I find toiletries and a change of clothes folded neatly on a luxe gray lounge chair by the bed. Thank god. I'm still in last night's dress, my hair is a rat's nest, matted down by sweat and tears. There's nothing I need more right now than a hot shower and fresh clothes. And to brush my teeth.

Rising, I cast a glance around the room. It's modern with clean lines. This place is no bachelor pad; it's designer chic with a simple white palette and bold black-and-white photographs along the walls. I honestly don't know what to make of Daniil other than he has a serious hero complex, and the ladies must love his roguish charm. His bravery was admirable, I suppose. Another woman may have even appreciated his efforts, just not me.

On top of the clothes and supplies, I find a note. It's from Daniil letting me know that a business matter called him away this morning, but he wouldn't be long. I hope this business has nothing to do with what happened last night. It's best for all if last night fades into a distant memory, never to be mentioned again.

A hot shower soothes my aching limbs and raw nerves. Bruises stain my arm from where Jorge took out his aggression on me.

Bile rises in my throat as I consider how my return to him will go. I hate Jorge with the power of a thousand suns, but I need him. I'm so close. So very close. And I'll make sure that *pendejo* gets exactly what's coming for him.

After my shower, I dress in the yoga pants and T-shirt that were left out for me and leave my damp hair down to dry naturally. My stomach rumbles, and I venture out of the room to find food and caffeine, something to rouse me after only a few hours of sleep.

"Good morning!" A petite blonde that, like me, appears to be in her early twenties stands in the middle of the kitchen holding up a carafe of coffee and a plate of croissants. "You must be hungry. Come sit. Don't worry, I'm harmless. Mostly," she adds with a wink.

She looks vaguely familiar, like someone I met recently, but I can't place her. "I'm Bianca," I say, sitting down at the breakfast bar.

"And I'm Kira, Daniil's sister. My brother asked me to bring some clothes and food over for you."

I gladly accept the cup of coffee she offers and help myself to a pastry. Leaning on the breakfast bar across from me, she flashes me such a wide friendly smile, she must have no clue what happened last night. She likely thinks I'm last night's hookup, which is probably for the best.

"Thank you," I say. "Do you know when Daniil will be back?"

Glancing at her watch, she purses her lips in thought. "Soon, I think."

Impatience thrums beneath my skin, but I don't want to be rude, so I force a smile and ask, "Were you at the casino opening last night?"

"Yes, although I left early. I was pretty wiped after working all day and dancing up a storm."

I nod and take a sip of coffee. "What kind of work do you do?"

A small smile lifts her lips. "I help run the family business. You know what the Kozlovs do I imagine?"

"I have a vague idea," I say, waving my hands in front of my face. "But I didn't think women were really allowed to work in that world. The bratva, I mean."

"It's not common. But my circumstances are different." She inclines her head, pausing for a moment. "My brothers are different from most *vory*. Made men in the Russian mafia," she clarifies when my brows pull together.

"Interesting," I mumble, unsure what to make of the Kozlovs.

She pours herself another cup of coffee. Carefully adding in sugar and milk before stirring for a while. "Aren't you with Jorge Días? I saw you two together last night."

Under the counter, my nails bite into my skin. "Yes, we're together." The lie tastes bitter on my tongue. If Kira wonders what I'm doing sleeping in another man's home, she doesn't ask, but to be safe, I change the subject. "So tell me what it was like growing up with three brothers. I imagine they were overprotective, no?"

A few heavy beats pass before she speaks. "I didn't grow up

with my brothers. I didn't even know I had brothers until a year ago." She chuckles at the surprised look on my face, but before she can say more, footsteps echo down the hall.

Daniil appears in the doorway, looking way too fresh for a guy who'd barely slept. He was hot as sin dressed in a tux last night but dressed casually in a fitted white T-shirt and worn-in jeans is too much for me to handle this morning. My attention is drawn to the expanse of his chest, the bulging muscles in his arms. He seems taller, more intimidating this morning. Or maybe it's that I'm not wearing heels.

"Good morning." His voice is a deep rumble, and out of nowhere, my core clenches. Or maybe not out of nowhere. Didn't I just spend a full minute ogling him?

Luckily, he doesn't seem to notice because he's too busy wrapping his sister in a one-armed hug and laying a kiss on the side of her head. She playfully bats him away, as any little sister would do.

His attention slides towards me. "Bianca," he says in acknowledgement. His deep baritone causes a little flutter in my belly. "How did you sleep?"

"Well. Thanks." I stand and push away from the breakfast bar. Swooning over Daniil will get me nowhere. "We should probably leave soon. I need to get back to ... my family."

He nods but doesn't look me in the eye. Kira collects her purse from the counter. Throwing it over her shoulder, she squeezes her brother's arm, and there's an entire conversation in the look they share. Sibling stuff, I guess. I wouldn't know. My sister didn't live to see her teens.

Kira's soft blue eyes flick my way. "Well, Bianca, it was nice meeting you. I hope our paths cross again."

Daniil's face looks tight as he shows his sister to the door. I hear him tell her Yuri is waiting downstairs to drive her back home. I wonder how it is that Kira didn't grow up with her brothers, didn't even know they existed. But it's none of my business, and frankly, there's no reason for us to get to know each other any better.

As I place my dish and mug in the sink, Daniil reenters the kitchen. "Have you reached out to Jorge yet?" I ask.

His lips flatten, but he nods. "There's been contact," he says vaguely. "I'll be going to Miami with you today."

"Really?" I run a restless hand through my still damp hair. I thought Jorge would still be in New York sleeping off his hangover, but maybe he headed home early. "You don't need to escort me, if you would just drop me at the airport—"

"I'm flying you over in our jet," Daniil interrupts. He won't look me in the eye, which I think is strange.

"What are you not telling me?" I ask, panic rising. Tension clouds the room, but his face remains stoic. "What's going on? Is it because I'm going back to Jorge? We talked about this last night—"

"That's not it," he sighs. "We can discuss it during the flight. Give me ten minutes to pack."

"Okay," I say, a sense of foreboding rising like a fog. "We can talk on the plane."

"WE ARE CRUISING at an altitude of twenty-two thousand feet. We'll be wheels-down in a little less than three hours, clear skies all the way. Enjoy your flight, Mr. Kozlov, and please don't hesitate to reach out to the crew for anything you may need. We are stocked with all your favorite foods and beverages."

The copilot salutes us and returns to the cockpit. Beside me, Daniil's face is cut from stone. He's not said one word since we left his penthouse.

Following in the copilot's footsteps is the overzealous flight attendant who has been circling Daniil from the moment we boarded the plane. She looks like one of the Jenner sisters, and I wouldn't be surprised if she's been his in-flight entertainment in the past, judging by the way she's throwing him hot and heavy glances.

"Can I get you anything, Mr. Kozlov?" she purrs. I don't warrant a second look from her.

"Mineral water, please, for both of us." And then he turns towards me. "Do you want anything else?"

I shake my head, and the Kendall look-alike saunters off, still eye-banging Daniil as she fetches our drinks.

"She seems friendly."

Daniil's lips tip up at the corner. "Sure. You can call it that."

He drums his fingers on the armrests, his stare fixed straight ahead. God, I hope he hasn't changed his mind. But that doesn't make sense. We're literally on the way back to my uncle's compound.

I wait until our drinks are in front of us before I turn to him, preparing to ask what's going on, but he beats me to it. "I'm not returning you to your uncle."

"What?" My head snaps back. "What are you talking about?"

He wipes a hand down his face. Exhaustion finally catching up with him. "Your uncle found out about what happened. I don't know who told him, but someone did, and he reached out to Andrei. The head of our family." I hold my breath. I know I will not like what he says next. He looks at me for a long, long time. "He wants us to marry."

The air whooshes from my lungs, my mind spinning in a million different directions. *Marry!* He wants me to marry Daniil!? When my brain finally catches up with my mouth, I slam my hands down on the armrests. "No. Just no. That makes no sense. He wants me to marry Jorge, not you."

He scoffs. "The feeling is mutual, *printsessa*." He takes a slow sip of his water, and when he puts his glass down on the tray, his eyes flick towards me, filled with contempt. "Apparently I compromised your honor, and it would be a great insult to your family if I don't put a ring on your finger." He cracks his neck. "Maybe your parents can intervene."

"My parents are dead." He flinches, but when he doesn't respond, I fill in the gaps. "I was sixteen. It was a car accident that took my younger sister as well. My uncle has been my legal guardian ever since," I add, the words coating my tongue in bitterness.

His eyes soften, and he gives me a look of pity that causes my stomach to clench. I fucking hate that look. But he surprises me by saying, "I'm sorry to hear that. I've lost both of my parents as well."

A normal person would say, "I'm sorry, too," but the last thing we need right now is a pity party, and I don't want to distract him from the point of this conversation. The point being—I can't marry him.

So, I take a deep steadying breath, and attempt to think rationally. "I'll talk to my uncle when we get to Miami. He thinks something happened between us, which obviously it did not." I shake my head, my words meant to soothe myself as much as Daniil. "He much prefers me to be with Jorge, he just needs to calm down and listen to logic. It'll be fine."

I hear how frantic I sound. Desperate. Because this will compromise everything, and I can't allow that. I'm so close, just a few more months, I can taste it.

"Good luck," he spits, "because we're supposed to get married tomorrow."

The water tumbles from my hand, soaking my pant leg, but I don't bother cleaning myself up. "No, no, that won't work."

Tension lines his shoulders as he eyes me carefully, studying me as if I'm a puzzle to be solved.

"I'm not saying this is ideal for either of us, but why in the world would you want to marry Jorge? I may not be perfect, but I'm gonna guess I'm a hell of a lot better than that scum."

"Maybe I love him," I shoot back.

His face darkens, and his eyes lock with mine. "No fucking way. I saw the hatred burning in your eyes. You don't love him. You don't even like him. Your uncle wanted you to become his wife, and now ... guess what. Plans have changed. Never forget, printsessa, we're both pawns in this underworld, and we just got played."

"He's never hit me before," I blurt. God, as if that makes it any better. I know it doesn't, I know Jorge is an animal, and I'll make sure he gets his. But right now, I need Daniil to be on my side. To fight against this marriage.

The sneer on his face turns ugly. "Like that makes it better? There's always a first time but never a last. Men who do shit like that don't change."

"You don't understand—" I start to clarify, then stop. Why bother? I can't explain myself to Daniil. He can't know the truth —it's better if he believes I hate him and love another. That I want nothing to do with him. Maybe he'll even back out of this arrangement when he realizes what a total brat I can be. Because the one thing I am sure of, I didn't suffer through years under my uncle's roof just to walk away now. Not when we're so close. Not when I almost have what I need to avenge my family's death. So I use my words as a weapon. "You think you're so much better than Jorge?" I scoff and shake my head. "Despite your silky words and unchecked hero complex, you're just another blood-thirsty mobster. Don't fool yourself, Daniil. Marrying Jorge or you ... there's no difference in my mind."

His eyes flash with a viciousness that he's kept under wraps so far. But he doesn't make a move, doesn't move a muscle. He merely runs his tongue over his teeth and flicks his wary gaze out the window, dismissing me as if I hadn't even spoken.

## CHAPTER SIX

### DANIIL

EMILIO'S COMPOUND is a gorgeous sprawling Mediterranean-style mansion in an exclusive gated community outside of Miami Beach. Secluded and well protected. I wouldn't expect anything less. Bianca and I exit the vehicle to stand on the stone driveway. Everything sparkles in the Florida sun—the marble lions flanking the stairs to the entrance, the black Range Rovers lined in the circular driveway, even the sunglasses perched on the noses of the mini army standing guard in the front of the home. Palm trees rustle in the warm breeze as a hulking guard with a shaved head approaches.

"Bianca," he says with a curt nod that she returns. And then to me he says, "Mr. Kozlov, I'll need to confiscate any weapons you have on you."

Is he fucking serious?

My hand instinctively flexes over the Glock tucked into my waistband. Bianca's eyes track the movement of my hand, and she raises an eyebrow at me. "My uncle is paranoid. It's a hard-and-fast rule for anyone entering his private residence."

I'd like to tell cue ball here to fuck off, I don't give up my

piece ever—especially when I don't trust the players involved—
but if I refuse, it won't be taken kindly. I might as well declare
war against the Zegas, and I'm not quite ready to take up that
mantle.

"I'd better get it back," I mutter, handing over the pistol.

Like most, I've never met Morales. With an ongoing war
with the Mexican cartels, he lays low, running his empire from
afar while Días attends to all in-person business. But his lack of
face-to-face time hasn't affected business. He's obviously doing
well, very well, judging by this prime piece of real estate.

A moment later, a stern-looking older woman, who introduces herself as Maria, the housekeeper, ushers us inside through
a wide set of steel doors.

"Your uncle will meet with you shortly. Would you like to
freshen up first?" Assessing eyes travel the length of Bianca,
taking in Kira's yoga pants and T-shirt.

"Yes, I'll go upstairs to change." Then to me she says, "Would
you mind waiting in the library while I get cleaned up? I won't be
long."

I nod and allow Maria to escort me to the library off the
main foyer. Settling into one of the velvet armchairs in the
corner, I take my phone from my pocket and text my brothers to
ask when they are arriving. This whole situation has me on edge,
and I'd feel better knowing my people are around.

"So, it's the groom-to-be?"

My eyes lift to find The Madman's eye, dark as night, staring
back at me. He looks worse for wear, with one eye swollen shut
and his right arm in a sling. Satisfaction melts through me to see
him hurt like this. He deserved far worse.

In a perfect world, Emilio would have him killed for
gambling away his niece, but since this world is far from perfect,
he stands before me still alive.

His lips tilt into a humorless smirk, and I remember the sight
of him hitting Bianca out on that balcony. How he treated her,
the terrible words he said to her. A sense of possession flares in

me now, a reminder that if I don't put a ring on Bianca's finger, this mudak will.

"I suppose I have you to thank for my upcoming nuptials." I allow a cocky grin to overtake my face. "I'm very much looking forward to making Bianca my wife."

"You think you're so clever, pendejo. You think you've won the prize, but don't be so sure," he growls, dropping any pretense of this being a friendly conversation.

"Take it up with your boss. His orders." I shrug, settling back in the armchair as if I don't have a care in the world. Then, with a conspiratorial whisper, I add, "Maybe if you didn't treat Bianca like the gum on your shoe, she wouldn't have come to me so readily."

Annoyance pulls his jaw taut, his scowl menacing. I've seen that look before. Right before guns are drawn or blades unsheathed. I may not be armed, but as far as I'm concerned, Días can choke on his rage. Unless he wants to invite the wrath of the Kozlov Empire down on his head—and I'm guessing he doesn't—he's powerless against me. And even better, he has no power over Bianca anymore.

"Rest easy, *parce*. I don't give a fuck about her. Never did. That bitch is your problem now." Despite his callous words, Días's jaw is locked so tight I think he might crack his molars.

"Say that again, I dare you." I raise my eyebrows. A clear indication that I don't give a fuck, but the hairs on the back of my neck stand on end. There's no way this half-cent gangster is going down without a fight. I took his golden ticket, the heir to the throne, and that marks me with an X between my eyebrows.

He'll come at me no doubt; the question is when. One thing I'll make certain of: when he strikes, I'll be ready.

A HALF HOUR LATER, Emilio summons us to a meeting. Bianca walks beside me, fidgeting with the neckline of her dress. She looks stunning, wearing a simple white shift dress and a stack of gold necklaces that sets off her golden-brown skin. There's a certain fierceness in her gaze, as if we're going to war rather than to see a beloved family member. I don't tell her about my run-in with Jorge. Doubt it would improve her mood.

Maria brings us out to an impressive veranda overlooking an Olympic-size pool surrounded by a neatly manicured lawn. Emilio is sitting waiting for us in a polo shirt and khakis, his dark hair brushed back from his tanned, handsome face. He looks like a business executive on his day off, not like the head of a deadly crime syndicate.

Emilio's hooded eyes track Bianca's every move with a quiet intensity that I don't fucking like. He looks at her like he hates her, and the feeling seems mutual. There's no affection in her eyes, no warmth towards her uncle, as she says, "Hello, *tío*," and plants a dry kiss on his cheek.

He doesn't rise to meet us, but he offers a nod in greeting. He gestures for us to join him at the patio table.

"Nice to meet you, Mr. Morales." I force a neutral tone. "My brothers send their regards."

"Call me Emilio," he offers with a false smoothness. "We'll be family soon."

"About that, *tío*." Bianca scoots forward in her seat, her usually golden skin pale. "We should talk about what happened this weekend."

"I know everything that happened this weekend." He doesn't bother to look at Bianca, instead he focuses on placing the napkin in his lap and helping himself to the fruit salad on the table.

"It was a misunderstanding. Daniil didn't know who I was. That I was your niece. Everyone was drinking … emotions were high … you can imagine. Daniil made a mistake."

Emilio's eyes snap to my own, but I keep my expression blank. I won't agree with Bianca that I made a mistake because I didn't. If

Emilio had better protected his niece, we wouldn't be in this situation. I doubt it was the first time Días had been rough with Bianca, and there's no way Emilio is ignorant of that. He appears to be a man who is aware of *everything* that happens within his organization.

But he's awaiting a response from me. I clear my throat, and say, "It's true, I didn't realize who Bianca was when I made the bet with Jorge." I pause for effect. "Nonetheless, a deal is a deal. And I intend to uphold my side of it."

Bianca lets out a frustrated groan and glares at me like I just ate her firstborn while Emilio nods, spearing a piece of papaya with his fork.

"Jorge made a mistake, but he is the man I want to marry." She practically chokes out the last part, and I wonder what game she's playing. That or she's scared of retribution from Días. "He's the man you wanted me to marry, tío, was he not?"

Emilio drops his cutlery on the table with a loud clang and glares at his niece. A wave of possessiveness has me on edge. This is no longer the face of the amiable CEO; this is the violent criminal drug lord who doesn't blink at the prospect of killing. "Your virtue was compromised by the events of last night. It made us look weak, and Jorge has been punished for his stupidity." His reptilian eyes cut to me, dead and flat. "You're lucky it was a Kozlov that claimed you. This marriage stands to benefit both families."

My lip curls in contempt, but I hold my tongue. I want Bianca to absorb his words. To understand how little regard her own flesh and blood holds for her. When she accepts that her family doesn't give a shit about her, she'll understand I'm by far the best option available.

Bianca releases a defeated sigh. "But why so quickly? Surely, we can delay the engagement by a few months. I don't even know Daniil, we need some time to—"

"*¡Silencio!*" Emilio seethes. "It's decided." He grabs her chin roughly and tilts her face towards him. "Do you want people to think you are a whore, dear niece?" She blinks at him and holds her ground, even as tears form in her eyes.

"Get your hands off her." My voice is low, but my words have a lethal edge that hangs heavy in the air. I don't move a muscle, but I'm all coiled energy, prepared to pounce if he doesn't release her immediately.

Emilio's jaw ticks, but his hand falls away from Bianca's face. His eyes, dark as night, continue to hold her captive. "Half the mafia families in greater New York saw you leave with Daniil last night. You don't think they'll talk?" Calmly picking up his fork, Emilio's attention goes back to the food in front of him. "Now we throw the wedding of the year, and we give people something positive to talk about. A union between the Colombians and Russians."

Bianca grits her teeth but holds her tongue this time. She won't look at me, but frustration ripples off her in waves. She's unhappy I didn't push back. Let her be unhappy with me, let her hate me. Frankly, I don't want this marriage either, but I don't want her in Días's grasp even more.

After a moment of blistering silence, Emilio stands, dropping his napkin on the table in front of him. Checking his Rolex, he frowns. "This is no longer open for discussion, Bianca. You will be married tomorrow. The wedding planner will be here momentarily to discuss the details with you."

With that he nods his head to me, the only sign of respect the *ublyudok* has shown me, and stalks from the patio, leaving us in tense silence. Tears trail down Bianca's face. I reach out and swipe at a tear, licking the salty moisture off my finger.

Her face falls, and she sucks in a shuddering breath. "Why are you going along with this? I thought you didn't want a wife?"

"I'm second in line to the Kozlov throne. I was always going to have to marry. The bratva is like royalty from the days of yore. We marry to create alliances and produce heirs."

She sneers, as if it's my fault the world is this way. "That's so fucked-up. You've never thought about marrying for love?"

"No." What I don't say is that I don't believe in love. It's a fallacy that we've been fed from day one, and I don't buy into the fantasy of happily ever afters. My parents married for what they said was love, and it ended with my mother in misery, eventually taking her own life. "You're as good as any other wet hole. Make me some babies and look good on my arm, that's all I need from you. Like your uncle said, it's a powerful alliance."

She flinches, but I don't care. She already hates me, now she needs to understand the terms of our arrangement. I brush invisible crumbs off my suit jacket as her eyes laser into the side of my face. Such an innocent thing. She can't even hide her feelings. It's written all over her face.

"*Hijo de puta*," she snaps.

While I don't speak Spanish, I know enough to understand I've been called a son of a bitch. Her arms are crossed in front of her chest, and she's twisted her body as far from me as possible. Fine. Let her be angry. But I do need her to hear what I have to say next.

I turn her face towards me, her jaw so delicate in my big hand, I could crush it without breaking a sweat. "But I want to be clear about one thing, printsessa. I'll never hurt you like he hurts you."

She gulps, and her eyes drift down to my mouth. An electric charge flares hot between us, lighting me up from the inside out. Even the air around us feels magnetic, the calm before a storm. She feels it, too. That I am sure of.

Before one of us breaks the spell, Maria emerges, announcing the wedding planner has arrived and that we are to meet with her in the study. It's the last thing I want to do, but as the old saying goes, in for a penny, in for a pound.

I stand and offer her my upturned palm. She stares at it like I just offered her a dead fish, before turning the other way, rising from her seat, and storming ahead of me.

Fuck. I like winding her up and watching her spin.

# CHAPTER SEVEN

## BIANCA

As I lie in bed, one thought alone echoes through my mind.

I failed.

Failed to convince my uncle not to marry me off, and even worse, failed to convince Daniil that I love Jorge, and our union is doomed. He doesn't care, he's made that clear.

His earlier words echo in my brain. *You're as good as any other wet hole.*

That pendejo. Beneath that charming facade, he's as poisonous as all the rest. A snake dressed in Armani. I won't marry him. Or anyone for that matter.

As quiet falls, I roll over, leaving the warmth of bed, and slip into the en suite bathroom. With the lights off, I open the lower vanity drawer and reach for the box of tampons I keep stashed at the very back. Thank god for period supplies. There is no better hiding spot.

Digging inside, I find the phone at the bottom of the cardboard box. Sitting on the cool bathroom tiles, hugging my knees to my chest, I make the call. It's the only thing I can do.

"I AM REALLY DIGGING this color on me." Kira sashays into the room and does a little spin for all of us. She's right, the forest green really does suit her well. I've joined all the ladies of the Kozlov clan—Kira and Georgia, whom I had already met, and now I've been introduced to Rowan and Alyona. They flew in earlier this morning, and it was decided by someone—the wedding planner maybe—that they would be my bridesmaids since I have no other female relatives or friends.

We're now gathered in a suite at my uncle's home trying on dresses for the wedding tonight. Everyone seems mildly shocked by the turn of events, but they are also putting on a happy face, assuring me how kind Daniil is when I know that to be a lie.

While the others are having their dresses altered, Georgia comes to sit with me, a glass of champagne in her hand.

"Hey," she says softly, "I bet you could use this."

"Thanks." I take the drink gratefully. "I definitely can."

"I can only imagine how you're feeling right now. Talk about an overwhelming twenty-hour hours. If there is something I can do to help, just ask." She squeezes my hand, her eyes shining with kindness I don't deserve.

Exhaling a shaky breath, I flash her a watery smile. "It has been crazy. I don't think I've absorbed it all yet."

"I know how insane this all is, but Daniil is a really solid guy. Yes, he's a swinging dick like all the Kozlov men, but underneath it all, he's as loyal as they come." I release a throaty laugh. Daniil and Andrei do seem to be cut from the same alpha-hole cloth. "And you're not *only* gaining a husband," she says, gesturing to all the women in the room. "You're gaining a squad. And a pretty awesome one at that."

Warmth blooms in my chest. If things were different, I might be grateful to have landed in this family. I watch Alyona fussing over her sister-in-law, Rowan's, dress while Kira takes pictures of everyone, and a wave of sadness bites at my edges for everything I can't have.

Georgia's hand covers my own, bringing my thoughts back to the present. "Want me to come to your dress fitting with you?"

"No need," I insist. "I'm sure you have a million things to do to get ready."

"Please"—she swats the air—"I can just slap on some makeup and call it a day. I'm happy to accompany you."

"No." The word comes out too forcefully, and I quickly plaster an apologetic smile on my face. "I insist you go with the others to get manis. The wedding planner is joining me, anyway."

"Well, if you change your mind, you know where to find me."

The next hour is a blur of cake tasting, finalizing the menu, and meeting with the florist to choose my bouquet. Madeline, the wedding planner, is like a dog with a bone. She isn't letting go until all her i's are dotted and her t's crossed. She literally has an army working for her, and the moment she decides something, her little minions scurry off to do her bidding. I almost feel guilty that so much work is going into a wedding that won't happen.

Daniil is nowhere to be found, and for that I'm grateful. I'd rather not look at his deceitful face ever again.

Just after lunch, as a team of decorators transform my uncle's home into a tropical-themed wedding paradise, Madeline and I head to an exclusive designer bridal boutique to get my dress fitted. I already picked the dress out online, now they'll do the final nips and tucks to ensure it fits like a glove. Or at least that's what Madeline thinks.

A staff of three women greet us as we walk into the luxe store. Only a handful of dresses are on display, and all of them look fit for a princess. Or a mafia queen, in this case. A pretty woman in her thirties with hair to her waist and the name Ming on her name tag greets me. "You must be Bianca," she says warmly. "The seamstress is waiting for you in the back. I'll escort you."

"Thank you." I turn to Madeline. "I'm sure you have better things to do than oversee my fitting. Why don't you stay out here and catch up on all the important details that need your approval."

Madeline's eyebrows pull together. "No need. It's best if I join you."

I don't move a muscle. The incessant ding of her incoming messages blares between us.

"I can handle this," I insist. I'll come out and show you the final fit." She looks unsure, but the hard set of my jaw makes it clear I won't be backing down. She glances at her phone once more as it starts ringing.

"I'll be right here," she promises me before turning and answering her call.

Ming takes me to a large fitting room in the back of the store where the dress is carefully hung beside a pedestal and a Japanese folding screen. Ming holds eye contact with me for a moment before nodding and exiting the room.

The moment the door closes, Deidre steps out of the shadows. Arms crossed in front of her, she looks as cool as ever. Her braids are tied back in a ponytail, a gun—as always—is tucked away in a holster under her no-nonsense sports jacket. Seeing Deidre fills me with both relief and a deep frustration that this is still ongoing.

"This is certainly an unexpected turn of events," she remarks in greeting. When we spoke last night, I'd only given her the most basic rundown of what happened. Though it wasn't a detailed account, it was enough to convey that everything we've worked so hard for is threatened. "Are you going to put on the dress?" she asks, gesturing to the elegant Vera Wang hanging beside the mirror.

"Forget that," I say, shaking my head in exasperation. "You need to get me out of here. Now."

She folds her arms over her chest, her expression unflappable as she stands stock-still. "I'm afraid we can't do that. Our investigation into your uncle is far from complete. Unless your life is in danger, I don't have the authority to transfer you into WITSEC."

I throw my arms in the air, frustration burning hot under my skin. "I've been working with the FBI for two years. I've provided you with damning evidence against my uncle and his cartel. How is it not enough to prosecute him or get me into witness protection?"

"Your uncle is careful. He has people help cover his tracks. He has the best lawyers at his fingertips, knows all the tricks of the trade. We need irrefutable evidence if it's going to hold up in court." Her eyes lance through me, piercing me with her uncompromising stare. "Like I told you from the start, these things take time."

My stomach twists violently. I don't have years, my life is about to implode *today*.

"You said you'd keep me safe," I accuse. "My uncle is marrying me off to a ruthless bratva head. I can't help you without access to Jorge and his loose lips."

"Sit down and take a few deep breaths," she coaxes, a wary eye on the door. She leads me to a chair by the window and forces a bottle of water into my hand. "Drink this, then tell me what's going on."

I drink, but it does nothing to steady my nerves. It's like my life is unraveling into a nightmare I can't control. Everything I've worked so hard for, sacrificed for, is slipping between my fingers like sand.

"What happened in New York?" Deidre's calm voice steadies me, and I recount the last twenty-four hours of hell I've lived through.

"And this Daniil that you're to marry, what's his last name?"

"Kozlov. He's part of a Brooklyn-based bratva family. They are a big deal on the East Coast. My uncle saw it as an opportunity, realized he'd get more out of an alliance with the Kozlovs than marrying me off to Jorge."

Her eyes are wide, as if I'd told her the juiciest secret in the world. "I know who they are. The Kozlovs are big-time." She grabs my shoulders, looking way too freakin' happy. "Shit, Bianca, this is gold."

"How is that?" My brows knit together in confusion. "Without Jorge and his nightly rum shots, I won't have any intel on the Zegas. I'll have to live in New York. Everything we've worked so hard for will be for nothing."

I want her to nod in agreement, but she's already off in her mind, scheming up a plan that will not benefit me. Burning awareness sweeps through me. She's not going to help. "You're not seeing the big picture. The Kozlovs are a major criminal enterprise. This could be huge."

I tip my head back in frustration, sighing loudly. "I don't care about the Kozlovs, I want my uncle behind bars. I want him to pay for everything he's done." I pound my chest, blinking back tears.

"I know," she says, frustration giving her voice a little edge, "but my point is the Kozlovs could be the key to putting your uncle behind bars. Two criminal organizations coming together to start something new. There is bound to be growing pains. People get greedy. Mistakes are made. This is your chance to get your uncle on something that will actually stick. We'll be able to build a powerful case against both crime families ... and you'll be the key."

"You're saying I should marry Daniil Kozlov." The words fall from my lips in barely a whisper.

She straightens to her full height and crosses her arms in front of her chest. "Yes. We have an opportunity here to put your uncle behind bars *and* take down another brutal crime family."

Crap, this is not going as planned. "He's not going to tell me anything. Daniil is hardened bratva, and he's not sloppy like Jorge. He's ... he's ..." Brutal, demanding, sexy as hell. "He's a monster who only wants me as arm candy."

She smirks and lifts a shoulder. "If he finds you attractive, that's a good start. You need to use everything at your disposal to get him talking."

My eyes narrow. "Are you saying what I think you are saying?"

"You're a beautiful woman, Bianca ... charming and clever. I think you understand—to get into his head, you need to get into his bed."

Squeezing my hands into fists, I try to will away the panic rising in my throat. I'm a virgin who's barely rounded third base. Seduction is not a tool in my arsenal, but my options are dwindling fast. "And then what?" I ask with a defeated sigh. "Do I pump him for information? Spy on him? Daniil will smell a rat from a mile away. He's sharp as a tack," I warn her, recalling how quickly he caught on to Jorge's poker fraud.

"And so are you." She pauses as she lifts the wedding dress from the stand it's hanging on. "You've fought so hard for this. Sacrificed so much. Trust me when I tell you revenge is within reach. We just need you to cooperate on this."

*Yeah, I've heard that before.*

"And the car accident?" I remind her. "The documents that I gave you ... Clearly my uncle was involved." Anguish climbs up my throat, but I swallow the emotions down. Five years has done nothing to ease my pain. It might as well have happened yesterday.

Her eyes flash with sympathy. "Again, all circumstantial. What we need is hard proof that your uncle was behind it. That's why you can't give up now."

My spine goes rigid as she holds the silky white gown up to my body, both of us staring at my reflection in the full-length three-panel mirror. She smiles at the sight while I choke down a scream.

I already regret the next words out of my mouth. "You need me to seduce him ..." The words stick in my throat. "Make him trust me? That's all?"

"For now," she confirms. "One step at a time. First, settle into your new life. When the time is right, I'll reach out about the next step."

I want to ask her what "the next step" means, but Deidre is busy carefully hanging the dress up. Her lips tip up at the corners. "Let's hope the dress fits you well because I'm a crappy seamstress." She winks and just like that, heads towards the back exit. "I'll be in touch" are her final words to me.

Holy shit. I'm getting married to a cold-blooded criminal I just met thirty-six hours ago, and there is nothing I can do to stop it.

# CHAPTER EIGHT

**DANIIL**

SHE'S LATE.

No bride is late for their wedding unless they don't plan on showing up.

I smooth a hand down the front of my tux and glance at Andrei, standing unflappable beside me on the altar. As if he can read my thoughts he leans in and murmurs, "She'll show. Probably."

"Thank you, but I don't need your reassurance," I respond through gritted teeth.

A low chuckle escapes under his breath. "You've checked your watch at least five times in as many minutes."

"I just want to get this over with." I feel like a circus oddity standing here on display amongst all these people gaping up at me. No doubt the story of our meeting has spread far and wide —how I bet on my future wife in a game of late-night poker— and now they all want to witness me claiming her in person. So fucking barbaric.

Part of me hopes Bianca did do a runner. That she managed to get as far away from here as possible, that she somehow found freedom. But it's an impossible dream. There is no escaping this life. Her uncle would hunt her to the ends of the earth rather than lose his prize filly.

The cello music drones on, grating on my nerves, and the smell of too much gangster cologne hangs heavy in the air. Even the priest keeps stealing quick glances at his watch, impatient to get the nuptials over with and flee this stifling room.

I raise my eyebrows at one of the wedding planner's minions standing off to the side of the podium. She huffs out a flustered breath and then slinks out the side door in search of the holdup.

It's a small wedding by mafia standards, only two hundred people, and other than my family, most of the guests are business associates. I feel a pang of something—sympathy, maybe—that Bianca had no friends to invite, and sadder still, that her immediate family perished in a car accident five years ago. There's no one she loves standing by her side today. Even if she wouldn't call this a happy day, it's a momentous one.

I think about reaching into my tux pocket and taking a nip of the vodka I have tucked away in a flask right above my holster. Some would say it's not classy to get married packing heat, but those are people that have never been to a mafia wedding uniting two very different factions. Better safe than sorry.

I look up to see Días slip into the back of the room, a buxom blonde on his arm. They take a seat in the last row. "What in the hell is he doing here?" I ask Andrei, motioning with my chin.

A little huff of air escapes his lips. "Invited by Morales. Ignore him. He's already moved on, judging by the blonde practically squirming in his lap."

Doesn't fucking matter. My collar feels too tight, and a bead of sweat drips down my back. I'm about to ask security to throw him out on his ass when the familiar notes of the "Wedding March" begin to play.

And just like that, Bianca is storming down the aisle, her uncle grasping her arm with no hint of subtlety. Emilio flashes a smile so fake on his overly tanned face it looks like he drew it on.

A long veil obscures Bianca's expression, but she holds her back straight, head high, wearing an elegant gown that hugs every dangerous curve perfectly.

She steps up to the altar, and a beat of silence passes between us. Tension ripples through the room like a thick fog, as if you can reach out and touch it. I lift her veil over her head so I can see her face. *That face.* Eyes the color of molasses shine brightly. Her makeup is subtle and tasteful, highlighting her fine features, delicate nose, and lush lips. My eyes fall lower, taking in her lovely long neck, and the graceful swoop of her shoulders. She's fucking magnificent, like she always is, and it's so easy to get sucked into her orbit.

"Thinking of doing a runner?" I ask, my voice barely a whisper.

We lock stares, and her narrowed eyes pull me in. Seconds tick by that feel like hours. Finally she whispers back, "Wouldn't dream of it."

And then it occurs to me—with all the delicacy of being hit by a Mack truck—that everything in my perfectly ordered and calibrated life is slipping from my fingers and has been since she walked into my life.

"THAT WAS A BEAUTIFUL FUCKING WEDDING." Kira's arms are wrapped around me, and she doesn't seem intent on letting me go anytime soon. Her small head rests on my chest. I wonder how many drinks it's taken her to get to this level of happy drunk.

Rowan smiles down at Kira before leaning in to kiss me on the cheek. "It really was a beautiful *fucking* wedding," she says quoting Kira. "Even if it is a wee bit unexpected."

I bark out a laugh. That's the understatement of the year.

"How does it feel to be a married man?" Yulian says, coming

up behind Rowan to wrap one hand around her waist in a possessive gesture.

"Who fucking knows?" I shrug, annoyed by all the fuss. We've been married for only a few hours, and in that time, I've barely exchanged ten words with Bianca. We sat beside each other at dinner, an electric silence pounding between us. Let her hate me. In fact, it serves my purpose if she does.

"Maybe you'll have a different opinion after your wedding night," Rowan teases, the length of her body practically molded to Yulian's.

"God, would you two get a room?" Kira makes a gagging sound.

"Gladly, but first I want to dance with my wife." Yulian pulls Rowan onto the dance floor as Kira mumbles something about needing to puke, even as she cuts a clear path towards the dessert table.

For the millionth time tonight, my eyes seek out Bianca. From across the room, I watch her greet an elderly couple. The woman leans in and kisses her right cheek, offering her congratulations before moving on.

Alone for the first time all night, I don't miss the way Bianca's shoulders slump, exhaustion seeping into her expression. I'm the reason for her misery, I'm the one that put all of this in motion, but I don't regret a thing. I may not trust her, and I certainly don't give a fuck about playing house, but when I look at her, a single thought echoes through my brain—*mine.*

Across the room, she lifts her head, and our gazes snag on each other's. She swallows, causing the little tendons in her throat to work overtime. It's not long before she blinks and looks away, spinning on her heel to leave the ballroom.

Before she can slip out the doors, a hand snakes out of the shadow and grabs her by the wrist. Días has her trapped in his hold. He leans close, whispering something in her ear. She doesn't respond right away, just listens, her body stiff like a board, her gaze glued to the floor. His hand is still shackled around her wrist when she turns towards him.

What fucking game is she playing? Huddled with Días, I watch as she glares at the man she claims to love but looks at with burning hate. Violence erupts in my veins, and in the span of a breath, I've crossed the room and have a gun pressed into The Madman's ribs. "Get your hands off her."

His shark eyes cut to my own, a sneer on his lips.

Bianca turns, her eyes nearly bugging out of their sockets when she sees I've drawn a weapon. "What are you doing?" she hisses.

"What's this mudak doing here? At my fucking wedding." I press the gun harder against his ribs. God, I have an itchy trigger finger right now, and nothing would bring me more happiness than blowing this guy's face off. A hush falls over the room, and heads snap in our direction.

"Put the gun away, Daniil," Bianca pleads. "You're making a scene."

I don't even bother glancing up, my full attention is lasered on Jorge, bristling with barely contained violence.

"Touch her again, and they'll need dental records to ID your remains," I spit.

Before I can make good on my threat, a familiar voice rumbles low in my ear. "What in the hell is going on?"

*Yeah, I should have seen that coming.* Andrei and Emilio intervene, pulling us both down the hall and into a study. Emilio pushes Días into a chair. Elbows resting on his spread legs, even with his injured arm still in a sling, he glares up at me, hatred rippling through every feature. At Andrei's insistence, I take the seat across from him, leaving my brother by my side, while Emilio remains standing.

"Care to explain what that was about?" Andrei motions between us.

"Happy to," I say, cracking my neck. "What's this fucker doing at my wedding, talking to my wife?"

"Easy, tiger," Andrei murmurs.

Emilio shrugs as if this is all a simple misunderstanding. "He's my top lieutenant, my right-hand. What happened between Jorge and Bianca is over. We're all adults here. Jorge understands that a marriage to you was best for everyone."

Días smirks at me. "Water under the bridge, *parce*. I was just offering Bianca my congratulations on her nuptials."

"Bullshit," I spit. Whatever words were exchanged between Bianca and Días, they weren't happy ones.

"*Enough*," Emilio growls. "You two are going to be working closely soon. Jorge will be in charge of laundering Zega money at the Bellair."

What the fuck? I glance over at Andrei. His expression remains neutral, but I don't miss the tightening of his jaw.

"That's not what we discussed." Andrei stands to his full height and buttons his jacket. "I don't think it's wise considering the bad blood between them."

Emilio doesn't flinch. "There's no one else I trust to oversee that level of operation. We're going to be pumping a lot of money into your casino, Kozlov. It needs to be handled by my right-hand."

A tense silence falls over the room. Andrei looks at me with a question in his eye—can I handle it?

I don't like Días; I don't trust him; I want nothing to do with him, but I also know the principles of *The Art of War*: keep your friends close and your enemies closer.

And The Madman is most certainly my enemy. But is Bianca? I plan to find that out.

I sigh, as if it costs me everything to agree to Emilio's terms. "As long as he doesn't go near Bianca, we won't have an issue." And I mean that. He can fuck with me all he wants, but the minute he comes near the woman bearing my ring and my name, he's a dead man. My eyes land on Días's smirking face, so I address him directly. "Any issues you keep between us. Between men. Understand?"

"Perfectly." He gets up and straightens his tie. "Bianca's all yours, my friend, I've already moved on."

"So it's settled." Andrei crosses his arms, blasting everyone with a don't-fuck-with-the-pakhan glare. "If my business suffers from your macho bullshit, you'll both pay."

"Of course," Días says between clenched teeth. I reluctantly grumble my acquiescence as well, but if my brother thinks it's that simple, he's dead wrong.

I don't trust the Zegas, and I never will.

# CHAPTER NINE

## BIANCA

THE SOUND of smashed glass from the terrace nearly makes me jump out of my skin. Whatever is going on outside isn't good. Daniil's been out there for the last hour, holed up with a bottle of Macallan, while I pace our hotel suite aimlessly, waiting for him to come inside and claim me as his bride.

Maniacal laughter nearly slips from my mouth when I catch my reflection in the bedroom mirror. I am in way over my head. Dolled up like a sex kitten, my hair cascades down my back in waves, strappy stilettos adorn my feet, and I'm wearing a black lace bra-and-panty set worthy of a Victoria's Secret runway.

I scream sex.

Talk about false advertising.

What I lack in skill, I'll make up in pure determination, because one way or another, I'll entice Daniil Kozlov to fall under my spell. Even if he currently considers me no better than gum stuck to the bottom of his shoe. Things were tense before the wedding, but something snapped when Daniil saw me with Jorge tonight. He mistook me being cornered by my ex for a cozy conversation.

Nothing could be further from the truth.

Jorge's fingers had dug into my wrists, holding me in place as he offered false congratulations. "Such a beautiful wedding, *chica*. And I have good news for you. Your uncle put me in charge of working with the Kozlovs, so I'll be living in New York, too. And don't worry, I'll make sure to keep a close watch on you and your Russian trash."

The fury I'd felt when Jorge grabbed me quickly transformed into fear. Instinctively, I sought out Daniil and found him across the room, his eyes flashing with violence. He had a pistol shoved into Jorge's side before I could blink, and words of possession slipped from his lips.

*Touch her again, and they'll need dental records to ID your remains.*

The thrill of his words sent shock waves to my core. I am his now. And that should scare me, not cause a little jolt of heat between my thighs. Because Daniil may want to possess me, but he also hates me.

"What are you doing?"

I spin at the sound of his voice, smooth and deep, coming from the doorway to the bedroom. He's leaning against the wall, wearing his suit pants and a bare chest that served as a canvas to some needle-happy tattoo artist. Bratva members often have tattoos that tell a story, or at least the old-school members did. I don't know what the swirl of colors covering his chest and arms represent, but I do know that no matter how much ink adorns his skin, there is no hiding the fact that his chest and upper body appear to be chiseled from rock.

I'm stuck in place, studying him like a mystery I can't quite figure out. Yet I want to. I want to unravel him, discover what makes him tick, why he's looking at me right now with hooded eyes, blazing over my exposed skin. It's almost as if I can feel little sparks all over my body where his gaze lands. I grab onto that flare of lust and desire, and with a confidence I do not entirely feel, ask him, "Are you coming to bed?"

He swirls the ice cubes in his drink, then polishes off the rest of his whisky in a long gulp. When he looks back at me, the hunger in his eyes just a moment ago is snuffed out.

"You think you can handle me?" His voice has a mocking lilt to it. He abandons the glass on a side table, and stalks towards me. "You wouldn't know what to do with my dick if I gave you an instruction manual."

I don't like the way he's looking at me with a challenge in his eye. As if he's testing if I have the guts to follow through on my invitation, calling my bluff only to remind me what a silly little girl I am. For that reason alone, I won't let him win.

I reach my hand out, fingertips following the hard planes of his chest and abs, trailing lower to where a light dusting of hair is evident above his zipper, but he stops me, his large hand curling around my wrist.

He bends low, the tip of his nose nearly touching my own. "We're not doing that, printsessa. Go to sleep," he bites before turning away from me. I've been dismissed.

"A marriage is not legally binding until it's consummated." I'm proud my voice comes out strong and clear.

He stops in his tracks, his shoulders forming a tight line. Turning, a hiss of air whistles through his teeth. But I can't back down now. He already thinks I'm a coward, and I won't prove him right. He's being purposefully cruel, attempting to scare me away, but his taunts only fuel my drive. I saunter towards him, reach down, and cup him through his trousers. I'm channeling some alternate-universe seductress, but part of me is reveling in this role. He feels impossibly hard, throbbing in my hand. Satisfaction pours through my veins as he releases an animalistic grunt.

"You can teach me," I whisper.

His eyes drop to my lips. "I don't fuck with virgins."

"Well, seeing as I'm your wife, you have little choice." His mouth thins, and I'm convinced he's going to push me away yet again, so I reach up on tiptoes to run my tongue along the shell of his ear. "Show me what you like."

I look up, our gazes colliding. Suddenly, I'm trapped in his very dark, very heavy stare. An energy spins between us, one that threatens to suck me in and never let me go, like a black hole. I could lose myself in this man. As it is, I can't drag my eyes away from his blazing irises.

When I remain still, his lips curve into a sinister smile. "Now I'm good enough for you? Are you going to think of Jorge while I fuck you?"

"I ... no." The words stick in my throat, his jealousy catching me off guard.

He smirks, forcing the back of my legs against the bed. His big body crowds me, and it feels dangerous, being pushed up against the edge in more ways than one.

"Want to know what I'd like? You on your knees choking on my big cock, using those beautiful lips to suck me dry. Still interested?" he taunts, dragging a finger down my cheek.

My core jolts, I'm both turned-on and wary, but fear doesn't serve me right now, so I stuff it down and put on a brave face. "Yes."

His hands drop to my ass cheeks, kneading them as his hard cock grinds against the flesh of my stomach. "Fine, you want to play, little wifey. Let's play." He suddenly releases his hold on me. "Take everything off and get on your knees."

His eyes light up when my tongue darts out to lick my dry lips. For a moment, I'm paralyzed in place, shocked at his sudden change in demeanor, but I brought this upon myself, so now I have to see it through.

Slipping the silky straps off my shoulders, I allow the bra to fall on the soft carpet, then peel my panties down my thighs. Earlier, I'd imagined myself posing seductively on the hotel bed in this fine French silk, now I nearly laugh at how different reality is from my stupid fantasy. The cool air causes my nipples to pucker, and his eyes linger, examining every inch of my body with unsettling interest. I use my arm to block my soft belly and heavy breasts. I'm proud of my figure, but I know I'm far from his ideal. He's probably used to rail-thin supermodels and actresses, and I'm all soft curves and generous hips.

But judging by his heated stare, maybe he doesn't mind after all. "Don't you dare hide yourself from me," he growls, drinking me in. "Every inch of you is perfect, and every inch of you is mine. Now ... Get. On. Your. Knees."

A thrill travels through my core at the way he claims me as his own. Following his orders, I kneel down, the carpet plush beneath me. Daniil takes obvious pleasure in my compliance; the corners of his mouth tip up in a taunting smile that makes him look brutally handsome. "I see you can follow orders. That's a good start, printsessa." His thumb brushes over my lips, pulling down the bottom one as far as it will go. "Now, undo my pants and take my cock out." His voice is husky and rough and betrays how worked up he is. Worked up for me.

My fingers land on his belt, making quick work of opening it, and then undoing his fly. I keep my eyes locked with his, an attempt to radiate confidence. A slight tremor in my hand is the only tell that I'm nervous—in way over my head. If he notices, he says nothing. His penetrating eyes stay glued on my own.

I reach into his open dress pants and take out his impressive length. His cock is big and thick, harder than I've ever imagined one could get. "Oh shit," I mumble.

He lets out a strangled laugh, then moves my hand away, fisting himself. He gives his cock a few hard strokes as a bead of pre-cum drips from his swollen head, and he wipes the moisture on my cheek.

He's doing this to punish me, to humiliate me—except that's not its effect. I don't find his actions demeaning; I find them hot as hell, and the smell of his arousal makes me shiver with pure need.

*What's wrong with me?*

I lean forward, trailing my lips against his length. I smile when he twitches beneath me. Fire lights my skin as I take a deep inhale, his musky scent consuming me from the inside out.

My seduction might be planned, but this moment is as real as it gets.

"Fuuuck. You look so beautiful like this," he whispers harshly. "My very own fuck doll. And that's all you'll ever be." His angry words pierce my consciousness. With my hair wrapped around his hand in a tight grasp, he rubs the head of his cock against my lips before thrusting forward. His erection breaches the seam of my lips, and he stuffs himself into my mouth, all the way to the back of my throat. I choke a little, and he strokes my face gently, a stark contrast to the harshness of his actions.

"That's right, sweet girl. Let me hear you gag on it. I want tears to run down your face and ruin your pretty make-up."

Fuck this man. He wants to prove I'm in over my head, that I can't handle him. But I'll prove him wrong.

I might be inexperienced, but I've read enough romance books to know I need to breathe through my nose while my mouth is full. His movements are rough and greedy. His hips buck and roll as I wrap my lips tighter around his cock and allow him to set the pace. When a groan rips from his throat and he tugs at my hair, a thrill shoots through me.

I may be the one kneeling, but I'm in control here. He's intent on my every move, his expression is almost pained as he throws his head back, a tremor running through his body.

Studying his face, I make note of every expression, every grimace and mumbled curse. I want this moment seared into my memory forever. The way he balances on the edge of agony and ecstasy. I did that to him. All me.

With a final anguished cry, he lurches forward, one hand holding me in place as his cock empties in my mouth. He doesn't warn me or offer to pull out. He's teaching me a lesson. Don't play with the big boys unless you can handle it.

"Look at me when you swallow my cum." Such a harsh demand, but I give him what he wants. My eyes are glued to his as he jerks in my mouth with a roar. I'm not ready for the flood down my throat, but he bucks hard, holding my head in place as I work to swallow every last drop. Even after, as his cock softens, he stays inside my mouth, breathing harshly. Fire erupts under my skin, and I squeeze my legs together, desperate for my own release.

One finger strokes over my cheek. "I see Jorge trained you well."

The heat I felt just a moment ago dies instantly. Doused like water poured over a fire. I flinch. I should have known this is where his mind would go.

He doesn't offer me his hand or provide any help as I push off the floor. He turns his back on me, as if I've been dismissed now that he's used my mouth. It's humiliating, although I think that's the point.

My blood boils, but even as I take my leave and head to the bathroom, I remind myself I'm playing a long game. And *playing* is indeed the operative term. Because as much as I enjoyed that moment, I came to him with one intention and one intention only.

I will use any means necessary to acquire his trust, and then I will use that trust for my own gain.

I catch a glimpse of myself in the bathroom mirror, shocked by what I see. The red from my lipstick is smeared across my face, and mascara has pooled under my eyes. My skin is blotchy, and I have sex hair, but damn if I don't feel a spark of satisfaction.

Daniil's unsteady breaths, guttural groans, loss of control—that was all because of me. His unaffected facade cracked like fine china on a stone floor.

I did that to him. A small victory.

It'll take more than cruel words and a rough blow job to break me. I have more at stake than he could ever imagine. I'd rather die than lose, and if that's what it comes to, I'm willing to make that sacrifice.

# CHAPTER TEN

## BIANCA

NEW YORK IS WASHED OUT, the sky a blanket of dark clouds as we make our way through morning rush-hour traffic, heading to Daniil's penthouse. It's a stark contrast to what we'd just left—sunny Miami, with its heat, vibrancy, and color. And now this drab city is to be my new home.

Daniil is beside me in the back seat of the Escalade, his face obscured by the newspaper he's reading. The man has been a wall of ice since last night. We slept in separate rooms and have barely said two words to each other since this morning.

From the corner of my eye, I discreetly take him in. Freshly showered and shaved, his suit neatly pressed. He looks expensive, and he smells divine, like citrus and sin. Flickers from last night come back to me unbidden. He hasn't mentioned what happened between us, but I wonder if he's thinking about it as much as I am.

Every filthy word, every debased act is branded in my memory. Me on my knees while he thrust into my mouth like I was his plaything. My seduction served a purpose, to get closer to Daniil, but it also left me hot and needy. *Aching*. Even after he left me rather unceremoniously on my knees.

"I'm dropping you off at the penthouse. Mikhail will stay with you." Daniil's gruff voice cuts through my heated thoughts.

"Okay." I smooth out my skirt, the unfamiliar heft of a honking diamond ring weighing down my finger. "What am I supposed to do with my time?"

"That's your business." He doesn't even bother to look up from the newspaper.

"Can I go into the city?"

He pauses for a moment. "For a purpose and only if you take Mikhail with you. Don't leave his side. Ever."

Great, the life of a cloistered mafia woman continues. We're one step away from the Bridgerton sisters who spend their days playing piano, reading books, and waiting for a husband. That was my precise existence when I became my uncle's ward, and now nothing in my life will change.

Except one thing. I need to get closer to Daniil.

As investigative journalists, my parents told me the key to breaking a story is to follow the money trail. Which is exactly what I intend to do. I settle back in the seat and clear my throat before asking, "Can I get a job?"

The paper crumples as he lowers it into his lap. He regards me carefully, his eyebrows pressed together. "Why would you want to do that?" he asks, genuinely confused.

"I'll be bored at home. My uncle never allowed me to do anything, but I was hoping we could do things differently. A fresh start."

He straightens his cuffs, looking beyond me at the rain-slicked city streets. "It's not a good idea."

Exactly what I expected him to say. I recross my legs, angling my body towards him. "What if I were to work for you? I can do data entry, crunch numbers, administrative tasks. Whatever you want me to do, I can do it," I offer.

"Have you held a job before?"

I pause. "That wasn't something my uncle would allow. But if you give me a chance, you'll see I'm quite capable."

"It's not what's done in this world. You know that. Wives don't work. They have hobbies." He huffs out a breath and taps his finger against his thigh. "Why don't you take tennis lessons or do a pottery class."

Whatever lady boner I had for him earlier deflates. I thought Daniil might be a little more forward-thinking. Guess I thought wrong.

"What about Georgia, doesn't she work?"

His jaw tightens. "That's different."

Now he's making me mad. I cross my arms in front of my chest. "How is it different? And Kira's a full-blown vor," I say smugly, using the Russian word she taught me when I met her in Daniil's kitchen. "I want to feel useful, not like some mafia princess banished to shopping sprees and mindless lunches."

Daniil hooks a finger inside his collar, stretching it wide. "Georgia is an art teacher and works in a private school where she can bring her own guards. And Kira is our sister, not to mention heir to two bratva fortunes. It's her rightful place. But you"—he spits out that word in a way I don't like—"your uncle practically kept you under lock and key. What do you know about working in our world?"

"You can train me," I snap back. "I am capable of learning, believe it or not."

"Just drop it, Bianca." His tone is softer than I expected, as if this conversation is draining him of energy.

Irritation morphs into resolve. I'm more capable than he could imagine. And when this is all over, he'll learn exactly how much he underestimated me.

We pull up to the curb of his luxury building. I barely recall being here the other night—it was dark, and I was half delirious —but now I take a moment and gaze up at what will be my home for the next ... god, who knows how long. My gilded cage.

Mikhail comes around and stands in front of my car door,

ready to spring into action. But I won't leave without a final parting shot. I swivel in my seat and narrow my eyes at Daniil.

"I'll make sure to get really good at spending your money. I believe Bergdorf is close by. And if I'm not mistaken, Louis Vuitton, too. Since I'm not good for *anything else* apparently, I'll shop till I drop."

Daniil presses his lips together as if he's tolerating the outburst of a petulant child. Then he reaches into his suit jacket and pulls out a sleek leather wallet. He removes a black credit card and holds it up between two fingers.

"Do your best, printsessa. This card has no limit."

I swipe for it, but he moves it just out of my reach. "Ah-ah," he warns. "You need to keep it somewhere safe."

The nerve of this stinking man. "My purse is in the back. I'm not a child, Daniil, I won't lose it," I tell him through gritted teeth.

He smiles but it's not friendly. It's predatory. He's taking way too much enjoyment in this little game. "I don't want to take a chance."

My eyes flick to the window, and I notice Mikhail has turned around so his back is now towards me. And in that moment of distraction, something thin and hard trails the length of my neck down towards my collarbone, then over the swell of my left breast.

I whip around and watch as his stupid card travels lower, headed for the spot between my legs. "C'mon, printsessa, somewhere safe?"

A shiver in my lower belly quiets the usual urge I have to sass him. "Alright," I challenge him. "I have the perfect spot." My fingertips find the hem of my skirt, and I slowly hike it up around my hips. His gaze falls to the space between my spread thighs, zeroing in on the strip of my red lace thong that's barely visible. He bites out a raspy curse. His tone is so crude, so feral it sends a spike of pleasure to my clit.

"Right here." I finger the lace thigh-high encircling my upper leg. I'm enjoying the sight of his tight jaw and rigid shoulders way too much. "Are you going to give me the card now so I can get on with my day?"

He swallows hard as one thick finger dips below the clip connecting my stocking and garter belt, and with a clean snap, the black plastic card is pressed against the skin of my thigh.

As if he wasn't just staring hungrily at my bare skin for the last minute, he pulls the newspaper open again, wordlessly dismissing me.

I step out of the car, a smile of victory playing on my lips. It doesn't falter as I breeze through the building's lavish foyer and step into the elevator, Mikhail trailing me the entire time. It doesn't even fall as I step into the penthouse that will serve as my new home and cage until I can bring not one but two criminal empires down single-handedly.

# CHAPTER ELEVEN

## DANIIL

MY FOOTSTEPS ECHO off the marble foyer, something I only notice because the penthouse is dead quiet at this late hour, or more accurately, early hour. The fact that I'm home before two in the morning is a near miracle; my schedule has been nonstop since the casino opened two weeks ago. But tonight, Leo took over managing the Bellair so I could attend to more pressing matters.

Like beating the shit out of a group of cheaters who were caught swapping cards under the table before the night was even in full swing. Their scam ran with two players switching cards to make up a winning hand, while a third person distracted the dealer with talk, and another acted as lookout.

There's only one way to deal with cheats: swiftly and brutally. And that pleasure fell to me tonight. It's a shame I couldn't have administered the same punishment to Días the night of the casino opening.

I flex my now busted knuckles. They probably need an ice pack, but I opt for the numbing effect of booze instead. Fixing myself a whisky from the bar cart, I discard my suit jacket and loosen my tie, allowing the liquor to settle my nerves. Dropping onto the living room couch, I lean back and release a tense breath I didn't know I was holding only to suck in a gulp of air that smells like *her.*

Fuck me, am I hallucinating? I turn and find a sweater of hers tossed along the back of the couch. I've seen pictures of her wearing it on the terrace, staring out at the city buzzing below. I'm barely around, but I know what she does every day—gym, shops, reads, paces, reads some more—because my men report everything back to me.

Everything but what is going on in that pretty little head of hers. That remains a mystery. Not that she knows me either. But it's best this way. Most bratva marriages are built on duty and nothing more—Andrei and Yulian are the exceptions to the rule. Even still, I can't help but pick up Bianca's sweater and take a deep inhale. Her scent, like cloves and vanilla, washes over me, making me want something I can't have.

I throw her sweater across the room, confused by my reaction. My cock twitches in my pants, and a feeling I have no words for blooms in my chest. In Russian, I would call her *zanoza* —a pain, a complication. From the moment she walked into my life, everything has been so damn *complicated.*

Starting with the fact that I now am required to work with her ex. Every night, under Días's careful watch, a handful of Zegas show up at the Bellair with wads of cash that they use to buy casino chips. Then they hit the tables and slot machines, winning a bit here, losing a lot there. When their loss is in the twenty percent range, Jorge signals his men. They cash out their chips and leave with fresh bills from the casino—dirty money now clean, and our casino is thriving.

Except seeing Jorge parade through the Bellair like he's the king of the fucking world is making me insane. Flashing an arrogant smile at the security cameras every chance he gets, he knows I'm sitting upstairs in my office watching him. Seething.

Yesterday, as I was walking out of the casino, The Madman

stepped into my path, a shit-eating grin on his face. "How's Bianca?" he asked with all the sincerity of a car salesman. "Please send my regards to her."

I was reaching for my Glock when Leo stepped between us. "Easy," he murmured. "He's fucking with you. Don't take the bait."

But it's too late. There's a buzz in my veins that won't be extinguished until Jorge is lying mangled at my feet, every bone in his body twisted unnaturally. "If I ever hear my wife's name on your tongue again, I'll cut it out and feed it to the dogs," I threatened, even though Leo remained between us.

"You mistake my intentions," Jorge claimed, a mocking edge to his tone. Then, with a little bow, he slithered away, and I was left with an acidic taste in my mouth and the intense need for violence.

I settled for shots of vodka.

But what I really need is a long, hard fuck.

And that won't be happening any time soon; my new wife and I are at an impasse. She doesn't want to be married to me, and I don't trust her. It's a funny thing though, I still want to bend her over a chair, and make her wet for me.

Ever since our wedding night, I've obsessed over how fucking good it felt to have Bianca's lips wrapped around my cock. The way she obeyed my commands, getting on her knees for me when I told her to ... Shit, that was everything. Her inexperience was clear, but it only fueled my hunger. I've been like a randy teenager since then, walking around at half-mast every time her lush curves and gorgeous face appear in my mind.

Fuck it, I'm hard as steel right now. I need a cold shower and a few hours of sleep before I do something really idiotic like visit the little traitor in her bed.

Abandoning my tumbler on the side table, I head towards my bedroom. I'm passing by the open door of the library when I hear it. A rustling sound, like papers being shuffled. I enter the room cautiously. The penthouse is secure, I'm not worried about an intruder, but I'm curious to see what a member of my staff is doing in here at this hour.

A moment later, Bianca steps out of the shadows, a small pen and notebook in her hand. Lit only by the moonlight streaming in through windows, she looks like a goddess as her full breasts swing gently under her loose tank top, and a tiny pair of sleep shorts show off smooth brown legs. Fuck. She's designed to ruin me.

Self-preservation makes me look past her to the rows of bookshelves lining the room. "What are you doing in here?" I demand.

She startles, pressing a hand to her chest. "Daniil," she chokes out. "I didn't hear you come in."

"That's the point."

I curl my toes into the Persian rug to stop myself from advancing on her. Instead, I cross my arms and lean against the wall behind me. With no makeup and her hair falling in soft waves around her face, she looks like an angel come to life.

Except she's no angel. I see the way she's trying to hide the notebook behind her back. "What's that?" I gesture to the contents in her hands.

"Nothing," she responds, her chin held high. "I was just ... journaling."

My eyes dart to the oak writing desk in the corner of the room. It's my mother's desk, a memento I took from my childhood home to remind me of her. The mother I lost way too fucking soon. I wonder what she would make of me now, a high-ranking vor who married not for love but for an alliance. Somehow, I know she'd be disappointed in me. Even though it's common practice in our world, she would have wanted more for me.

*She would have expected more.*

Yet here I am, standing off with my wife that I treat no better than the hired help. I imagine I'd be a disappointment to my mother in more ways than one.

"Were you going through the desk?" I ask. Truthfully, there's nothing to find. I never work here. And for that reason, I don't bother locking the desk drawers. I keep nothing related to the family business in the penthouse. It's Mafia 101, if our homes ever got raided, the authorities would find nothing of use.

"Of course not," she fires back all too quickly. "Why would I go through your desk?"

"Care to share what's in that little notebook of yours?"

"Now why would I do that?" She scowls at me but continues to stand her ground.

Amusement curls my lips. For some reason, I'm enjoying her bravado. But I want to see if I can make her sweat. Pushing off the wall, I take a few steps and close the gap between us, stopping just shy of touching her. Her own arms wrap tightly around her waist, her wary gaze bounces around the room, as if looking for help or a way to escape me, but that's not possible. Time is suspended as I listen to her quickened breaths, waiting to see how she'll react.

"I think you're hiding something from me," I whisper breezily in her ear.

She looks up to my face and our gazes hold, locked in battle. Most women would stand down at this point, but not Bianca. She meets my fiery look with a scathing one of her own.

"Fine, you want to read about how bored I am, how useless I feel here. Be my guest." She holds the book up, but I don't make a move for it, preferring to graze my thumb over the hammering pulse in her neck.

"What are you really looking for?" I ask, my lips brushing against the shell of her ear. A little shiver dances down her spine.

"Nothing, pendejo. You ignore me for weeks and then you accuse me of ... of what exactly? Snooping? As if I care to find out about your business. You mean nothing to me." She pushes hard against my chest, but I don't move an inch. Instead, I grab both of her hands and hold them captive in mine.

"Why do you hate me so much?" I ask, dipping my head to

run the tip of my nose down her neck. She turns her face away from me, but I don't miss the way her breath catches in her throat. "You made it clear you didn't want this marriage, so I'm giving you space," I growl. "I haven't forced myself on you. I haven't asked anything of you. I let you live your life, just as I'm living mine."

"Exactly," she seethes. "We live like strangers. Having nothing to do with each other. Not even sharing a bed."

A shaky laugh escapes my throat, and I release her hand that still clutches the journal. Reaching down, I twirl a piece of her silky chestnut hair around my finger. "I didn't realize you needed to be fucked so badly."

She snorts. "You're clueless if you think that's what this is about."

"So enlighten me." My thumb traces over her lips. A slow back and forth. Maybe I do it to see how she'll respond ...

A gasp escapes, causing her mouth to open, and those full lips parting reminds me how well she uses them. It's all I can do not to lean in and taste her. The only thing holding me back is her fierce expression. "I'm not allowed to do anything except shop, work out, and watch TV. I'm dying a slow death over here, and you don't even know or care."

Tears spring to her eyes, and my chest squeezes, a strange tightness wrapping around my lungs. *Blyad*, I've gone soft. Since when am I moved by a woman's tears or bothered by their emotions? Bianca has a hold over me. I'm drawn to her. I crave her. Need her. Even though she's keeping something from me. I'm sure of it.

I step back from her, dragging a hand through my hair. Abruptly, I turn away, not wanting her to pick up on the conflicting emotions playing out inside me.

"Daniil." Her voice is scarcely a whisper.

"I do care," I say tightly.

Light footsteps shuffle towards me, but I flinch before she

can make contact. I can't stand her touch right now. I can't bear to hear how much I'm disappointing her.

Not waiting for her response, I leave the room in a fog of confusion.

SITTING DOWN HEAVILY on my bed, I grab my cell off the desk and dial Kira's number. She picks up after the first ring.

"Daniil! Nice to see your name pop up on my caller ID, even though it's the middle of the night." In the background, a car horn honks and yells ring out. The familiar sounds of New York City streets.

"And what are you still doing out at this late hour?" I chide jokingly.

"I could ask you the same thing!"

I snort. "Alright, fair point." I lie back on the pillow and stare up at the ceiling of my bedroom. "I'm sorry I'm calling out of the blue. I know we haven't spoken in a while. I've been busy."

"Hell yeah, you have been. You're a married man now, I hope you've been living in bed, having a shit ton of sweet newlywed sex—"

"Not quite," I interrupt, rubbing the back of my neck. "That's why I'm calling."

"Oh ... 'kay." There's rustling and the sound of keys jangling as she enters her loft. "I'm all ears. What's going on?"

Kira has only been in our lives for about a year—hell, we didn't know we had a sister until shortly before that—and yet she's become an integral part of our family. The best part, if you ask me.

"Fuck ... I just ..." I stumble, at a loss for how to explain myself. "I don't know how to be married. What am I supposed to do?"

"I'm sorry?" A stifled laugh on the other end of the line. "You mean like, how to treat her?"

I close my eyes and pinch the bridge of my nose. I sound like such a loser. "She's bored and lonely and told me as much. I'm working all the time, cause that's what I do. She's not like other mafia wives—she doesn't want to shop and go to the gym all day. She wants to work, and I don't know ... be useful somehow." What I don't mention is how shitty I've treated her. Purposely.

There's silence on the other end of the line before she asks, "So you didn't even take time off for a honeymoon?"

"It's an arranged marriage, and I'm busy with the casino." And she hates me. But there's no point in sharing that.

"Right. Well, first things first, you gotta make some time for her. Take her out for dinner. Nowhere fancy or too stuffy. Somewhere down-to-earth where you can both relax and get to know each other as people. Bianca does not strike me as a cartel princess, so don't treat her like one."

I scratch my chin. "I can do dinner. Anything else?"

Kira huffs out a laugh. "Start with dinner and not working all the damn time. She'll tell you what to do next."

I grin to myself. Yeah, she probably will. Bianca is no shrinking violet. "Can you organize a girls' night out for her? I think it would help if she had some friends."

"Already on it. We just need to settle on a date, then we'll whisk her away for a crazy night on the town."

"What!? I meant a quiet dinner, maybe a lounge or something ... somewhere that we own. No crazy night!"

There's a loud cackle on the other end of the line before she hangs up.

Shit. I have a feeling I just opened a big box of worms.

# CHAPTER TWELVE

## BIANCA

"WHAT KIND OF BREED IS THAT?" I point towards the boisterous black puppy running circles around my feet on the lawn.

"That's a black Lab, ma'am. He's a month old."

"So cute," I exclaim. "What's the temperament of this breed? High-energy?" I ask the breeder hopefully.

"They do require quite a bit of activity, but they are highly trainable and make for wonderful companions," she assures me with a smile. "Labs are very gentle."

*Well, forget that.*

"I love a dog with a little spirit," I say with a laugh. "Lovably naughty, you know. Can you recommend a dog like that?"

"Oh." The breeder's eyebrows pull together in thought. "No one's ever asked for that before."

Mikhail, my ever-present shadow, clears his throat. "I don't think Daniil would—"

I hold my hand up to stop him from finishing that thought. "You let me take care of Daniil, okay? Can't a wife surprise her husband?"

Mikhail rolls his eyes and mumbles something in Russian. He'd looked none too pleased when I'd announced this morning that we were off to see a dog breeder in New Jersey. He may have said something about Daniil being allergic to furry animals, but honestly, not my problem. This dog will serve a much greater purpose.

I bring my focus back to the breeder. "So, any recommendations?"

She takes her glasses off and wipes them on her shirt, shaking her salt-and-pepper bob.

"I know someone not far from here that breeds Japanese Spitz, but honestly, you don't want that kind of dog. Don't get me wrong, they're cute and affectionate, but they're hyperactive. Always getting into things that they shouldn't, practically untrainable if you ask me."

*Bingo.*

"I'd like the name of that breeder, please."

There's more Russian cursing behind me that I willfully ignore.

Three hours later, we are back at the penthouse with Mikhail nervously smoking on the terrace, eyeing me like I'm the devil incarnate while I lie on the couch being smothered in excited dog kisses. Eris is what I've named her. She's a big bundle of white fur, an aggressive cuddler, and she can't sit still for more than a minute. She will serve her purpose well.

When I was nine years old, my parents bought me a dog. My sister, Celeste, had just been born, and apparently, I'd been acting up, unaccustomed to sharing my parents' attention. Molly, named after my great-grandmother, was a gentle golden retriever, and all the jealousy I felt towards my sister fell away with her appearance. Mom had a new baby, and I had a baby of my own.

As Celeste grew, she also fell in love with Molly, and the dog became both of ours. I already adored my younger sister, but this shared love of our pet brought us closer. We spent many afternoons in our pool, swimming and playing in the backyard together.

The memories spark a swell of emotion that catches me in the chest, tumbling me back into the waves of grief, the undertow so strong that my lungs burn with the need for air. My eyes sting with tears, but I refuse to let them fall. Instead, I'll channel that grief into the reason I'm here. The only reason.

The close call from a few nights ago—when Daniil caught me snooping unsuccessfully in his library—was a wake-up call. I can't risk being caught poking around where I shouldn't be again. Daniil was clearly suspicious of me. I threw him off by having a mini meltdown, but that was a one-time Hail Mary.

Heat thrums beneath my skin just thinking about my humiliation in the moment. I'd been looking for a way to distract him; I hadn't meant to speak the truth, to admit being bored and lonely.

Even if I am.

Truthfully, I've been bored and lonely for years. Ever since I moved into my uncle's home at the age of sixteen. But to admit it to Daniil was beyond humiliating, and then his response, turning his back on me and walking out with barely a word made it so much worse.

The fact that he looked as gutted as I felt is the one scrap of satisfaction I've taken from the exchange. The only thing I'm sure of is the sooner I get Deidre the information she's looking for, the sooner I can get out of here and never see Daniil Kozlov again.

Which is where Eris comes in.

My father always said that Molly was the best damn distraction there was. And so, I'm picking up on that line of thinking. Eris—named after the Greek goddess of chaos—is going to do exactly as her namesake promises. This ball of white fur and unbridled energy, currently chasing her tail on the couch next to me, will be my excuse to get into places that are normally off-limits, like his bedroom and office.

I have no plans to train Eris. I'm going to let her run wild. I'm not backing down until I find what I'm looking for. Whatever that is.

# CHAPTER THIRTEEN

## BIANCA

"IS THAT A DOG?" Daniil's deep voice reverberates in the large open space of the penthouse kitchen.

I glance up at him in surprise as I feed Eris a piece of chicken under the table. It's barely after sundown, and Daniil rarely makes an appearance while I'm still awake.

"Why, yes, this white fluffy beast that walks on all four legs is a dog," I don't soften my sarcastic tone, he doesn't deserve it. "Daniil meet Eris. Eris, Daniil."

He blinks rapidly, staring at Eris as if he's convinced she's an illusion and will disappear if he wills her to. No such luck, buddy.

"But why is it in my house?" he asks sourly.

I stand and meet his challenge head-on. Well, as head-on as I can get considering I come up to his chest. Our stare off attracts the attention of Eris, who jumps up and paws at Daniil's Gucci-clad leg. I nearly burst out laughing from the expression of horror on his face.

"It's a *she*, actually. Her name is Eris. And she's here because she's mine. I adopted her today."

"Out of the question." His jaw snaps together, teeth grinding as often happens when he's irritated. But I won't back down.

Taking in a lungful of air, I steel my spine. "Oh, it was never a question. I didn't ask because I'm a grown-ass woman. I don't need your permission. This is my dog, not yours."

"This dog is not staying here, and that's final."

Through narrowed eyes, I take in Daniil's hardened expression. He's an asshole of the highest order, and I don't know why I ever thought differently. A storm rages behind his eyes; he's as stubborn as I am.

He advances on me, and although I want to hold my ground, when a mountain of a man comes close, it is only natural to retreat. He seems to enjoy this game, the one where he uses nonverbal forms of intimidation to get his way, but I'm not having it.

Clearing my throat, I use the strongest voice I'm capable of. "If you kick Eris out, you kick me out."

He's on me before I can stop him, pushing me back into the breakfast bar. He holds the back of my neck and forces me to look up at him. Magnetic whisky eyes meet mine, and I'm suddenly aware of how big and powerful he feels against me.

Jesus, what is happening?

As if he can sense how he is affecting me, his attention lowers to my pulse hammering in my throat. My breaths are shallow and too quick. I swear, he doesn't miss that either. Nor has he released me from his grasp.

"Explain the dog to me," he commands, this time his tone is less biting.

"I got Eris to keep me company."

His eyebrows pull together and for a moment he looks ... shattered. He tilts my chin up until I meet his gaze. Now his mouth is dangerously close to mine, so close our breath intermingles.

"I don't want a dog in my house." His jaw tightens, and he

looks at a point far in the distance before his eyes return to my own. "But I also don't want you to be lonely."

He's so close, holding me in a way that doesn't feel aggressive anymore, it feels like something else entirely. I draw in a breath and try to convince myself that the crazy beat of my heart is from the fight alone, not from his hand cupping the back of my neck or the way his eyes dance when my tongue darts out to moisten my lips. I try to wiggle out of his grasp, but he stops me. His skin blazes against mine, and I'm so painfully aware of his presence—his jawline sharp as an arrow, and that masculine scent of his, spicy and musky with a hint of sweet underneath.

"Your dog pissed on the floor."

What!?

Mikhail leans casually against the far wall, pointing to a puddle on the tumbled-stone kitchen floor.

"Eris, no!" I yell, although it's hardly the dog's fault she had to relieve herself in the corner. That blame sits squarely on my shoulders. I break free from Daniil's grasp and get some paper towels to mop up the mess.

"*Chto za chert*," Daniil grinds out as he and Mikhail talk in rapid-fire Russian, likely arguing over why Mikhail allowed me to get the dog in the first place. The poor man had no choice. I threatened to tell Daniil he's smoking cigarettes again if he didn't keep his mouth shut. Apparently, it's a point of contention.

Scooping up Eris, I brush past the men and head out to the terrace where I've set up a little potty training spot for the pup. New York is lively at dusk as the setting sun glints off the water below and the Brooklyn Bridge fills with both humans-on-foot and car traffic. After living in Miami for most of my life, New York is a revelation. But living here feels like I'm only a bystander, observing it from high above rather than as an active participant.

As I settle into one of the outdoor lounge chairs, watching

Eris rambunctiously rip up one of her toys, Daniil steps outside. I can feel his eyes roving over me from his post by the door.

"Why did you name the dog after the goddess of chaos?"

Goddammit. How does this man know about Greek mythology?

"Because." I gaze towards the horizon, a breeze rustling my hair. "It's an analogy for my life, isn't it? Chaos, strife, discord."

He runs his hands through his thick, messy hair, his features hardening. "It doesn't have to be that way."

If he only knew.

"Whatever you say." I release a heavy sigh, not wanting to continue this pointless conversation. "Why are you home so early?"

He opens his mouth to say something but seems to think better of it. "Fuck." It's the barest of whispers, but I still hear it. I train my eyes on Eris, and from the periphery, I see Daniil studying me closely. "Because ... I'm trying something new here."

"And that is?"

"Dinner. I want to take you for dinner."

I sit up straighter and face him. "I'm sorry. What? Like a business function? I-need-to-be-seen-with-my-new-wife kind of thing?" Because honestly, we haven't shared a meal since we moved in together. The only reason for us to go out would be for show. "What's the dress code?"

"The dress code is whatever the hell you want it to be." He shrugs, a smile playing on his lips. Gone is the stern mafia boss, and in his place is Daniil, the roguishly sexy man I met at the poker bar on our fateful first night. "It's not a business event. I figure if you're going to live in Brooklyn, you should try the best pizza the city has to offer."

"Oh." I sound like a moron, but this is so unexpected I don't have the presence of mind to question his motivations. "Give me a few minutes to get changed."

He nods. "And for the love of all that is holy please leave that animal in her crate." But he surprises me by bending down and ruffling Eris's fur, rubbing behind her ears as she wriggles all over him. Shit. Didn't expect that.

"Aren't you allergic to dogs?"

A huff of laughter passes between his lips. "Is that what Mikhail told you?"

"Yeah."

He gives me the barest of smiles, his eyes roving over my face. "Yeah, I'm really fucking allergic." With that he stands and leaves me to my increasingly turbulent thoughts.

# CHAPTER FOURTEEN

## BIANCA

DANIIL IS DRIVING, and I can't stop stealing glances at him. This is the first time I've seen him behind the wheel of a car, and it shouldn't be this sexy, should it? But the way he steers the Audi like it's an extension of himself, maneuvering through the streets of Brooklyn with exacting control, looking like a cross between a movie star and a motorcycle gang member—no, like a movie star *playing* a motorcycle gang member—is hot as hell. He's dressed down in ripped jeans and a white T-shirt that hugs every hard plane of his torso, leaving his full arm sleeves on display.

I swallow hard, and look out the window, distracting myself from ogling Daniil by watching Brooklyn come alive at night. This place has such a different vibe than Miami, but I like it. More edge, less glitz and glamor, which suits me fine. Not like I'll be here forever.

But this dinner is a step in the right direction. For whatever reason, he's softened towards me, and I'm going to take full advantage of the chance to have him open up.

Beside me, Daniil clears his throat. Turning towards him, I

catch him dragging his gaze down my body. "You look nice," he says, adjusting his position on the buttery leather seat. But the way he's looking at me doesn't suggest that *nice* is the most accurate word. More like smoking hot.

I suppress a smile as I wave my hands in front of me in a this-old-thing gesture. I'm wearing a sky-blue halter dress with the fitted top showing the perfect amount of cleavage while the defined waist gives way to a flared skirt with a slit on one side. It's not over-the-top sexy, but it shows enough skin and flatters my hourglass figure.

A rush of warmth floods my veins as I carefully cross my left thigh over my right, so he can get a peek of smooth brown thigh. If this is my only chance to seduce my husband, I am going to make the best of it.

He cracks his neck and brings his focus back to the road ahead.

Score one for me!

Daniil pulls to the curb in front of a little restaurant tucked away on a nondescript street. This is no grand steak house or five-star Michelin eatery that I imagine he frequents. Then again, looking at him tonight, he seems like a regular guy. Minus his souped-up Audi with bulletproof windows, he looks like any other handsome young Brooklynite going about their evening.

Entering the restaurant, we're whisked from the front door to a cozy table on the charming back patio. Fairy lights twinkle overhead, and red checkered tablecloths are draped beneath empty wine bottles that function as candleholders. While we're the only ones on this patio tonight, which I know was Daniil's doing, it still feels like a night out.

A waiter comes over to us, bearing water and wine, and Daniil says to him, "The usual, Sal."

"You got it, kid."

"Kid!" I scoff as Sal trudges towards the kitchen. "I take it you're a regular here?"

"You could say that." His lips turn up at the corners, and he adds, "I've been coming here for half of my life. It's one of the few places where I can relax and not feel like the world is breathing down my neck."

And yet, he brought me here. To his haven. I shouldn't read into it, but I can't help the rush of warmth that floods my system. I still don't understand what's going on here. He's attracted to me, that much is clear, but weeks of ignoring me, and now an intimate dinner? Maybe I'm being paranoid, but why the change of heart?

"So ... what gives?" I ask, taking a sip from my wineglass. "What are we doing here?"

He huffs a little laugh and runs his thumb over his bottom lip. "We're having dinner." His voice is low and sexy, like the purr of an engine, and my thighs clench together in response.

"You know what I mean," I counter.

He's quiet for a moment, staring off into the distance before his eyes find mine and something in his expression changes. "I didn't like hearing that you're unhappy, that you're lonely."

I bite back the wave of emotion his words bring on. How long has it been since someone's actually cared how I feel? I almost don't know what to do with his concern.

"It's not that I'm miserable here, or with you in particular, it's ..." *This life*. But how can I tell Daniil that? He's fully entrenched in the world I want to get far away from.

"I get it, more than you know," he says, focusing on swirling the wine in his glass.

The weight of his full attention settles heavily on me, even as a team of waiters delivers what seems to be half the menu to our table. There's pizza of course, but also eggplant Parm, Caesar salad, and spaghetti and meatballs. It all looks so good.

"Why did your uncle raise you after your parents died?" he asks, putting a slice of pepperoni on my plate.

"I didn't have a choice." I smooth the napkin in my lap and lift the slice, but don't actually eat it. It's simply an excuse to keep my hands busy while I consider how much to reveal.

"Emilio was the only living relative I had, and I was still a minor. It was either become a ward of the state or live with him."

He brings the glass of wine to his lips, and studies me over the rim. "Were you close?"

"No," I say a little too quickly, venom coating that one word. "I hadn't even met him before I was sent to live with him. My mother left Colombia when she was young. *Abuelito* had a great love for my mother and didn't want her tainted by the ugliness he was involved in. It was only getting more violent as the Colombians went to war with the Mexicans. My mother wanted out, and Florida made sense. She enrolled at the University of Miami and met my father in their journalism program, fell in love, and the rest is history. She never went back home."

A tragic history.

"Did you know about the Zegas? That your uncle ended up taking over the cartel?"

"Not really," I shrug. "My mother hinted that her brother was involved in some shady stuff, but no details. I only learned all that after ..." After it was much too late.

Daniil nods, and then holds a slice up for me to take a bite. "Here, try it. Brooklyn-style pizza. Thinner and crispier crust."

"You don't need to feed me!" I protest.

"I want to," he insists. "Open up."

I do as he says, opening my mouth and leaning forward to take a bite. His intent eyes watch me closely. Damn, as promised, this pizza is amazing.

"Printsessa," Daniil murmurs, his presence cutting into my thoughts. I press a napkin to my lips as I swallow the saucy deliciousness. "Have I told you how pretty you look with your mouth full?"

"Oh my god," I choke, reaching for my water, but he's clearly enjoying making my cheeks warm.

"Come on," he chides. "You have to admit, this pizza is pretty unreal."

"It is," I agree, though I look away from his heated stare. I try to distract myself by taking in our surroundings, the string lights twinkling overhead, the picture-perfect little table all in a row. Such a quaint place. When was the last time I had done something like this, something so normal? Just a casual dinner out. Not since coming to live with my uncle.

"So, your parents were journalists?" He leans forward, and the intensity of his attention burns my skin.

I suddenly feel exposed. I hadn't meant to share all that I had, but something about *this* Daniil—the one who takes me to a casual red-sauce joint and listens intently when I speak—is different. Still, I'm on dangerous ground here. My parents were investigative journalists, the best at what they did. But I don't want him looking too closely at them, because if he does, it won't take him long to connect the dots.

"I don't like to think about the past, to be honest." He nods, not pushing the issue. Somehow, he's asked all the questions tonight, when I'm the one who should be doing the deep dive into his life. But I'm tired of always playing this game, rather than living my life, so I ask something I am genuinely curious about. "You don't like my uncle, do you?"

The glow of candlelight glints off his light-brown hair, casting a shadow under his cut cheekbones as he takes a slow sip of his drink. "I don't know your uncle enough to dislike him."

"You don't trust him or Jorge. Our wedding was proof enough. I want to know why."

"I don't trust anyone," he says with a frown. But there's something behind his words I don't buy.

"Including me?"

With a finger under my chin, he tilts my face up. "You most of all, printsessa."

"Just because I didn't want to marry you? Because I wanted to stay with Jorge?" I lean in close, so he doesn't miss my words. "Better the devil you know than the devil you don't know. Ever hear that expression? For all I knew, you could have been the worse choice."

His eyes drop to my lips. "And am I?"

I swallow hard. "No." Not even close.

The truth of my words hits me directly in the solar plexus. Whatever Daniil is, and I haven't made my mind up about him yet, he's not what I expected. And I mean that in the best possible way.

WE'RE both quiet in the car on the way back to the penthouse. But as we approach his building, I feel his eyes on me, studying me with interest.

"What?" I say finally.

"I have to tell you something," he says, pulling up to the curb. "I'm working with Días, laundering money through the casino. It was part of the deal made with your uncle when he insisted we marry."

"Oh," I say, keeping my voice steady. A weight pushes down on my chest as I meet his heavy gaze.

My arms break out in goose bumps. I've refused to think about Jorge being here in Brooklyn. It was easy to put it out of my mind while locked up in the penthouse all day, but Daniil's words are a reminder that I haven't escaped Jorge's grasp. Not yet.

Should I warn Daniil to keep his guard up around Jorge? If I do, will he be more protective about sharing information with me? Diedre's advice comes back to me; there are growing pains in any new partnership, a higher chance of them screwing up and revealing something. And that's what I want. The sooner they mess up, the sooner this will all be over.

I take a deep breath, ignoring all the thoughts churning in my head like a twister. "It's business," I say with a shrug. "Jorge is my uncle's most trusted lieutenant."

"I don't like how he looks at you." His gruff voice catches my attention. I meet his gaze, and good god, he is sexy when he's angry. *Smoldering* might be the word for it. "He doesn't get to touch what's mine. And you are mine, never forget that." His hand shoots out to wrap around the nape of my neck, holding me in place.

The air between us is charged, as combustible as a flick of a lighter in a dry forest, and our inferno would rage bigger and hotter than a hundred-acre wildfire. I try to suppress the shudder that moves through me, but it's no use. He doesn't miss a thing.

"Say it, printsessa. Who do you belong to?" His breath fans across my lips like a warm breeze as he awaits my response.

"I belong to no one." I won't say the words even as I wear Daniil's ring on my finger.

"Wrong answer."

And then his lips are slanted over mine. His kiss is hard and demanding, like he's testing me. But I kiss him back, digging my fingers into his back. I feel half out of my mind. Drugged by him. Seduction may have been part of my plan, but right now, my only thought is getting the sweet relief my body craves.

My heart rate ratchets up at the way his lips brush over mine, his tongue invading my mouth. Shit, he can kiss. I may not have much experience, but whatever he's doing feels really good. As I release a moan, he captures my bottom lip between his own, sucking hard, nearly to the point of pain. Just when I can't take it anymore, he groans and licks my lips. The sound of his enjoyment is enough to make me claw at his chest, trying to bring him closer, wanting more of him in a way I barely understand. All I know for sure is that my panties are soaked, and I need him. Need more of him.

But an aggressive horn blast brings me back to earth. We've been making out like two horny teenagers in the front seat of his car on a busy Brooklyn street. What was I thinking?

Daniil pulls back with a satisfied smile. "It's okay," he assures me, "the windows are tinted. Now, let's try that again. Who do you belong to? And, printsessa, if I don't like your answer, I'll be taking you over my knee."

*Alrighty then.* The logical thing to do would be to agree, I mean, I'm trying to seduce the man for Christ's sake. But my stubborn pride won't allow it.

"Can I think about it?" I smooth my dress down my legs and attempt to fix my hair. For whom, I don't know. I'm simply trying to put myself back together after ... well, whatever that was.

He shifts in his seat, running a hand over the back of his neck. His voice is rough and husky when he says, "Don't think too hard. There is only one right answer." He glances towards the windshield before his gaze locks back onto me. "I have to go to the casino now, something came up."

Disappointment hangs heavy on my shoulders. He has to go *now*? After what we just started? I'm not sure what possesses me, but I find myself turning in my seat, notching up my chin. "Can I come with you?" He shakes his head, but I press on. "Please. Don't make me go back up there. I won't be a bother. I'll stay in your office, or wherever you tell me to stay, I just don't want to be alone."

He blows out a heavy breath and lifts his eyes to the ceiling. "It's not a good idea."

"Please," I say with all the sweetness I can muster. My voice might be pure sugar, but my hand lands in his lap, grasping his still hard cock through his pants.

"Fuuuuck," he hisses. I feel him twitch and my confidence grows with his heated response, so I grab him more forcefully. Whatever I'm doing now, he seems to like. He groans, as if in pain, and then stills my hand with his own, he says, "If you keep doing that, printsessa, I'm going to shoot in my pants."

Fire lights my skin at his words. At the thought of how we'd taste together, smell together, just the thought of our juices mixing. I clench my thighs and hope it's enough to calm my raging hormones. Daniil's finger trails down my neck to land at my pulse point. He smiles a big genuine smile when he feels my blood pounding through my veins.

"I'm gonna regret this, but fuck it," he whispers before reaching over to buckle me in. Then, throwing the car into drive, he tears away from the curb. City lights illuminate Daniil's Adam's apple and defined cheekbones. My pulse stutters as I realize that for a brief moment, he wanted me as much as I wanted him. And it was real.

Tonight, I'm happy not to be alone, trapped in a glass cage in the sky. It hadn't occurred to me until now that this is a way to get closer to him, a way to unravel his secrets. That is, if I can stay awake long enough to find anything out. Between the carbs, wine, and excitement of that kiss, I'm feeling drowsy and relaxed. Maybe for once I'll let myself just be and appreciate the night for what it is, a chance to let down my guard and enjoy the company of the man I'm married to.

# CHAPTER FIFTEEN

## DANIIL

I SCRUB a hand over my tired face and allow myself one more tiny glance at Bianca. It's only the millionth time I've snuck a peek at her, but she is especially beautiful when she sleeps. Scratch that, I find her breathtaking all the time.

Blyad. When have I ever waxed poetic about someone's beauty? I sound like fucking Romeo over here. Pathetic.

The door to my office opens and when I see Leo, I wave him in, putting a finger to my lips and pointing to Bianca curled up on the couch, my jacket draped over her. His eyes understandably widen in surprise, because only a day ago, I was actively avoiding anything Bianca. But that was before.

Before she broke me down. Before I *let her* break me down. Because if I'm going to be honest with myself, the minute I saw her from across the casino floor, something inside me knew she was mine. I've been fighting the magnetic pull between us for so long, it's impossible to resist anymore.

More than that, I don't want to.

I know she's keeping secrets from me. Hiding skeletons in

her closet that one day I will unearth. I just hope they aren't big enough to break us apart.

Leo sits across from me at my desk. He takes a cigar out of his pocket, but then glances at Bianca and seems to think better of lighting up.

"This is an unexpected sight." He gives me a little smile. "I take it to mean you're on better terms."

I kick my feet up on my desk and avoid his question. "It's unexpected for me, too. She didn't want to be alone."

When I'd agreed to let her come to the casino with me, it was under the condition that she didn't leave my office unless escorted by me, a condition she happily agreed to. We got here around midnight, and after five minutes of looking around my office, she settled in front of the television, eventually closing her eyes and drifting to sleep.

A pang tugs at my chest at how content she seems to simply *not* be alone. She must have been left alone a lot in her life. At least after she went to live with her uncle.

Leo nods in understanding, his intense gaze fixed on me. " Días just got here," he says, gesturing to the large monitor on my wall. "VIP poker room." I pick up the remote, and flip to the correct security camera. Jorge and his posse of Zegas appear on-screen. There's nothing unusual about this, the Zegas are in here every night, but the knowledge Días is near makes the hair on my arms stand on end. "You still don't trust him." It's not a question, Leo is stating a fact.

"Not even a little. I don't know what his endgame is." Bianca releases a little sigh in her sleep, and both of us look over at her, still curled up peacefully. "No, fuck that. I do know his endgame. It's her."

"Fuck," he mutters under his breath. "You think he would cross Emilio to get her back? He's not that stupid, is he?"

I scratch my neck in thought. "He's not stupid, he's vengeful —which is worse. Much worse."

My eyes flick to the monitor. The VIP room has gotten

increasingly rowdy since the last time I looked. Tonight is a party night. The Zegas are letting loose. Drinks are flowing, girls are milling about in various states of undress while a poker game is underway in the middle of the room.

As if we have a psychic connection, Días looks up at the security camera, a wasted stripper on his lap. He smirks, holding eye contact with the camera as if he knows I'm looking right at him in this moment. It sends a chill down my spine. This guy is a fucking loose cannon, and I don't want him in the same building, much less the same city, as Bianca ever again.

With a final menacing grin, Jorge turns back to the game in front of him, pushing the girl off his lap like the dick he is.

"He might be slippery as fuck," Leo says, interrupting my thoughts, "but he hasn't actually done anything yet. We have to bide our time and wait until he screws up before we can deal with him properly."

Leo might be right, but when I look over at Bianca, hair fanned out behind her, parted lips, looking even younger than her twenty-one years, I decide I don't like that idea very much. *Wait and see* means we're vulnerable, like sitting ducks, and that's not my style. "No, fuck that. We need a different approach."

Leo leans back in his chair, folding his hands behind his head as he observes me. "I'm listening."

"We need to set him up. If he has intentions of messing with us, let's make it happen sooner than later."

Leo raises his eyebrows. "Are you suggesting using Bianca as a lure?"

"That's not at all what I was suggesting," I respond, jaw clenched.

He chuckles, holding up a hand. "Shit, don't bite my head off. Deny it all you want, but if he's going to do something stupid, it's gonna be over her."

"I don't like it," I grind out, but I also know my brother is probably right. There's a reason he's in charge of spying and intel for the family. "But let's say for argument's sake I agreed, what would you suggest we do?"

He sighs and swipes a hand over the back of his neck. "You told me that Kira is organizing a girls' night out for Bianca. We leak the time and place to the Zegas." I shake my head, but he holds up a finger to let him finish. "We send them to one of our clubs, we have the place surrounded by our men, we'll be there. If Jorge shows up ... well, that says something."

I hate this idea, but I hate sitting back and waiting for him to make a move even more. It's true what they say—the best defense is a good offense.

"We keep this between us," I say tightly.

Leo stands and straightens his tie, his eyes flicking towards Bianca. "Then don't tell her."

"I don't want Andrei to know either. He thinks I'm overreacting about working with Días as it is."

Leo pauses with his hand on the doorknob, turning towards me. "Are you sure? Georgia will be there. If anything happened to her, Andrei would rearrange your face."

Rolling a pen through my fingers, I cock an eyebrow. "There's no risk to them ... you said so yourself."

"Crazy motherfucker" is the last thing he mumbles before exiting my office.

He's right about that. I am feeling crazy.

Pouring myself a whisky, I get up and perch on the coffee table beside the couch where Bianca is sleeping. We should get out of here, but I don't want to wake her. More than that, I'm not sure what's supposed to happen next. Judging by tonight, she doesn't hate me as much as she once did.

And fuck, I like it when she doesn't hate me. That kiss was everything I thought it would be and more. Way more.

It was deep and hot and wet. Eager and hungry. Jesus, feeling her body against mine ... soft, pliable, so fuckable ... it took every ounce of willpower not to throw her in the back seat and rail her silly.

But I didn't.

Call it a crisis of conscience or just plain stupidity on my part, but whatever grain of trust has sprouted between us needs time to grow, and fucking her, especially the way I like to fuck, would only complicate our fragile bond.

Watching her sleep now, something foreign squeezes in my chest. I'm protective of her. That's all it is, I'm sure. She wears my ring after all.

Whatever is about to go down with Días has the potential to be messy, and I don't want her caught in the cross fire. I sweep a hand through my hair as reality hits. The best way to protect her is to keep her at arm's length until I've worked out what the hell is going on. And that means putting a stop to whatever we started tonight.

Downing the rest of the amber liquid, I settle into my office chair and turn my attention back to the VIP room's monitor. Jorge is still deep into the game, a new half-naked woman gyrating on his lap.

All I can do now is play the game and wait for Días to fuck up. And when he does, I'm gonna take him down so hard he won't know what hit him.

# CHAPTER SIXTEEN

## BIANCA

"Your dog is a menace."

I look up from my book to find Mikhail in front of me on the terrace, his face as sour as if he'd been sucking on a lemon.

"Oh, no," I sigh audibly. Putting my book down on the chaise, I lift my sunglasses up off my face. "What did she do this time?"

"She got into Daniil's office." Mikhail hits me with a warning look. "Made a real mess. He won't be happy."

"Of course," I say acting contrite. "I'll deal with this. It shouldn't be Nadia's problem." Nadia has neither the time nor patience for my "mutt," as she not very affectionately calls Eris. Who can blame her? It's not the first time Eris has gone somewhere she shouldn't and flipped on her mini-weapon-of-mass-destruction button. In truth, it's not Eris's fault. It's entirely mine.

"Nadia is out running errands. You have fifteen minutes before she returns and tattles on you." He lights a cigarette and heads to the edge of the balcony to watch the world and smoke. I smile at his back. He might try to deny it, but Mikhail—a hardened bratva with a sense of humor as dry as toast—has a soft spot for Eris.

"That dog," I mutter as I wander into the apartment and track down Eris in Daniil's office, still rummaging through his garbage.

"Oh, Eris," I exclaim, loud enough for Mikhail to hear. But when I enter the room and drop down beside her, I whisper in her ear, "Good girl. You really nailed it this time." She wags her tail and buries her head into my lap. I must admit, this dog might be naughty as hell, but she really is worming her way into my heart.

Giving her one final pet, I start the laborious cleanup process. She really did trash the place but cleaning up gives me an excuse to be in his office for longer than a few moments. Daniil rarely works from home, but after weeks of being here, it's the only room I haven't been able to search in earnest. I was able to go through his bedroom earlier this week after Eris went on a real spree, apparently garbage cans are her enemy. But honestly, his bedroom is like a mausoleum. Or maybe a hotel. The point being it's barely lived in, contains few personal effects, and there's nothing of use to the FBI unless they want to know what kind of shaving cream or deodorant the guy wears.

And let's be honest, while the feds don't care what he smells like, I admit to taking a healthy sniff of his delicious aftershave —musky, citrusy, masculine. And all Daniil. His scent makes me lightheaded; like a hit of drugs, it blasts straight through my veins.

I force myself to pull it together, internally chiding my libido for going around craving his scent. Here I am swooning over his aftershave when he's decided I'm not even worth the effort. He's gone back to being ice-cold after our date. Working all the time. Barely seeing or speaking to me, other than in passing. Stupid me, I thought we'd shared something that night, something unexpected. The worst part is at some point during that dinner I stopped focusing on what I need to learn about the Kozlovs and just focused on getting to know Daniil as a person. And I like what I saw there. Behind the stern bratva mask, there is someone real. Warm. Compassionate. Sexy as sin.

And that kiss ...

Jesus, I still see stars when I think of his mouth on mine.

But I also know it meant nothing to him.

I give my head a little shake. He doesn't deserve a moment more of my thoughts. Tossing a squeaky toy towards Eris, I kneel down to collect the papers strewn across the floor. I make quick work of it, glancing at each piece of paper as I pick it up and add it to the pile in my hands. I'm not sure what I'm looking for, but I hope I'll know when I see it.

But they all contain numbers. Random numbers that do not make a lick of sense to me. The numbers are organized into columns and rows, but with no words, how is anyone supposed to interpret what they mean? After ten minutes of organizing and sorting, and doing some extra tidying up, I have found nothing of value. Or at least what I think could be of value. I decide to take a few sheets anyway, folding them in quarters, and stuffing them under the back waistband of my pants.

Deidre contacted me last night and asked for an in-person meeting this week. While we communicate using the FBI's encrypted messaging platform, face-to-face meetings are preferred and much less risky. She wants an update, and I'd like to give her something—anything—to go on. Because as it stands, not only do I have no leads for her, I also don't really know Daniil. He's still barely more than a stranger to me.

"What's going on?"

As if I conjured him with my thoughts, he stands in the doorway to his office, all six-foot-something of him, looking stern and menacing. I startle at his presence, pressing a hand to my chest. The reaction is one hundred percent real, but what I say next requires all my acting skills.

"The dog," I say rather breathlessly. "She got into your office. Sorry about that." A muscle ticks in his jaw as his eyes land on the stack of paper in my hand. "Just tidying up the mess she made."

He's quiet for a few moments. Staring at me. Assessing. It takes major willpower not to allow my eyes to wander from him. Looking away would be an admittance of guilt. Maintain eye contact, don't swallow, keep your breathing normal—it's what Deidre instilled in me right from the start.

I must be convincing enough because Daniil nods and purses his lips. "This dog needs training," he gestures towards Eris, now pawing at his leg. "Nadia texts me daily updates about his bad behavior."

My back stiffens. I don't know what I find more offensive, that Nadia texts him on the regular, or that she tattles on my dog. "Is that why you're home in the middle of the day? To check up on my dog?"

His lips twitch. "That's not why. But you have to admit, Eris is trouble."

"It's not her fault." I straighten, feeling stupidly defensive of my dog who I *named chaos*. "She's still a puppy. The breeder said she would calm down when she's older."

He moves farther into the room, like a panther stalking through his kingdom, and pointedly takes the papers from my hands, laying them on the desk. "Her behavior will improve when you send her to obedience school. How did she get in here, anyway? I always leave the door closed," he grumbles, but his eyes are on me. My throat, my mouth, my entire face. This master poker player is studying me, watching for my tells.

I fight the urge to swallow. "Nadia must have left the door open when she was cleaning earlier." *Lie.*

"I'll talk to her about that."

I smile even as a nervous shiver trickles down my spine. "I'm sorry if Eris messed up anything in here. I'll watch her more closely," I promise, hurrying to scoop up my dog.

Daniil seems to accept my explanation at face value, which is both comforting and alarming. Have I become that good a liar?

The papers shoved down my pants are burning a hole in my lower back, and I need to head to my room so I can compose myself, because right now, I'm feeling way off balance.

Before I can make a hasty exit, he crooks a finger at me and growls, "Come here."

I turn slowly, my mouth dry, my heart in my throat. "Why?"

"Because I want you to."

A bead of sweat runs down my back. "That's not a good enough reason," I challenge, fighting to keep my voice steady. I hug Eris tighter to my chest knowing if I put her down, he'll see the tremor in my hands.

But then he does something surprising. He buries a hand in his hair and gives it a little tug. That's his tell. He's nervous about something. "Fine," he grits. "I'm sorry I haven't been around more. I told you I was working with Días, and ... there's stuff going on."

I wait for the other shoe to drop. For him to call me out on my subterfuge. But instead, he blinks down at me, waiting for a response. Shit. Is Daniil nervous about apologizing to me? He doesn't strike me as a man who says sorry very often.

I lean against the doorframe and rub behind Eris's ears. The motion is as soothing for me as it is for her. "Like what? What stuff is going on?"

"Nothing you have to worry about."

I roll my eyes. I hate that *don't worry your pretty little head about it* bullshit. "That's not helpful," I say before huffing out a breath of frustration.

"Fuck," he bites out under his breath. "I'm not good at this. I ... I can't tell you everything that's going on. It's the way it is being married to a vor. I'll tell you what I can when I can."

I nod because I don't trust my voice right now. Concerned my eyes are mirrors into my lying, scheming soul, I let my gaze drop to his lips. And what a fine pair of lips they are, that defined Cupid's bow. Just pouty enough to still be masculine.

And soft. Perfect, really. The memory of his lips on mine still plays in my head often.

Too often.

"One more thing," he adds, shuffling the papers on his desk. His attention had already moved on. "Kira is organizing a girls' night out this weekend. She'll fill you in on the details. Just wanted to give you a heads-up."

"Really!" I didn't expect to be so excited about plans to go out, but I suppose that speaks to how freakin' bored I am here. "This calls for a shopping spree. I wonder where I left your no-limit credit card?" I tap a finger on my chin.

Daniil leans forward, two hands spread wide on his desk as he drinks me in from head to toe. "I remember exactly where I left it. Let me know if you need a reminder."

I raise one saucy eyebrow before spinning on my heel and leaving him to his memories.

# CHAPTER SEVENTEEN

## BIANCA

MY EYES PEEL OPEN, and I shoot out of bed as if it's on fire.

Holy shit. How could I forget?

I'm supposed to meet Deidre today. Our first in-person meeting since I became Daniil's wife, and it completely slipped my mind for no good reason other than my bed is extra warm and cozy and I'm curled up with Eris. She might be a demon during the day, but at night she is a pure angel, snuggling with me like the only thing she needs to survive is my body heat.

See, who needs a man when you have a dog?

Rousing Eris beside me, I let her out of my room while I shower and hurriedly dress, then head to the kitchen to find Mikhail and Timofey sitting at the breakfast table with mugs of coffee. Eris, for once, is calmly playing with one of her chew toys in the corner.

"Good morning," I say cheerily, pouring myself a cup of coffee. "I'd like to go shopping today. There's a little boutique on the Upper East Side that does private fittings. They'll close the shop for me."

Stoic as ever, the two guards nod, and Timofey asks for the

name of the store so they can run it through their database. I don't even know what that means, but I'm happy to oblige. They'll find no threats. Deidre will have made sure of it.

An hour later, we pull up to the curb in front of a boutique called Boutique Amber. Located in a former architect's townhouse, it's both glam and funky at the same time. I step out of the car, flanked by my two guards. Wearing an above-the-knee Diane von Furstenberg wrap dress, tall heels, dark sunglasses, and blood-red lips, I feel every inch the mafia printsessa that Daniil accuses me of being.

As planned, the store is empty except for the manager, a man who introduces himself as Marco. Stepping forward, he takes my hand. "Madam Kozlov," he says in a thick Italian accent, "a personal stylist is waiting for you in one of the private fitting rooms."

I nod, and allow him to lead me towards the back, both guards hot on my heels. Right before Marco opens the door to the room I'm to meet Deidre in, I turn towards my hulking shadows. Pointing at two luxurious armchairs near the door, I say, "Best to wait for me here." Mikhail and Timofey exchange a look, unsure how to handle my suggestion. "I don't think my husband would appreciate you watching me change," I say, eyebrow arched, but Mikhail stands his ground.

"We need to clear the room first," he insists. "It'll only take a minute."

"Of course," I grumble. Perhaps my uncle's guards were less careful, but this has never happened before. Still, when Mikhail enters the small, elegant space, Deidre turns from the mannequin she is dressing and greets him with a friendly smile.

She's looking all New York high fashion in leather pants, a gauzy gray blouse, and high boots. It's a far cry from her usual jeans and blazer. Her braids are pulled back into a sleek bun, and her majestic cheekbones are highlighted with a swipe of blush. I never noticed how lovely she is, but it turns out Deidre is a babe.

As Mikhail clears each corner, I go through the charade of

introducing myself to her and explaining some outfits I'm looking for.

"Wonderful," she replies, taking me over to the racks of clothes laid out against one wall. "I think you'll find much of what you're looking for here."

As I rifle through the racks of designer clothes, Mikhail gives me a tiny nod. "We'll be right outside," he says, and it sounds like a warning as much as it does an assurance of my safety.

Once he exits, Deidre's expression loses some of that effortless charm, and the hardened FBI agent emerges. "How are you?" she asks, getting straight to the point.

"I'm doing ..." Man, I don't know how to finish that sentence. Confused by my feelings for my new husband, bored, lonely, unsure if I can really be useful to the FBI, though I'm still desperate for revenge. But I say none of that. I settle on, "I'm doing alright."

"Good," she says, carefully eyeing me. "Is Daniil treating you fairly?"

I feel myself blush, so I quickly look away. My eyes land on the decorative tin ceiling before I can meet her gaze again. "Yeah. He's actually not that bad."

A small smile stretches across her lips. "I see. So that's how it is," she teases, lifting her eyebrows suggestively. "Good. Whatever brings you closer. Did you learn anything of interest?"

Her questioning gaze meets my own, and a sheen of sweat breaks out at my nape. "We haven't done that ... yet," I validate, my cheeks blazing. "He's still wary of me. But we'll get there soon."

Unable to stand the awkwardness of this moment, I turn around and busy myself hunting through the contents of the rack in front of me. I tug out something silver and shiny, holding it up in front of me in the mirror.

"Shopping for an event?" Deidre comes up behind me. We lock eyes in the mirror, and I know she's studying me, weighing everything I'm not saying.

"Look, I have something for you," I say, remembering the papers that I stole from Daniil's office earlier this week. Retrieving my purse, I offer Deidre the crumpled papers with the random numbers running in columns throughout. "I managed to get into his home office," I explain.

She stares at the papers, her brows drawing together. "What is this?"

"I don't know." I shrug. "I thought you could tell."

Her mouth drops into a frown. "We're going to need more than this, Bianca."

I tug at my hair. "Like what?"

Her lips twist in thought. "I understand Jorge is in town and working with the Kozlovs. What's he doing?"

I hesitate for the barest of moments, and Deidre notices. But I force myself to blurt out what I know. "The casino. The Kozlovs are laundering Zega money."

She nods. "As we thought. But it's nearly impossible to prove. The dirty money gets mixed up with the clean so fast in a casino there is no way to know where it all came from. It's not enough."

I rub my temples, feeling oddly defensive. "I'm doing my best," I argue. "I even got a crazy-ass dog so I'd have an excuse to poke around in places I wouldn't otherwise have an excuse to poke around in."

"I understand, and I know you're doing everything in your power to be useful"—she levels me with a sobering stare—"but now the real work begins."

I knew this was coming. They want something more concrete to go on, but that can't fall completely on my shoulders, can it? Grabbing the papers had already been too close of a call. My breath catches remembering how Daniil nearly caught me stuffing the sheets of paper down my pants.

She hands me a small black case. I grip it with hands that have gone cold and clammy. "What is this?" I ask, but even before the words are out of my mouth, I know.

I open the case only to find exactly what I expected. Four

tiny black listening devices lay encased in gray Styrofoam. I don't know what I expected them to look like, but it's not this. They're smaller than a baby's fingernail.

"A micro spy bug," Deidre confirms. "Tiny but it has hundreds of hours of battery power and, most importantly, is undetectable by electronic sweeps."

All I know is if I'm found with it, I'm a dead woman. "You want me to bug our home?" I ask, dread coiling low in my belly. For some reason, this seems worse than anything I've done before. "I'm sure they use some sort of audio jammers to avoid this kind of thing. Can't you tap their phones?"

She shakes her head. "We tried, they gave nothing away. You'll need to plant them in his home office, casino office, anywhere he conducts business that you can gain access to."

"You don't understand," I breathe, grabbing her arm. "I don't have access to anywhere Daniil works. He keeps me separate, locked away from his world. He doesn't trust me as it is. Me demanding to visit his office or slinking around where I'm not supposed to, it'll be obvious I'm up to something."

Deidre's face is impassive as she leads me to the couch in the corner of the room. We sit side by side, and she gives me a moment to compose myself.

"I know it seems like we're asking the impossible of you, but you are a strong woman. I know what you're capable of. You've lived through your uncle and Jorge, and now you'll live through this." She pauses for a moment. "I wish I could help you avenge your family's death without expecting anything in return, but that's not how we work."

"But the Kozlovs have nothing to do with my uncle. He's a monster ... they're not like that." I swallow hard and cross my arms over my chest, feeling self-conscious that I'm defending the Kozlovs.

"They are cold-blooded killers, Bianca. Make no mistake, they aren't good people." She stands and smooths down her stylish ensemble. "Your uncle and the Kozlovs, they're a package deal now. If you want to see your uncle behind bars, I suggest focusing on what you can learn from your husband."

My hands curl by my sides, nails digging into my flesh. I knew this was coming, so I can't comprehend why it feels so scary. In the early days, Deidre trained me on the basics of planting bugs and other necessities. I thought I'd never have to employ that skill, but I guess I thought wrong.

"How am I supposed to use these?" I ask, defeat weighing on my shoulders.

"Instructions are in the case. I'll have Marco pack them into one of the many boxes of designer clothes you'll be taking home. Make sure you insist on unpacking them yourself."

Diedre stands, clapping her hands and loudly exclaims, "That dress looks beautiful on you, Mrs. Kozlov. The royal blue really sets off your complexion."

I take the hideous dress she pushes into my hands. "Yes, thank you," I say, my voice flat. "It's perfect."

"I'm glad I can be of service." She nods, catching my eye. "Until we meet again."

"Until we meet again," I echo.

It's me against the Kozlovs. I'll have to find a way to get right with the way the feds need this to play out. If Daniil and his brothers walk free, so does my uncle. It's all or nothing.

Time to ante up.

# CHAPTER EIGHTEEN

## BIANCA

THE CLUB IS DARK, loud, and filled with beautiful people dancing, talking, posing, and trying to get the attention of other beautiful people. I'm high above it all, watching in fascination from the open balcony of Stereo's VIP area. I've never been to a nightclub like this, and I've never been on a girls' night like I am now with Kira, Georgia, Alyona, and Rowan.

It's a night for firsts. *Yeah, first time partying in the name of pumping my new family for info.* I hate myself a little bit for it, but what choice do I have? I've planted two of the bugs in the penthouse—one behind a bookshelf in the study where Daniil often nurses a late-night whisky and another under a lampshade in his bedroom. A room I have yet to be invited into.

Truth is, bugging his penthouse is useless. Daniil is barely home, and even when he is, I sense he's careful to never utter a word of bratva business within the penthouse walls. Maybe his car would be a promising spot, but even that he rotates regularly, so I never know which vehicle he'll be in. And perhaps he talks freely in the casino office, but it doesn't seem like I'm getting an invitation back there anytime soon.

With limited choices, and Deidre breathing down my neck, Kira's invitation may be my best bet at learning something—*anything*—that I could feed to the feds. God knows alcohol loosens lips sufficiently.

"Tequila time, bitches!"

I turn away from the balcony to find Kira approaching with a tray of shots that she lowers onto our table. The plan is for all of us to get stupid forget-your-worries drunk ... except that's not what I'll be doing. I need to keep my wits about me, and to do that, I need to be sober, but I don't see how I can turn down the first shot of the night without seeming like a total stick-in-the-mud.

As we crowd around our table, Kira raises her glass and locks eyes with me. "To Bianca becoming a Kozlov and finding a man that I hope makes you happy. Even though he's my brother and it's gross, I hope you are having a lot of amazing newlywed sex."

I nearly choke as cheers erupt, and the girls do the ritual lick, sip, suck. If she only knew. Not only have we not had sex, but Daniil hasn't touched me in a week, not since our date. He's gone back to treating me like a guest in his house. I thought we were past him freezing me out, but apparently not.

Well, screw him. I made sure to buy the teeniest, tiniest, most risqué dress I could find, spending his money like it's going out of style, like I'd promised I would the day I moved to New York. Not that he'll blink at the twenty-thousand-dollar charge but seeing me all done up and ready to hit the club sure made him do a double take.

Triumph slams into my gut recalling how his eyes darkened to a shade of onyx, his jaw held so tight I thought it would break when he opened the door to the penthouse tonight as I applied a deadly shade of red lipstick in the front hallway mirror. I'd put a short Burberry trench over it, so all he saw was my fishnet-stocking-covered legs and four-inch red Louboutins.

As he'd stood in the doorway with a beastly presence, his

words came out low but with an edge of danger. "You need to change."

My eyes cut to his in the mirror. "I don't think so," I replied breezily, purposely applying another layer on to my parted lips, moving in slow-mo. A thrill cut through me as his hands balled into fists. He eyed my coat like he had X-ray vision and could see what was underneath.

Dropping my lipstick into my clutch, I turned towards the doorway he was blocking with his considerable frame. "If you don't mind, I'd like to get through," I hissed.

"By all means." He moved over an inch, giving me maybe half a foot to squeeze by him. Fucker. But this was my opening, and I was going to take it. Facing him, I pressed my back to the doorway in an attempt to squeeze through, but a brutal hand shot out to grip my hip and his powerful leg pressed up between my thighs, halting my progression. My breath caught in my throat. He was watching me, just as I was watching him.

"What do you have on under there?" he growled against my racing pulse.

"Wouldn't you like to know."

My snappy response earned me his leg pressed tighter into my core, setting my blood to steam, not in anger, in pure lust. The trench, along with my dress, was now hitched up around my waist, and I was riding his thigh. Not by choice, but he had me trapped.

My spine went rigid against the frame as something sizzling and needy filled the space between my legs. My clit throbbed with the pressure his leg provided, and I moaned against my will. His lips twisted, and a smile like sin grew on his handsome face. Slowly, so slowly, he raised his leg further, rubbing it firmly between my thighs, threatening to crack my resolve.

But he doesn't get to play hot and cold with me. My mother always told me to never chase a man, to let him come running after me. So I forced myself back down to earth. "Fuck off," I hissed.

For the briefest of moments, I thought Daniil might keep me trapped there until I took my orgasm on his leg, but the ding of the elevator and Mikhail's presence in the hallway seemed to stir him awake.

I pushed off his leg, and twisted from his grasp, eyes trained straight ahead on my escape. As I looked past Mikhail, I busied myself by smoothing down my dress, praying that my makeup was thick enough to hide the deep blush I was sure must be straining my skin.

Before I could put any proper distance between us, Daniil's giant hand reached out and collared my wrist. I stopped in place but didn't turn to make eye contact. He could say whatever to my back. "Be careful tonight. Don't go anywhere without Mikhail."

I hadn't bothered acknowledging his words before stomping into the elevator, my heart beating an unsteady rhythm.

Kira's voice in my ear brings me back down to earth. She sits beside me, half shouting over the thumping electronic music. "I haven't known my brother that long, but seriously, I never really took him as the marrying type. It's nice to see him, you know, settle down."

"Right, you mentioned that the morning we met," I say, although that morning in Daniil's penthouse feels like a lifetime ago. "What's the story there?

Kira tilts her head my way. "Daniil didn't tell you our family history?"

"No," I mumble, feeling foolish. I'm grateful the others are too wrapped up in their own conversation to overhear. "We haven't had much time to discuss family history."

"Shit, right." Kira brushes a hand through her hair and raises her voice over the thumping beat. "My brothers and I share a mother. My biological father—I'll call him *the seed* because that's the only recognition he deserves—was actually a rival of the Kozlovs. He seduced our mother and got her pregnant with me. When I was born, he sent me to Europe where I was raised by my aunt or in boarding schools. Anyhow, it's a long and fucked-up history. I didn't even know I had siblings ... but when Andrei, Daniil, and Leo found out they had a half sister, they went searching for me. Didn't give up until they found me."

"Whoa." I sit back in my seat, stunned. "That must have been quite the reunion."

She laughs and shakes her head. "You don't know the half of it.

I owe my life to my brothers ... and Georgia," she adds, tipping her head at our sister-in-law talking animatedly with the others.

"Really?" I'm a bit shocked that Daniil has told me none of this, but of course, I haven't asked. And maybe it's because there's a teeny tiny part of me that's hurt by his rejection—which makes no freakin' sense considering the only reason I'm even married to him is to bring him down. And yet, my body throbs for something I can't quite put into words.

"It's true," Kira confirms. "But all that matters is we're together now, and life is pretty good."

I nod, making a mental note to share this detail with Deidre. I consider pumping Kira for more details but think better of it. The night is young, still plenty of time to get them talking.

Kira leans heavily into my side. "I know the whole arranged marriage thing is weird, but Daniil is crazy about you, I can tell."

I shrug and reach for the mocktail I'd ordered earlier, stirring the drink with a straw. "It's been an adjustment," I admit. Total understatement.

She nods knowingly. "It'll take time. These arranged mafia marriages are kind of nuts."

Beside Kira, Alyona leans towards us, having picked up the tail end of our conversation. "Now what is this about arranged marriages?"

I laugh. "We're talking about me. I assume you are a modern and liberated woman, free to do whatever you please?"

Alyona's beautiful arched eyebrows pull together. She looks

like she's fresh off a catwalk with her feline features, lithe body, and insane style. In the limo on the way here, she'd explained how she lives in Paris as a fashion buyer for a major European luxury store but visits her brother and sister-in-law in New York whenever she can.

"I have no plans to get married, and if I did, it definitely would not be to someone connected to the brotherhood," she says, her eyes growing dark as her ruby lips fall into a frown. "I stay far away from all this nasty business."

Alyona holds her body tense; something about this conversation has struck a nerve, maybe because her father died in the line of duty, having served Daniil's father when he was the pakhan.

Rowan throws her arm around Alyona and smiles. "My super independent sister-in-law, if you only knew what you were missing. Marriage is not *all* work … there's lots of play as well." Rowan flashes a devious smile, her red hair spilling around her shoulders like the vixen I suspect she is.

"Oh my god, enough talk of marriage." Georgia stands, flipping her nearly black waves behind her shoulder. "Tonight is about us, not them. And I think it's time we broke a sweat. Down there." She points to the mass of writhing bodies on the dance floor below. It's like a snake pit when compared to the sparse and orderly dance floor in the VIP room.

But it certainly looks more fun … not that I'm here to have fun.

All eyes land on Georgia.

"You sure that's a good idea?" Alyona looks doubtful. "Might Andrei have something to say about that?"

"He might." Georgia's Cheshire grin suggests she doesn't care. "But he's not here. Besides, it's his club, only someone on a suicide mission would try anything here. And don't forget our ever-present shadows." She gestures to the half dozen guards surreptitiously surrounding us.

"I like it!" Rowan pipes up. I can practically see the devil horns sprouting from the side of her head. These women are trying to goad their husbands on purpose, and not only do I like their style, but it gives me an idea.

Running my hands down the length of my miniature sequined dress, I announce to the group that I'll be back in a moment, and head towards the luxuriously appointed ladies' room, all smoky mirrors, gold accents and dark velvet wallpaper. There is a full-length mirror on one side of the restroom, and I take a moment to pose, finding the perfect position that shows off my assets. My legs aren't in fact long, but this itty-bitty dress and sky-high heels give the appearance of length, and of course, Daniil never got to see the plunging neckline on this sparkly number. Perhaps it wouldn't be quite as revealing on someone else, but with my curvy figure, the dress looks sexy as hell. Something Daniil will not appreciate judging by our earlier exchange.

Having found just the right pose in the mirror, I snap a selfie, and text it to Daniil. No words needed. He wanted to know what I was wearing tonight, here's his answer. I smile to myself. Let him try to ignore that! I might be a few drinks in—especially if I count the champagne we had in the limo—but it's not liquid courage fueling me right now. I'm sending him a message that he can't freeze me out.

Arriving back at the table, Georgia greets me with a sweep of her hand. "You're just in time," she announces, gesturing to the fresh round of shots on the table. "It's called the Big O."

"That's certainly how I hope my night's going to end," Alyona quips. As the only other single woman in our group, Kira throws her arm around her friend's shoulder, agreeing in not-so-subtle terms.

I hesitate for a moment. What's one more measly shot? This one seems more like dessert anyhow. It's creamy and a little pepperminty, and it goes down so damn smooth, I can't say no when Georgia thrusts the next shot in my hand.

We stake a claim on the dance floor right under the DJ booth—I swear I can feel each drop of the bass shoot up my spine. I've been to state dinners and refined cocktail parties with my uncle, but this is something else entirely. This club is full of people letting loose, relinquishing their inhibitions, allowing the music to wash away their Monday-to-Friday worries.

When I look around at our group, everyone's cheeks are flushed, arms up in the air, eyes closed with big smiles on their faces. And so I join them—enjoying this moment to the fullest. I don't think about what comes next, or my endgame, or how I need to ply them with more drinks and pump them for information.

Stretching my arms up to the ceiling, I completely let go, screaming into the wall of sound, jumping up and down with Kira's arm around my shoulders, her laughter in my ear. We're swept up in the same euphoria, and it feels better than I could ever have imagined. I missed out on years of this living with my uncle, so I will make up for it right now. Fuck it.

With the music a deafening roar, my hair plastered to my forehead, surrounded by hundreds of people, it all sinks in, in one perfectly clear moment.

I'm having fun.

Real fun.

The kind of fun that girls my age *should* have with their friends.

This is what life is. This is what my life *could* be, but it's not. And never will be.

An hour later, I'm dying for a cold drink of water and my feet feel like they're encased in cement. The rest of the group is still going strong, so I catch Georgia's eye and gesture to let her know that I'm going to cool off upstairs in the VIP section. She gives me a thumbs-up, still lost in the beat.

My eyes travel toward the wall closest to us. I wave at Mikhail to let him know I'm ready for a break. Through the dry-ice fog and strobe lights, I'm not sure if he nodded in response or not. I try again, but this time I lose him as the crowd shifts against me. The buzz from the shots has worn off, and now I'm tired and ready for a break.

I give one last glance over my shoulder at my new friends on the dance floor before setting off in the direction where I last saw Mikhail. And crash smack into a wall of muscle, or maybe he crashes into me, I'm not sure. All I know is giant hands come up and grab me around the waist.

"Sorry, beautiful," a strange man smirks down at me. He doesn't look sorry at all. "I guess I need to pay more attention to where I'm going."

"Yeah, I guess so," I snap, removing his hands from my waist. There is something oddly familiar about this guy, but who knows, maybe all creeps are cut from the same cloth. "If you'll excuse me—" He grabs my wrist and pulls me against him.

"Where are you running off to?" He presses himself firmly against my body. "What? You too good to dance with an average Joe like me?"

Unease presses down on my chest. Something feels off about this exchange. I don't bother to respond. Lifting my foot, I bring the pointy end of my heel down hard on his leather-clad foot. "What the fuck." He howls in pain. Twisting out of his grasp, I push the crowd aside, and fight my way towards the VIP section.

With the crush of bodies, it's not surprising Mikhail lost track of me. I don't want to get him in trouble, but I also know I need to get the fuck off this dance floor now.

A bouncer nods in greeting as I jog up the stairs to the VIP section, sore feet be damned, and beeline straight to our booth. I'm grateful for the jug of ice water I find at the table, and gulp down two glasses. My creepy interaction with that man is still fresh, and my skin crawls just thinking about it. Women have been putting up with unwanted attention from assholes for millennia, but when a guy's aggressive like that, it can leave you a little shaken up.

I remove my heels and knead my foot, trying to soothe my aching soles, but the man's face keeps flashing in my mind. Was he actually familiar, or was he a carbon copy of some other dude that couldn't take a hint? Something about this feels different, more palpable.

Panting, I stand and hurry towards the washroom, hating the heavy feeling that's settled over me and the way the room spins slightly. I push open the door to the ladies' room and head to the sink. Splashing water on my face, I hope to calm my overheated flesh. With my eyes closed, I take deep, centering breaths, calming my nervous system. When my nerves settle, I push off the sink, preparing to go back out to the lounge. But I can't move. A wall of heat locks me in, while a dark heavy material comes to rest over my eyes, obscuring my sight.

"No, please don't!" I scream, terror jolting through me.

My attacker ignores my pleas, reaches under my dress to jerk my thong down my thighs, and pushes my dress up to my hips.

My heart thrashes in my chest. Who would do something like this? The man from earlier? I try to fight, but my arms are locked in vice grips, and the cruel presence delivers a brutal smack to my ass. I choke out a sob, but I can barely get any words out. I feel like I'm going to suffocate.

"Please," I beg. "Please don't hurt—"

My words are silenced by another hard spank, this one on the other cheek.

I cry out for help, but in one fluid motion the blindfold is ripped away. For some reason, I still keep my eyes pressed shut, not wanting to gaze into the eyes of a monster. That is until I hear a deep, angry voice in my ear.

"Hello, wife."

# CHAPTER NINETEEN

## DANIIL

I AM SO FUCKING mad I could scream. Not at Bianca, though. At myself. I should have fucking known better than to go along with Leo's plan. Everything has been off tonight. The club's packed to the gills, and a restless energy permeates the dance floor. This crowd is looking for trouble. Whether the fucking or fighting kind remains to be seen, but trouble nonetheless.

Leo and I had been watching their girls' night unfold on the surveillance monitors from the manager's office. One moment I had her in my sights on the packed dance floor—the dance floor they never should have gone down to—and the next she was gone, swallowed by the crowd. When I saw her again, she was back in the VIP area *without* a guard, looking rattled.

I'd lost her. Just for a minute, but it was long enough to make my blood sing in my ears and dread drip down my spine. As Leo predicted, Jorge showed up with an entourage tonight, though he's not on the main floor. He and his crew have decamped to the champagne room in the basement, a secret lounge equipped with stripper poles and private alcoves. And girls. Lots of girls.

I had no intention of letting him through the door, but Leo

insisted the whole point is to see what he's going to do. And so far, it seems he's done nothing other than let a bunch of naked strippers grind on his lap. It's cold comfort, though, since I know what he's capable of.

It's this riot of emotions in my chest that compels me to follow her into the bathroom, to spank her, to teach her the consequences of ditching her guard. It might be twisted, but I want her to feel genuine fear. Anyone could have attacked her. Anyone who wanted to hurt me through my wife.

She is still shaking in my arms when I take her blindfold off and reveal myself in the mirror.

"Hello, wife."

"Daniil," she gasps, her eyes flashing with anger at my reflection. "Why are you doing this? Is it about the picture?" I have her rammed against the sink, caged in by my hard body. I smell her fear, taste it even.

A cold, dark laugh escapes from my lips. "The picture was a nice touch, I must admit, but that's not what this is about. This is about teaching you a lesson, printsessa." I wrench her back by her hair and press my lips to her ear. "I warned you before you left tonight not to go off alone. And you didn't listen. Why?"

Her thong is still stretched around her ankles when I deliver another hard strike to her gorgeous ass, watching tan flesh jiggle after I deliver my punishment. It makes me hard as hell. Tears leak from her eyes, but I'm immune to them. With the next spank, she cries out again, but this time I notice she closes her eyes and releases a groan of approval.

"Do you like when I punish you like a slut, Bianca?"

Anger swirls in her glare, and she attempts to nail me with an elbow, but I anticipate the movement and block her before she does any damage. I chuckle, low and mean, as I restrain her wrists with one of my hands while I use the other to slap her clit. Her answering moan tells me how much she's enjoying my discipline, even if she continues to buck and snarl in my grasp.

"I want a divorce," she seethes. "We're not even legally

married since we haven't consummated the marriage. I will seek an annulment."

"Interesting," I grumble into her ear while sneaking my hand between her legs. Moisture greets my fingers, and it's clear that while she may hate me, her body clearly doesn't. "Maybe we need to rectify this oversight. Maybe I need to fuck you right here and now."

My fingers continue to work her pussy, playing with her clit before I give her the full-length of my fingers, working her tight virgin hole open for me. A shiver ghosts down her spine and I know she needs this as badly as I do. "Look in the mirror, printsessa. Look at the pleasure I'm giving you."

She does as I say, her rapt expression and half-lidded eyes betray how turned-on she is. I continue to work her clit with my thumb as my fingers work her body open for my cock. She pushes back into my hand, groaning as the sound of her wetness fills the small space of the bathroom. One more hard circle of her clit has her coming around my fingers like a champ.

"Such a good fucking girl," I praise her as she cries out her release. "Look how wet you made me." I bring my glistening fingers up in front of us, and when they land in my mouth, I lick them clean as she releases a full-body shudder. She tastes as good as she looks—sweet, with a salty edge. "Are you ready for my cock? As you so aptly pointed out, we still need to make this marriage legally binding."

Her eyes meet mine in the mirror. She looks conflicted, a debate warring inside her, but I make the decision easy.

"Spread your legs," I command, bending her over the vanity. This isn't about punishing her anymore; this is about making her feel good and taking what's mine. The marble digs into her hips, but she doesn't complain. Instead, she arches her back, presenting her pussy to me. My naughty girl wants this as much as I do.

I stop for a moment, realizing I haven't tasted her yet. I pull her chin around and take her mouth. Her lips are warm and insistent, and she tastes like tequila and heaven. I grunt as her head tilts back further, allowing her tongue better access to tangle with my own. I palm her breast with one hand and grip her hip hard with the other.

When I release her, she wiggles her ass against my fully clothed cock. "Well, Daniil, are you going to make good on your threat to fuck me?" Her voice is throaty and raw with need. For me.

I lean in and nip at her neck. "Is this how you want to lose your virginity, printsessa? Shoved against a sink in a public bathroom."

Her pulse hammers in her neck, and she takes a deep breath before answering, "Yes."

My hands shake with urgency as I undo my pants and free my cock. I line myself up at her soaked entrance and, staring into her eyes in the mirror, shove into her with one firm thrust. She releases a hiss—a noise of half pleasure, half pain—as my hand collars her throat. This is a fucked-up way to lose your virginity, but she doesn't seem to care, too lost in the moment. I give her a minute to adjust to my size as she braces her hands on the mirror in front of her.

"Eyes on me," I instruct her reflection. And then I let go, fucking her hard from behind, each slap of flesh reverberating through the small private bathroom. There is no intimacy involved in taking her virginity, it's not sweet and gentle as she probably pictured her first time, I'm sure. I thrust into her like a man possessed, my blood still boiling from finding her alone, vulnerable to attack.

Harsh pants fall from her lips as her fingers slip down the mirror. I press my face into her throat, breathing in her sweet scent, licking the sweat from her skin. "I never want to see you without protection like that again," I grit against her flesh. "As it is, I'm going to have to kill Mikhail."

"What, no!" she cries out, giving a little jerk. I assume it's an effort to turn around to look at me, but I force her back in place, drilling into her. "Please Daniil, don't. It wasn't his fault."

"Promise me," I say, licking the back of her neck. "Promise me you won't disobey me again." I've never negotiated during sex, but it seems as good a time as any.

"If you won't kill him, I promise." Her fingers slip farther down the mirror until she's supporting her weight on the sink. I love the little desperate sounds she's making. Circling her clit with my fingers, I drag her closer to release.

I go still for a second before slowly tilting her head up so she can see my reflection. My inked fingers collar her throat. "Look how good you're taking me," I croon. "Your pussy was made for my cock."

Through the smudged mirror, I see her flushed cheeks, and how her eyes keep fluttering closed with every brutal thrust. We're both on the verge, I can feel her the walls of her cunt clamping hard around my dick, ready to explode on me.

"Fuck," I cry out as a blinding orgasm overtakes me, and I spill my seed into my wife. I grind at her clit mercilessly, and it's all she needs to come with me. Her pussy pulses around me, milking every last drop of my cum. Her knees go weak, and I support her with an arm around her waist until our breathing calms and the reality of the situation intrudes.

I pull out of her, turning her around to frame her face with my hands. "Did I hurt you?" It's a bad time for a crisis of conscience, but I was rough with my virgin bride. I look down at my cock to find it's smeared in her blood. *Shit*.

But she shakes her head and instead does the most unexpected thing. She pulls my mouth to her own and drops a sweet kiss on my lips.

I'm suddenly consumed by the need to care for her. I wet a towel and do my best to wipe up the mess between her legs, gently swiping so as not to irritate her sensitive flesh. Silently, I straighten her dress and help smooth down her hair. When we're both looking more presentable, I pull her into my chest.

"I'm sorry I was so rough with you," I say into her neck. It's time to come clean. Well, not entirely clean. She doesn't need to know it's Jorge I'm taking issue with. "An enemy of ours is here, somewhere in the club. I lost it."

Her eyebrows press together. "What? Who?"

"No one you know," I insist. "But I fucking lost my mind when I saw you wandering on your own. Unprotected." She looks conflicted, not sure how to react. I release a tense breath. "What happened on that dance floor? When you came upstairs you were upset."

She pulls back to look up at me, her eyebrows raised. "How do you know that? Were you watching me?"

"All fucking night, printsessa. Watching you shimmy and shake on the dance floor in that slinky dress ... fuuuck " I release a strangled groan. "I could spank you all over again ... but I think you'd enjoy it too much."

A sheepish expression creeps over her face, and I know I'm right. "I was trying to get Mikhail's attention, but it was so wild down there." My palms close into fists, but I try to keep my expression neutral. "I just wanted to get some air, but as I moved through the crowd, I bumped into someone ... or maybe he bumped into me, I couldn't tell. He wanted me to dance with him, but I refused. He was pushy and gave me the creeps. That's why I hightailed it back upstairs alone. Finding Mikhail wasn't my top priority."

I catch my bottom lip between my teeth and resist the urge to punch the mirror. Barely. "Describe him."

"I don't know." She shudders at the memory, and I can tell it wasn't a pleasant exchange. "He was a big guy, tall, kind of built. Bald. It was dark, but I think he had some tattoos on his neck."

My ears instantly perk up at that detail. "Cartel tattoos?"

"I couldn't tell, but why would that be an issue?" I don't miss the way she twists her wedding ring in thought. Possession blooms in my chest. A reminder that she's mine. Wearing my ring.

"It's not. I'm going to sort this out," I promise her. "I'm sorry I wasn't there to protect you from him," I say. "I should never have allowed tonight to happen. It was so fucking stu—"

She cuts me off with a hand to my chest. "It's fine. We've actually had a lot of fun." She lifts onto her toes and, again, kisses me softly on the lips, letting me pull her close. God, what this woman does to me is fucking insane.

Ultimately, I know she'll be my downfall, and I can't find it in me to care.

"Let's go home," I tell her, knowing I need to feel her in my arms again tonight. "Together." I stroke her face, her skin soft beneath my fingers. Something has shifted between us. Beyond the sex. I can't fight my feelings for her anymore. She may have secrets, but that doesn't mean she's untrustworthy.

She looks up and gives me a nervous smile. "Okay."

"Why don't you say goodbye to the others. I have one thing to take care of."

I lead her out of the bathroom and give her ass a final squeeze before heading in the direction of the champagne room.

"GET THE FUCK OUT OF HERE." My Glock is aimed straight at Jorge, even though I'm talking to everyone in the room. "All of you. Leave right the fuck now."

There's a tense silence for a moment. A few of Jorge's guys look at him in question, reaching for their pistols—I'm just one guy, after all, and I didn't come with backup—but Jorge angles his chin, a sign to stand down. He pushes away the girl on her knees in front of him, zipping his fly as he stands to face me. A shit-eating smirk plays on his lips, testing my patience to the limit.

When his dick is put away, he holds up his hands in faux surrender. "What's the matter, Kozlov? We're just minding our business down here, having some fun. I thought we were cool?"

I grind my teeth and consider blowing his dick straight off. As I take aim, I feel a hand on my shoulder. "*Brat, ne delay etogo.*" Leo's voice of reason filters through the red that's clouded my vision, warning me to hold back. "*Poterpi. My skoro unichtozhim yego.*"

Fuck patience. Leo wants to take the cautious route, but I'd rather take care of Jorge right here, right now. Man-to-man. I know the dance floor exchange wasn't an accident. Jorge was behind it. I consider his presence tonight to be shots fired.

Jorge gestures for his entourage to wrap it up. "We'll leave, *parce*. I know when I'm not wanted." His eyes meet mine, and he laughs, dark and cruel. It makes my stomach clench.

I lower my gun but continue to shoot daggers his way. "Why are you here? You weren't invited in the first place."

"Do I need an invitation to enjoy the finest club Brooklyn has to offer?" As his entourage filters out the door, I don't move a muscle, forcing them to squeeze around Leo and myself. Jorge and his enforcer, Rio, remain the last two in the room. "Since you've never offered to play host while we're in New York, we've had to make our own fun."

"Yeah." I take a step closer to him, rising to my full height. Jorge is no pip-squeak, but I'm even bigger. "Tell me why you think it's fun to provoke me. To come into my club when you know my wife will be here ... You're digging your own grave."

His eyes go wide with false innocence. "Bianca? I don't know what you're talking about. Haven't seen her all night."

My fist connects with his jaw with a sickening crack, knocking him on his ass. Rio reaches for his gun, but Leo is one step ahead, a pistol already trained on him. "Don't do it" is all my brother has to say before Rio freezes, moving his hand away from his holster.

"You so much as look at my wife ever again, and I will personally see to your torture."

Jorge is back on his feet in an instant and lunges for me, but this time Leo steps in between us. "Leave now," he grits out, fury evident in his expression. "Before I put a bullet through your brain."

Jorge spits at my feet and calls me something nasty in Spanish. I'd like to end this once and for all, but Leo's enormous frame is in the way, and I know he's holding me back from making this an international mafia incident. Personally, I'm ready to rip him limb from limb with my hands. But Jorge and Rio smartly exit the room before I can make a further move.

Leo whips around to face me, and I can tell he's not impressed. "What the fuck was that? What happened to the plan to build a case against him that we can take to Andrei? We're gonna have a war on our hands."

I pace around the room which still reeks of booze, sweat, and cum—it's fucking gross. "He will not tattle to Emilio. This will stay between us, trust me."

Leo crosses his arms in front of his beefy chest, pinning me with a doubtful look. "How are you so sure?"

"Because this is personal. He wants the chance to get revenge, and he won't get it if he snivels to his boss. He's not going to give up."

"Maybe not," Leo finally agrees. "We should go to Andrei and put an end to it."

"Not happening." I shake my head, dying for a whisky to calm the adrenaline pumping through my veins. "This is between Jorge and me now. He's gonna keep coming at me, and I'm gonna be ready for him."

"You still have to work with the guy," Leo points out.

"All the better to watch him closely." I shrug. "I'm not backing down, Leo. Are you on my side?"

"Always, but ... let's be smart about this. No more acting like a cowboy."

I crack my neck. It would be useless for me to make a promise I can't keep. Instead, I say, "I have to get back to Bianca. Thanks for having my back."

He slaps a hand on my shoulder as we turn to leave. "The fun never ends."

I release a dark chuckle. Definitely not, not as long as I have any say in the matter.

# CHAPTER TWENTY

## BIANCA

"WHAT HAPPENED UP THERE?"

We're in Daniil's sporty Bugatti doing six hundred miles per hour, and he's been vibrating with an intense energy since we left the club ten minutes ago. Something happened after our bathroom tryst. Something that has him on edge, and I deserve answers—especially because it's likely about me.

He flexes his hands around the steering wheel, his knuckles going white with tension. "I had to take care of a matter," he says cryptically.

"Yeah, I got that." I want to press him further, but the hard lines of his shoulders and the tightness of his jaw suggest now is not that time. I reach over and rub my hand down his leg. "It's okay, whatever it is." My hand dips to his crotch, rubbing over his hard length. I'm drunk on our sex, on how good it felt, how much I liked it. I'm no expert in this department, but I'm pretty sure no one would argue that his cock is glorious.

"Shit." He hisses out a breath. "That feels so fucking good, baby."

When I notice his eyes practically rolling back in his head, I steal my hand away. "Let's continue this when we're not in a moving vehicle."

"Mm." He grunts in agreement. "Take off your underwear, printsessa."

I give him a shy smile. "I'm not wearing underwear." His eyes shoot to mine in question. "After the bathroom, they were soaked in your cum."

He takes in a deep breath through his nose as if to steady himself. Satisfaction tightens my core. I love that he's so turned on by me he can barely hold himself together. I never imagined I'd have that power over a man, but now I can see how addictive it is.

"Looks like we're gonna make the car seats filthy as well. Spread your legs for me." His voice is hoarse, coming out in a strained whisper. I do as he asks, hiking my skirt so he has unfettered access to my pussy.

Within seconds, two of his fingers plunge inside of me. I should be so sore—I just gave the man my virginity, and it wasn't gentle—but I'm soaking wet, and it helps soften the underlying bite of pain. He's also using his thumb to rub my clit in delicious little circles that push me to the brink.

He's driving with one hand on the wheel and one hand deep inside of me, doing all sorts of delicious things to my self-control, and yet the man doesn't break a sweat as he speeds down the Belt Parkway.

"I can't wait to stuff my cock inside this tight little pussy again. I hope you're not too sore, because—" His filthy words are cut off by the sound of a siren behind us, the flashing lights of a police car illuminating our vehicle.

Sitting up straighter, I grab Daniil's arm in an attempt to push his hand away.

He tsks at me. "Not until you come, baby."

Daniil pulls the car over to the side of the road, and the police car comes to park behind us.

"I can't—" I argue but he only moves his fingers deeper

inside of me, his thumb brushing against my clit, making me buck up to meet his hand.

"Better make it quick." His voice is low and smooth like silk. "He's getting out of his vehicle."

"Daniil," I half moan, half gasp. I hate him for what he's doing to me right now, but I'm also so damn turned-on. I'm pleading with him for something I have no words for. I never knew my arousal could be so thick it would echo through the car every time his hand moves inside of me.

"Please," I beg. He grunts and crooks his fingers, hitting a spot that nearly lights me up from the inside. I cry out as an orgasm slams into me, riding out each pulse on his fingers until I'm wrung out and sore.

He pulls his hand from me, brings his still wet fingers up to his mouth, and licks my arousal clean from them. My blood roars in my ears. I'm sure I've never seen anything quite so hot before.

"What a good fucking girl you are, coming on my command," he praises, and then a second later, he rolls down his window and greets the man now standing beside the car. "Good evening, officer."

My cheeks flame, and I'm so intensely embarrassed I don't even look at the cop. Thank god I had the presence of mind to shove my dress back down my legs, but I'm still all shaky and flushed from the most mind-blowing orgasm of my life. And despite my overwhelming shame, I can't deny that the risk of being caught was intensely erotic.

The cop's breath catches when he gets a good look at Daniil. "Mr. Kozlov," he stutters. "I didn't recognize the vehicle."

Daniil releases a throaty chuckle. "It's new," he confirms.

"Apologies. If I'd realized it was you—"

"Of course," Daniil's voice is all breezy, like he's almost happy that we got pulled over.

"Thank you for your understanding," the cop grovels. I can't help but look over at him to see what this is all about. A middle-aged man with a neatly trimmed beard tips his hat to me with a respectful smile. "I'll let you get on with your evening ... er, morning," he corrects himself, slinking back to his car.

Daniil closes his window and leans back in his seat, drinking me in. "You were exquisite," he breathes.

"And you got pulled over on purpose." I cross my arms in front of my chest, narrowing my eyes at him.

"Maybe," he admits, starting the car and pulling back onto the road.

"I'm going to get you back for that," I swear with false heat. And then I laugh out loud at how ridiculous that was. "Do you literally have every cop in the tri-state area on your payroll?"

"Pretty much," he confirms, smiling at me. "It's a good thing," he adds, revving the engine, "because I'm going to break every speed limit between here and home since I need to bury myself in your cunt again. Hold on, Bianca."

Goddamn, this man is going to be the death of me.

THE MINUTE we enter the penthouse, he pushes me against the wall, sweeping his tongue inside my mouth. His hands knead my breasts before settling at my nipples, pinching and rolling them until they stiffen to hard points beneath my dress.

I never really believed sexual chemistry was real, I thought it was some fictional state that only people in romance novels experience. But holy hell, turns out I was *very* wrong about that.

His lips are on me, hot and unrestrained, as his hands tug at my hair for better access to my mouth. "You taste so fucking sweet," he gasps between drugging kisses down my neck. "You're going to be so sore tomorrow, and I don't care. I want you to remember what you feel like after being so full of my cock."

Not waiting for an answer, he yanks my dress up, his fingers seeking my wet heat. I'm still tender from earlier, but his touch is everything. It lights up every nerve ending in my body, each and every sense sharper than before.

I reach for his belt, undoing the buckle and lowering his zipper, pulling out his thick cock. On our wedding night, I didn't get a chance to explore him, but now I'll take my time with him. Palming his length in my hands, I admire it in all its glorious splendor. Long and hard and thick. I've never really had an appreciation for cocks, having seen few in my life, but I could start a fan club for Daniil's.

"I'm going to explode if you keep doing that," he says in a hoarse voice. "Do you want me to paint you in my cum?"

A rush of sensation hits me, making me feel out of control in the best possible way, like I'm about to jump out of a plane. I've never skydived before but I imagine it's the same dizzying blend of excitement and nerves.

He lifts me up and, in one thrust, slams inside of me, filling me up so completely, so perfectly it's like his body was designed for mine. Or vice versa. The perfect match. My arms wrap around his neck and my legs encircle his waist, as he drives into me like a man possessed. I want everything he has to give me. This darkness, the way he holds nothing back, stretching me to a breaking point. This sweet release. I never want it to end.

I scratch his back while sucking his neck, whispering desperate pleas against his skin. Daniil pulls back to check in with me, and I give him a smile and urge him on by squeezing my legs tighter around him, coaxing him deeper inside of me.

"Are you going to come all over my cock, my beautiful printsessa?" I moan, my head thrashing against the wall as he continues to bounce me on his dick. His eyes are glued to my breasts spilling out of my dress. "Just like that, baby."

He leans in, sucking my neck as his thumb focuses on my clit, and I go off like a Fourth of July firework. Holy hell. Colors swim behind my eyelids as the most intense pleasure I've ever experienced streaks through me. Just as my orgasm subsides, Daniil drives into my body one last time before he stills and then cries out. Warmth gushes deep inside me, and I'm boneless in his arms.

We're both panting and cursing, drenched in sweat, but also, there's a lightness between us. Like we'd just fucked away any of the lingering awkwardness.

Still inside me, he carries me to the bedroom. His bedroom. A room we've never been in together. And I don't know what to make of it as he lays me down on the bed, takes off my dress and then removes all of his clothes before coming to lie beside me as our heaving pants fade into even breaths.

Before either of us ruin the moment by talking, I turn on my side, desperate to touch him now that he's finally fully naked. I run my hands everywhere, worshiping his hard planes and bulging muscles.

Scars mark his skin, but he's still perfect. Daniil hisses as I lean in and run my tongue over his chest and abs. He buries his hand in my hair, and I wonder how things have changed between us so drastically in such a short amount of time. Pulling me to him, he settles my head on his chest, and trails his hand down my back before resting it on the swell of my ass.

"I'm on the pill. For period cramps," I clarify, considering he came inside of me unprotected, twice now.

He sighs and stares up at the ceiling. "I should have asked."

I laugh. "Tonight was ... unexpected."

"That wasn't supposed to happen." He takes a moment, as if looking for the right words. "But I lost it when I realized you were without a guard. And that fucking dress." He sucks in air through his teeth. "Never wear that again."

"Oh, was there a problem with that dress?" I ask, batting my eyelashes.

He huffs out an annoyed breath. "Don't make me take you over my knee, Bianca."

A flurry of butterflies erupt in my stomach, desire coiling low in my belly. Apparently I've discovered a new kink.

"Considering you practically ripped it off of me, there's no chance of me wearing it again."

"I don't like other men looking at you, printsessa. You are mine."

"You don't treat me that way," I say, confused. "I know you regret this marriage, but—"

"I don't regret it." He props up on one elbow, my chin held firm in his powerful hand. I'm silent, unsure how to respond, so I go with sarcasm.

"Could have fooled me."

"This is all new to me. I'm learning. And there's definitely been growing pains." His hand travels down my neck, over my breasts, and lands between my legs, his fingers brushing against my slit. He leans forward and whispers in my ear. "But does this seem like I regret it?" *Okay, point made.* I wiggle into his hands, my breathing already becoming erratic ... then he pulls his hand away. "Not so fast. I'll give you more orgasms soon, but first we need to talk about tonight."

That sobers me up quickly. "What about?"

"Your safety. I can't focus on anything when I'm worried about you. I need to know that you won't ditch your guard again."

A sliver of guilt moves through me, but it's not like I'd ditched Mikhail on purpose. "It was so crowded," I explain, "and I thought because it was one of your clubs, I was safe."

"Unfortunately, that's not the case." Daniil lies back down, pinching the bridge of his nose. "I have enemies, Bianca, lots of them. I'm second in line to the Kozlov Bratva. If someone wanted to hurt me, they'd come at you. That's the way it is in organized crime ... you must have been a target when you lived with your uncle."

"Hardly," I say. My uncle would have to care about me for that to be true, but I keep that to myself. "Is something going on?" I ask, rising on one elbow. There's something he's not telling me, and I don't know why.

His jaw hardens. "Not exactly, but with the casino now, and

with plans to open another one soon, it makes us even more of a target. We're high profile. I don't want to take a chance, printsessa."

Is he saying he cares for me or cares about being vulnerable to his enemies? I don't know, but the tenderness in his eyes is confusing.

"I'll be more careful," I agree, lying back down. At that, he sweeps me into his arms and pulls me close against his body. I can feel the thump of his heart beneath me, and it's such a comforting feeling, to be close to someone like this, being intimate with someone—not just sexually but in other ways.

"Hey," Daniil's voice interrupts my spiraling thoughts. "What are you thinking?"

"Nothing." I flash him a watery smile. "Why do you ask?"

He huffs out a laugh, looking so sexy I avert my eyes at the ceiling to avoid melting. "Something is going on in that head of yours to make you frown." He touches a point between my eyebrows. "Which makes that little line form right here."

Ugh! I attempt to smooth out my features. "What do you want from me?" I ask, exasperated.

"I know I've been an asshole, and honestly I have no clue how to do this relationship shit." I snort at his choice of words, and he returns my wry grin and lifts his free hand to trace the line of my cheekbone. "But I know I want you sleeping in my bed with me every night."

I smile and thread my fingers through Daniil's. He brings his face to mine and plants a sweet kiss on my lips. Daniil is offering me something I haven't experienced in so long. Someone in my corner, someone who cares for me, who has my back. And yet, I can't allow myself to get swept up in our connection.

He might do bad things, but I believe he is a good man and doesn't deserve my betrayal. But none of that matters. I sealed my fate the moment I crossed enemy lines. I have one purpose, and that is to avenge my family's death.

No matter the cost.

No matter the sacrifice.

I've made up my mind, and nothing can stop me.

## CHAPTER TWENTY-ONE

**DANIIL**

THE ROAR of the Thunderbolt whooshes past me as a bunch of kids high on sugar and fun careen past us on the way to the Wonder Wheel spinning in the distance. Bianca's laugh as she veers out of the way of the grubby monsters is clear and bright. I turn towards her to see her face turned up, soaking in the afternoon sun and general revelry that is Coney Island's Luna Park.

An unfamiliar pleasure ripples down my spine. Sensing my eyes on her, she returns my smile, and a sweet, comfortable energy settles between us.

I'm not in the habit of blowing off work for a woman. As in I've literally never done it. But here I am, on a Thursday afternoon at Coney fucking Island with a personal SWAT team of security around us, all because Bianca told me she's never been to an amusement park outside of one family trip to Disney World. I suspect there are a lot of things she missed out on in her life, and I don't know why, but it makes me want to give them to her. To give her everything.

Of all the ways this crazy arranged marriage could have gone, I never imagined it could be *this*. A spark of light in the darkness. It's been two weeks since I took her into my bed. Two weeks since I stopped fighting the magnetic force that draws us together.

"Another round of bumper cars?" I offer.

"Ugh, I think I need to let that hot dog settle first." Her hand lands on her belly, as a lopsided grin splits her face. "But I wouldn't say no to an ice cream cone."

We meander over to the nearest ice cream vendor and order waffle cones with soft serve, then take the cones to a quiet area where a picnic bench sits under a willow tree.

Watching her devour the cone in delight, a slow smile spreads across my face. Bianca catches me staring with what's got to be a stupid grin on my face. "Penny for your thoughts?" she asks, parroting the question I'd asked her the first time we met.

"Nothing really." I shrug. "I'm just good." I mean it. For the first time in a long time, I don't have the restless feeling that's usually bubbling under the surface. "You know my parents used to take us here when we were young—before the Kozlov Bratva was so powerful, and we could leave the house without an armed militia—and we'd spend weekends making ourselves sick going on ride after ride. Andrei wouldn't want anyone to know this, but he has a glass stomach. The first swoop of a roller coaster he'd be retching into his lap."

"Ugh," she grimaces. "Gross." Then softly she asks, "Tell me about Kira?"

Her question fills up the space between us. "What do you want to know?"

"All of it."

I stroke my chin, hoping to stall for a moment. Her question is complicated. I haven't shared this story with anyone outside of our immediate circle. But she is my circle now, my everything. With a jagged breath, I say, "My father revealed we had a half sister as he bled to death in Andrei's arms."

Her hand reaches for mine, threading our fingers together. "Shit. I'm sorry." She cringes.

"Yeah, well ... it's the world we live in. And in some fucked-up, twisted way, there is a happy ending. We found Kira after months of searching. Or rather, she found us, though she had no clue we were related. Her father, Oleg Antonov, was a sadistic fucker, and our family's biggest rival. To hurt our father, he'd seduced our mother, gotten her pregnant, and when she was at her lowest, took the child from her. That baby was Kira." Pain swirls in my veins like a drug, the untouched ice cream melting in my hand. I toss it into a garbage bin nearby.

Bianca's face falls. "I get it, you don't have to go on."

But I need her to know everything. I *want* her to know. A humorless smirk touches my lips, and I reach out to run a thumb over the edge of her jaw, admiring her beauty in the early afternoon sunlight. "Kira didn't know the truth of her past. She just knew that her father was a monster." A dry laugh escapes my throat when I think back to my pint-size sister's boldness. "She devised a plan to take over as the head of the Antonov Bratva, and that plan included abducting Georgia as leverage so Andrei would agree to help her take down her father. Our reunion was rather ... dramatic. She learned we were her brothers with her father's gun pointed at her head."

"Holy shit!" Bianca's eyes widen dramatically. "And I thought my family history was fucked-up."

"Yeah, well, we all have our skeletons, don't we? What matters is we're together now. And if it wasn't for our quest to find Kira, Andrei would never have met Georgia. Maybe things turn out the way they do for a reason."

"Do you really believe that?" she asks, head tilted to the side.

"Maybe," I scoff. "I don't really know what I believe. I don't buy that my mother deserved what happened to her. Seduced by the enemy, left to deliver a child in secret in a mental hospital, then having a newborn ripped from her arms. It's what led her to take her own life."

Bitterness drags through my veins as I run a shaky hand over my jaw. Bianca doesn't respond with words, all of them useless right now. Instead, she comes to me, nestles in my lap, and presses her tits into my chest so she can put her lips on mine. "I'm sorry," she whispers against my mouth. "For all of it."

"You have nothing to be sorry for. It's the men in my mother's life who need to repent." My father paid in the end—assassinated by Oleg, the same man who'd seduced his wife once upon a time. "What about you?" I ask. "Tell me about your family ... before your uncle."

She tenses in my arms. I know this is a difficult subject for her. How could it not be? She lost her entire family in a car crash. I've faced my fair share of devastation, but I can't even fathom that kind of loss all at once. It makes me admire her even more than I already do.

Bianca clears her throat, her gaze landing on the thrill rides in the distance. "My dad was funny. He was kind of like the family jokester, the class clown. He always made us smile, lightened the mood wherever he went. But my mother was my best friend, really. She didn't have my sister, Celeste, until I was nine years old, so it was just me and my parents for a long time. When Celeste was born, it was amazing, it was like I had my own little doll to take care of. God, I loved her so much." She swallows the ball of emotion, and I bring her closer to me. "We lived a nice, normal life in Miami, and then it all went to hell." She shakes her head like she's trying to free herself of the flood of memories. "It's just a painful history I'd rather leave in the past."

"Okay," I say, kissing her shoulder. I certainly understand the need to leave the past where it belongs. If not, it has the potential to haunt your every waking hour.

I run a hand over her ribs and down the flat of her stomach. "If you keep doing that ..." she rasps before trailing off. Her gaze sparks black, and then the mood changes instantly even though we are outside in a very public area.

"That's okay," I say, nipping the flesh of her neck. "I've always wanted to fuck in public."

"You dirty, dirty man," she chides. "Do you want your men to see? Cause I count at least fifteen—and that's without looking behind me."

Fire shoots through my veins, and I lift her to a standing position. Reaching for the nape of her neck, I bring her against me, whispering into her ear, "I'm gonna do a lot more than fuck you. In private."

Her answering gasp is all the invitation I need to drag her to the back seat of the Land Rover and pound her into oblivion.

# CHAPTER TWENTY-TWO

## DANIIL

"EMILIO WANTS to use our shipping routes to start moving his product."

My head whips up from my phone as I absorb Andrei's words. It's just Andrei, Yulian, Leo, and me in the cigar lounge we keep private for our own purposes. Mainly drinking, gambling, and talking shit.

Swiping my vodka off the bar, I shoot it down like vodka is meant to be consumed. Ice-cold and in one gulp. Whisky is for savoring, not vodka. Andrei is tracking me closely, reading my reaction to his announcement. I clear my throat and slam the shot glass down on the bar. "It's too risky."

Only our most-trusted associates have access to our shipping lines, which span throughout the globe. We've stayed out of street sales—and all the headaches and pressure that comes with it—by getting into the lucrative business of smuggling and transportation.

Unnerving silence falls as Andrei takes a cigar out of his pocket and cuts the tip off, lighting the Cohiba with slow, sure movements. I knew this day was coming, that the Zegas would want to exploit our connection, but I'd hoped for more time to figure out Jorge's endgame. It's clear he's out for revenge, but what his version of revenge entails, I don't know, and I'm not willing to sit around and find out.

"Why?" Andrei's voice is smooth as silk, but lurking beneath, a hardened pakhan is out for blood. "Everything has gone smoothly at the casino with the Zegas has it not?"

My jaw ticks in annoyance, dread pressing down on my shoulders. I'm not ready to share with Andrei everything that has happened with Jorge, partly because he warned me to play nice, but also because I can't sound the alarm until there's something to report. And right now, I have nothing solid to go on. Just a bad feeling in the pit of my gut.

"It's barely been a month. Cleaning their money on our turf is one thing, allowing them to use our ships to move their product gives them power over us. Are we ready for them to know exactly what ships we own, the ports we have deals with, the right hands to grease along the way? It's fucking reckless."

My brother's eyes narrow as he releases a ring of smoke into the air. "Why is that?"

I sit up straighter, unease pressing down on my chest. "They're not my family, and I don't trust them yet. One wrong move, and we'll have the DEA all over us."

Yulian's chuckle is low. "If we waited for you to trust the Zegas, we'd be shit out of luck. Unless we have a problem you're not telling us about."

A pulse flickers in my jaw. "You saw the shit he pulled at my wedding."

"You mean daring to talk to Bianca?" Andrei takes a slow sip of his drink, unimpressed with my reasoning. "All I saw was how you overreacted ... especially for a wife you claimed not to want."

"When did I fucking say that?" I growl, even though I know it's the truth. But fuck him for throwing it back in my face. Because my life would be a hell of a lot easier if I felt nothing for the chestnut-haired beauty with the crazy-ass dog running around my penthouse.

But that's the problem. I feel *everything* for her. It's like she put a spell on me and I'm helpless to resist. I'm Daniil Kozlov, and I'm an addict.

Leo's eyes meet mine over Andrei's head, and he gives me a subtle shake of his head. "Drop it," he's telling me, "we'll deal with this in our own way." My younger brother and I have always had an understanding that not all our business must concern the whole brotherhood. Some things are better left to be dealt with by our own hand.

I can't help but get in one more jab. "If I recall correctly, we walked into a derelict warehouse without backup or arms when Georgia was abducted based on nothing but blind trust. Call this a hunch, too."

Andrei's eyes soften at the corners, no doubt remembering how Leo and I were willing to do anything necessary to get Georgia back.

"We have an opportunity here," he presses. "The feds have the US-Mexico border on lockdown these days, it gives the Zegas an advantage. They're producing more powder than ever in Colombia since they don't have to share as much of the market with the Mexicans. We have a fleet of empty container ships circling the coast of Urabá, ready to be loaded." He drags a knuckle over his jaw, his gaze sharp despite a night of vodka shots. "And you're telling me we shouldn't move forward because you don't like your in-laws?" A sour laugh peels from his lips as he stubs out his cigar.

I bristle, feeling the weight of everyone's stare on my skin. "I'm asking you to trust me on this, brat."

Andrei's chair pushes back with a loud squeal. "I need proof that we have an actual problem with the Zegas. Bring me something solid or put whatever personal shit you have aside so we can make some goddamn money."

Yulian is the next one out of his seat. "If you need me, *bratan*, you know where to find me," he says in parting, following Andrei out, which leaves Leo and me alone.

My younger brother smirks at the closed door, slumping in his chair. "Well played," he says, loosening his tie, and throwing it on the seat beside him.

"What kind of proof does he expect? This is bullshit." I huff out a dark laugh and lean back in my chair, fishing my phone from my pocket. Three swipes on my screen, and I'm looking down at a live feed of my wife asleep in my bedroom in Brooklyn. I've lost the fight with myself to keep Bianca at arm's length.

We've settled into a new routine these past couple of weeks where she takes Eris to dog obedience school during the day—a hard-won negotiation on my part and still a work in progress—and during the afternoon lull at the casino, I go back to the penthouse to spend time with her. It's new to me. The need to be near her. To touch her skin, to talk.

The one hard limit I have—she can't come to the casino with me. Because if Jorge or any other enemy wanted to make a move, the casino would be an obvious place to hit.

"Who the fuck are you and what have you done with my brother?"

My head whips up at the sound of Leo's voice in my ear. He's watching me watch Bianca on the camera feed, amusement coloring his smile.

"Shut up." I swipe to turn off my phone and drop it on the table in front of me. "You don't understand what it's like because no one wants your ugly ass."

"If you say so." Leo smirks at me.

I can't sit any longer. Fire ants burn under my skin as I pace the carpeted floor of the lounge. If Jorge was only after me, I'd say bring it on, but my pound of flesh won't be enough.

"We have to provoke him," I say, an idea taking shape in my mind. "Give him a reason to come at us properly, none of this pissing-in-his-Cheerios shit to get a response. He wants to fight it out, let's do it."

Leo tilts his head, a cocktail toothpick between his lips. "Sounds like a bad fucking idea." He launches the toothpick across the room. "I'm in. Have anything specific in mind?"

Smiling at my brother's absolute fucking recklessness, and mine too, I pour two shots for each of us. "Yeah, I have something in mind. Drink up, and I'll share all the dirty details."

# CHAPTER TWENTY-THREE

## DANIIL

It's a three-hour trek between Brooklyn and my family's estate in East Hampton, but I choose to drive it rather than take the chopper. I'm craving time alone with Bianca. Just us, no distractions—unless you count Eris softly snoring on her lap. But for once, that crazy dog is still, and the only sound in the car is Morcheeba on my stereo system and the dog's sleep sounds.

Beside me, Bianca's wearing a short leather jacket over an elegant wrap dress and naughty wedge heels that do fantastic things to her thick legs. I am a sucker for killer curves, and she has those in spades.

When she notices my roving eye, she attempts, rather uselessly, to pull her dress down over her legs. "Shouldn't your eyes be on the road?" she snaps playfully.

"Don't worry, I've driven these roads a million times. And those legs are mighty distracting. Although I'd have a better view if that furball wasn't spread out all over your lap."

"Don't talk about Eris that way," she jokes, covering the dog's ears. "She'll get offended."

"That dog has the best life of any animal I've ever known.

And thank fuck for allergy meds or else she would have been loaded into Mikhail's SUV."

I glance up in the rearview mirror to get a view of Mikhail behind us, transporting not only our clothes and personal effects, but a boatload of dog stuff too.

When I first told Bianca that I wanted to move us to the Kozlov estate, I expected her to fight me on it, but she didn't. Maybe because our family's property offers more space to move around or because Georgia lives there and Kira is a regular visitor, but she was open to the idea. She had a fuckload of questions I did my best to answer without revealing the truth. Which is I'm ready to provoke her ex into revealing his true colors.

I'm protecting what's mine at all costs. Bianca doesn't need to know the shit that Jorge is pulling. He'd done enough damage to her psyche during the time they were together; he's now my problem.

So I'd told Bianca a half truth: Living at the estate is safer, at least for now, while we grow our casino business. It's a move which is sure to piss off more than a few organized crime families, so she accepted my reasoning and hasn't asked about the night at the club again, which is a relief. I don't want to lie, I just don't want to worry her.

AN HOUR LATER, we pull up to the grand mansion my family calls home. I softly shake Bianca awake. Like Eris, the winding roads lulled her to sleep. Her gorgeous deep-brown eyes open, taking me in. For a moment, she looks at me unguarded, affection and warmth evident in her gaze. I don't get to see this side of Bianca often.

The energy has changed between us. The sex has definitely played a part. Our physical attraction is sizzling. And even though work and the situation with Jorge takes up most of my waking hours, I also make an effort to spend more time with her now.

I lean in and kiss her lips softly. She opens her mouth and I suck her tongue, hungry for her, as I always am. "We're here," I whisper.

Leading her into the foyer, Bianca looks around in wonder with Eris trailing behind, probably wondering what corner she should piss in. She's still the worst-behaved dog on the planet, but I have a soft spot for the hyperactive torpedo.

"You weren't kidding about this place being a fortress. You grew up here?"

"Not exactly." I chuckle. "We grew up in Brighton Beach, but my father moved us here when we were young. Once he established the Kozlov Bratva, he needed a well-guarded estate. Lots of good that did," I mumble, the words falling out of my mouth. "Our enemies still found a way to get to us."

Her warm hand lands on my back, and she presses herself into my side. I don't need to say anymore because Bianca understands the world I was born into. It's late and we're both tired, but I show Bianca the basics—library, kitchen, dining area, the pool we keep heated to bath-like temperatures until the first snowfall just in case she wants to take a dip tomorrow.

She settles herself on one of the pool loungers, gazing up at the brilliant stars in the sky. In the city, the stars are muted and seem so far away, but out here, it's as if they burn more brightly.

"Amazing, huh?" I ask, enjoying her look of wonder.

She smiles. "Are Georgia and Kira around?" she asks.

"They're dealing with business out of town, everyone will be back tomorrow."

She nods in response and stares out at the pool before a naughty smile overtakes her face. "I think I'll go for a dip."

I focus on the crazy sexy woman standing before me, leisurely stripping off her dress to reveal a tiny black lace thong and bra.

"Holy shit," I breathe. "Are you stripping for me, printsessa?"

"No," she answers. But a flutter of her eyelashes communicate something entirely different.

My blood goes hot, desire for her flaring in my chest. "Mm, I like that."

Her head tilting to the side, chestnut curls falling over her shoulder, she purrs, "Are you going to join me?"

I sit up straight, my hard cock suddenly throbbing in my pants. She has my full attention now, and she knows it. "No," I rasp. "I want to watch you. Take the rest off for me, printsessa. Go slow."

Her eyes flash with heat, as she reaches around to unhook her bra. Her ample breasts slowly fall out, bouncing as they are released, and my mouth waters. I can't wait to suck on her nipples properly.

"Now the thong," I command.

She swallows and looks nervous for a moment, scanning to see if any staff is milling about. "Don't worry. They know to give me privacy. Especially when I'm with my hot-as-sin young wife."

A soft moan escapes her lips. She likes when I talk dirty to her.

"Panties off now," I remind her harshly. She complies. Peeling the scrap of lace over her hips and down her golden thighs until she steps out with one foot, then the other. "Good girl," I praise. "Now stuff it in your mouth."

Her eyes nearly bulge out of the sockets, but she doesn't refuse me. Because she likes this kind of play. I sense it in the taut lines of her body, in the way her eyes light up at my commands. She opens her mouth wide and as instructed, wraps her lips around the small piece of fabric. The sight is so erotic I need to adjust myself in my pants.

"Turn around and bend over for me. I want to see the goods I was forced to purchase."

She hesitates for a moment, and that won't do at all. I tsk and shake my finger at her. Then I'm on my feet, stalking towards her. "You need to listen to my commands," I breathe, "or else you get punished."

She moves now, turning around and touching her toes. Her hair grazes the ground while she lets me glimpse her most intimate parts.

"Better," I say. "But you still earned this." I smack her pussy, the punishment coming out of nowhere. She's not prepared for it, and her body nearly buckles, but I catch her with one hand around her waist. "Should have listened the first time." One more smack to her clit, but she braces herself this time, and stays in place, waiting for further instruction.

As a prize, two of my fingers slide into her already soaking cunt, and she releases a needy mewl that is music to my ears. Our appetites line up perfectly. She's so wet, her juices slide all the way down my hand, igniting a shot of lust through my veins. "Hold still," I warn before corkscrewing my fingers inside of her.

This time, she obeys without question, and I drop to my knees. Gripping her ass cheeks, one in each hand, I spread her wide to feast on. I press my face into her soaked pussy, my fingers circling her clit while I bury my tongue in her slit. I don't go easy on her, easy is not what she really wants. I can tell my printsessa wants me to be rough with her.

"Take your panties out of your mouth. I want to hear my name on your lips," I command.

She does as I ask, a gasp escaping her mouth as I continue to lap at her without restraint. My tongue is buried inside of her as spasms rock her body, and she squirms against my face. I deliver a stinging slap to her backside. "Hold still," I remind her.

Her knees buckle, but I force her back into position. She'll stay like this until she comes. Kneading the flesh of her ass, she opens her legs a little wider for me so I can continue playing with her. My teeth gently pierce the most delicate part of her flesh, and she reflexively cries out—in one breath begging me to stop, the next coaxing me to continue. I'm driving her wild, and it's fucking hot watching her surrender to me.

"You are going to come on my face," I demand. "And you're going to love it."

"No. Not like this," she sobs.

"Yes, like this." There's no compassion in my tone as I lean forward to suck her clit between my teeth, taking her to the edge of pain, and then easing off.

She gasps as I feed her two of my fingers, twisting them in and out, causing her breath to shallow and her limbs to tremble. I love watching her surrender. Every inch of her body is on fire as I work her bundle of nerves, her slickness dripping down my arm.

I go all the way now, my fingers and tongue wringing every ounce of pleasure from her sweet pussy until the surge of bliss crashes over her like a powerful wave. "Fuck, yes," she cries out, before lowering to her hands and knees, unable to remain standing any longer.

Now she's truly mine. Broken, exhausted, spent.

"Remember this," I tell her, leaning down into her ear. "You're my printsessa in public, my whore in private, and my good girl always."

She sighs hard, reminding me there's still so much I want to do to her.

## BIANCA

I'm barely able to stand on my own two feet when I float back to earth after the most devastating orgasm of my life. Damn, what this man is capable of with his mouth alone is mind-boggling. I never in my life imagined I would bend over and do that for any man ... present myself in such a vulnerable way. Having his eyes on the most intimate parts of me, soon followed by his fingers and his tongue, was such a potent turn-on.

Daniil helps me up, and I sag against his chest. His fingers delve lower, between my thighs, avoiding touching my too sensitive clit. He's feeling the wetness that's currently dripping down my leg into a filthy puddle.

He kisses my forehead. "Such a dirty girl. Look at the mess you've made." He brings his glistening fingers up for me to admire. "Taste yourself," he insists. Despite my earlier orgasm, I'm still crazy turned-on, loving the little games that we play together. "Go clean yourself up in the pool." He slaps my ass as a way to get me moving, and I huff in response, my hands landing on my hips.

"Only if you come in with me."

He chuckles at my demand. "I'm the one who makes the rules when we fuck."

*Fuck*, the word sounds so baseless, especially in the context of marriage. I stand on my tiptoes and nip at his jawline before I whisper in his ear, "We're not fucking right now, we're talking."

"And whose fault is that?" He smiles down at me, his arms still holding me close. Despite his dirty talk, I feel protected; like someone is looking after me for once.

But it's not a feeling I can allow myself to get used to. "It's your choice." I push off his chest and saunter towards the dark water. "You can join me, or you can watch me from the deck." I sink into the water, releasing a happy little sigh as I float weightless in the pool. It's fall, and the air has a definitive chill to it, but the water is warm like a bath. "I think you'd have a lot more fun in here."

I give a few lazy backstrokes, allowing my dusky nipples to peek out of the water. With a cocky smile, he unbuttons his ever-present white dress shirt. I've certainly spent time appreciating Daniil's form before but watching him undress, I'm taken aback by his raw masculinity. His shoulders are so broad, every muscle bunched and defined as he abandons his shirt on a lounger, revealing impeccably defined abs.

Strong and lean, he's covered in ink, and I take my time, shamelessly staring as he reaches for his belt, snaking it through the loops. He drops his pants to reveal muscular thighs with a smattering of light hair. I already knew what he was packing between his legs but seeing his body like this is addicting.

Catching my slack-jawed expression, he smirks. "Like what you see?"

There's no point in denying it, so I just give him a sly smile. "Yeah, it's alright."

He wades into the pool, his eyes on me the whole time. I continue with my lazy backstrokes, teasing him with the bounce of my breasts above the waterline. He's standing in the shallow end, definitely paying attention to my little show.

"Get your ass over here," he growls. His voice is intense and demanding, but I don't want to play by his rules.

"Make me."

"Oh, printsessa." He pushes off from the floor of the pool, fast as lightning. "There's nothing I would enjoy more."

He's feral now, like a beast stalking its prey. My response is instinctual, like any innocent being hunted, I swim the other way. But he's fast. His powerful strokes cause water to slosh over the edge of the pool. I make it to the ledge and am hauling myself out of the water, when one giant hand wraps around my ankle and pulls.

"Get off me." I thrash in his grasp, fighting as if my life depended on it.

"Make me." He throws my bratty words back in my face. I'm fighting in earnest, kicking and bucking in an attempt to escape his grasp. He waits for me to tire myself out, his hand still gripped tight around my ankle, and then, like a creature from the Black Lagoon, he gives one firm yank, and I'm submerged. When I break above the surface of the water, his rock-hard body crowds my much smaller form against the ledge.

"You shouldn't have run." His words ghost over my ear. "I'll always chase you. Never forget that." He doesn't give me time to respond. In one unforgiving thrust, he's inside of me. My pussy wraps around his cock, his front pressing tight to my back.

"Hold on sweetheart," he rasps in my ear. "I need to look at what's mine when I blast my cum inside of you." He pulls out long enough to turn me around, my arms coming around his shoulders and my legs wrapping around his waist. If it wasn't for his tight grip on the ledge, we'd both sink to the bottom of this pool. But he's got us.

I don't know why, but I also need that face-to-face connection.

His tongue enters my mouth at the same time his cock thrusts up inside of me. I'm so full of him, my senses over-whelmed by his taste, his smell, everything about him. His fingers dance over my clit as he fucks me like it might be our last time together. He doesn't go easy on me. Biting my ear, sucking on my throat, tweaking my nipples. I moan and thrash in his arms, crying out as the orgasm sears through my body. The sensation is so strong it's almost violent, like shock waves moving through my core.

Daniil joins me soon after, grunting as he pulses inside of me. Then, as if sharing a secret with me, he whispers in my ear, "You're going to be my ruin, printsessa."

My stomach dips. "What do you mean?" I ask, hesitantly.

"This pussy, these tits, this ass," he rasps, still fully seated inside of me. "You are fucking made for me. I'll never get enough." Relief fills me. He's just referring to sex.

When he sees that I don't yet have control over my limbs, he lifts me out of the pool, then hops out after me. In one quick move, he has me thrown over his shoulder.

"Daniil, put me down! What are you doing?" But he doesn't stop. Doesn't even respond as he carries me to the poolside hot tub nestled in a rock grotto with a cascading waterfall overhead. "Damn, this is nice," I exclaim as I lower in, the hot swirling water soothing my muscles.

"Andrei had it installed after he married Georgia. I don't want to think of all the shenanigans that have gone down here."

"Gross!" My eyes pop open, and I nearly bolt from the water, but I catch the naughty gleam in his eyes, as he breaks out in laughter, I flick water his way. "Hijo de puta," I hiss.

"Mm, I love it when you speak Spanish. How come I only ever hear you speaking it to Eris?"

"I'm more comfortable speaking English. My Dad was American, didn't speak any Spanish, so it's the language we mostly spoke in our household."

"And your uncle?"

I groan. "A mix, I suppose. English when we were in the States, Spanish when we were in Colombia. But that was me mostly talking with the staff. My uncle and Jorge were always busy doing whatever it is that they do."

He cocks an eyebrow at me. "Do you know what they do?"

"I know the basics. They produce and sell drugs." I shrug, sinking deeper into the bubbling water. I'm quiet for a minute, gathering courage to ask the question I don't really want to know, but have to ask. "What are the Kozlovs involved in?"

Daniil shifts uncomfortably. My words fill up the cavernous space, and the question hangs between us like an anvil.

"I trust you, but this is not something that we can ever discuss." Something squeezes in my chest at the word *trust*. Such a loaded word between us. His fingers brush over my chin, and then continue upwards, tracing my cheek up to my brows. Studying my face in a way he hasn't done before. "I can tell you this. We don't deal in the flesh trade."

"You mean prostitution?"

He nods. "Not just that. Any human trafficking. We won't touch it."

"Drugs?"

He looks towards the cascading water falling directly in front of us like a privacy screen. "Not directly. We control major supply routes to the East Coast. That's one of the things that makes us so powerful." I open my mouth to ask another question, but he shakes his head. "Why so many questions?"

"Don't I have a right to know, as your wife," I say, putting emphasis on the last word. "My uncle treated me like a child. I had no say over my life, my future. I can't do that again," I warn him. "What's the real reason we moved here?"

"There are threats above and beyond the usual," he admits. "I can't share details, but I don't want you worrying about it. You'll be safe here."

Safety. Such a false promise. Because if Daniil ever discovered what I am really after, he'd be the person I'd need protection from.

But living here is the opportunity I've been waiting for. The Kozlovs conduct at least some of their business from the estate. This might be my one real chance to give the feds something they can use before they lose interest in me, my case, and my family's death.

"Does it have to do with my uncle?" I ask. Daniil has said suspiciously little about working with the Zegas, even though I know he must be interacting with Jorge and other high-ranking cartel members regularly. He hates Jorge, that much is clear, and maybe it has something to do with me. A thought that creates a satisfied ripple over my skin.

His gaze cuts to mine, as he sinks deeper into the bubbling water. "What makes you say that?"

Because my uncle is the slimiest two-faced bastard I've had the misfortune of knowing. But if I reveal such hatred for my uncle, it opens the door for questions I'm not willing to answer.

"I don't know," I say. In an attempt at distraction, I stretch, allowing my breasts to float above the water. "You told me you're working with Jorge, and you *did* pull a gun on him at our wedding." I grin at the memory.

A hiss of air escapes between his lips. "We're working through our differences." But I notice the way his jaw tightens, and I file away this information for later.

"And what about your safety?"

His laugh is cold and hard. "My life is always in danger. Nothing's really changed."

Unease blooms somewhere deep inside, and I don't like it. I'm getting lost in Daniil, consumed by these moments of connection between us, and if I let that happen, all will be lost.

Because in the end, he'd betray me too. Bratva business above everything else, that's always the way. I tell myself he's different from my uncle, but how could he be? He was born and raised in the brotherhood, and it's no fucking different than any other organized crime family.

I rise from the water, steam curling around me like tendrils of smoke. "I'm beat," I say. "Let's go upstairs."

He stands, pulling me against him, allowing our naked bodies to slide together. Despite the warmth clinging to my skin, all I feel is the icy burn of my betrayal.

## CHAPTER TWENTY-FOUR

### BIANCA

"So, how have you been settling in here?" Georgia sits back in her seat, lifting her face to the sun in an attempt to soak up the fading afternoon rays. We're enjoying pre-dinner cocktails on the terrace, the sounds of the ocean mingling with the distant call of seagulls.

I can't help but break out in a grin. "It's going well," I admit. "Being out of the city has been good for me and being by the ocean is a dream." It's true, I've found a rhythm living here that's been good for my soul—soaking up the beautiful early fall weather; walking along the beach with Eris playing in the surf; spending hours in the library getting lost in a book; and of course, Daniil.

He's still as busy as ever, but he's making more time for me. My hand reaches up and trails the delicate chain of the necklace he gifted me last night. He'd blindfolded me and made me stand naked in front of the full-length mirror in our bedroom. His heavy chest pressed into my back, as he slipped something cool and delicate around my neck. Removing the blindfold, his fingers traced the chain all the way down to his initials which fell squarely between my breasts.

I couldn't help but laugh. "Your initials?"

His eyes snagged with mine in the mirror. "So everyone knows who you belong to."

Even now, a smile still dances on my lips, and Georgia flashes me a sly grin. "Mm, I bet it's going really well," she says, taking a sip of her oversized margarita. "I've never seen Daniil so ... relaxed."

"Yeah well ..." I slip my hair behind my shoulders. "I suppose I have that effect on him."

She holds out her drink to me, and I raise my glass in cheers.

"I'm sorry I haven't been around more," she says with a grimace. "Between teaching and Andrei's schedule and the fundraiser I'm planning for a Brooklyn-based art school, I'm always so stretched."

"No need to apologize," I wave my hand dismissively. "You have a life, and I'm happy for you. Now tell me about this fundraiser you're planning."

"Oh, I hope you'll come!" she squeals. "It's at the Bellair, and it's going to be epic ..."

As Georgia continues on, I can't help smiling to myself. I've come to really like my sister-in-law. She's no bullshit, and although her and Andrei had a very unconventional beginning— starting with him taking her captive—they've somehow managed to make it work. Even better than that, judging by the perma-glow she's always sporting. I wonder if Daniil and I could ever be like Georgia and Andrei. If we could beat the odds to become a real couple. But it's a useless thought, and I dismiss it quickly.

"What about you?" Georgia asks, perching her sunglasses on her head and wrapping her shawl tighter around her shoulders. "Now that you're settled in, have you thought about what you want to do with your time?"

"You say that as if Daniil would let me work. I don't know

what kind of good pussy voodoo you pulled on Andrei, but Daniil doesn't seem keen on me having a job."

Georgia nearly spits out her drink. "Damn. I didn't even think about that. Maybe my pussy is magic." We both burst out in laughter. "More likely, I just made Andrei realize if I'm not happy, he won't be either."

"Honestly," I tell her, "I don't even know what I'd do. I haven't given my passion much thought."

Emilio forbade me to go to college, claiming it was useless as I would be a mafia wife and well taken care of. Of course I went along with his demands, not only because I had little choice, but because I wanted him to believe I was on his side, willing to do whatever needed to be done for the cartel.

"You have some time to think about it now," Georgia says, swiping at the salt on the rim of her margarita.

"I tried to talk Daniil into letting me work for him when we were first married. He was not open to that idea," I add, frowning at the memory.

She huffs a laugh, tilting her head. "What exactly would you want to do for the brotherhood, anyway?"

"I don't know," I say, shrugging self-consciously. "Just something. I have a good head for numbers, I'm organized, I'm business-minded, at least I think I am." I've always had ideas, I just had no one to take me seriously. When Jorge used to get tipsy and let Zega business slip, beyond gathering intel, I'd also analyze the strategy behind certain decisions. While my uncle is shrewd, so am I.

I shake my head, trying to stay on track. Because as much as I enjoy sitting outside in the fresh air and sunshine talking to someone close to my age, I'm starting to lose focus on the real reason I'm here. My mother would often talk to me about the need for investigative journalists to stay cool-headed and objective, not to get wrapped up in their sources and the story that they're covering. And yet here I am, doing exactly that.

It was easy to focus on exacting revenge at my uncle's home, surrounded by terrible men, but here, life is different. I'm content here, and I wonder if my parents would want me to focus on revenge, or just being happy. Deep inside, I know the answer, but I can't give up now.

"Are the guys always so busy?" I ask, navigating the conversation back to the brotherhood. "Daniil works constantly."

"Yes, but ..." She waves her hand in front of her. "I've never seen them work like this. Their empire is growing, especially with the casino." She sighs heavily. Georgia doesn't come from the mafia world like I do. I wonder if it's still weird for her.

"How do you manage that?" I ask. "Never seeing Andrei."

"Oh, I wouldn't say I *never* see him." Her head tips to the side, and she twirls a piece of hair around her finger. "I have the means to get his attention. And it usually includes busting into his office wearing no panties."

I nearly spit out my drink. "Oh my god." I laugh. "That's brilliant."

"You should try it sometime. They're never too busy for a little fun ... or the right kind of fun."

BINGO.

An idea forms in my head. Now I just have to wait for the perfect moment to carry out my plan.

"I think I'll try it," I agree, sitting back in my seat, and bringing my cocktail to my lips. After a beat, I ask her something I've been genuinely wondering. "Do you ever have a hard time with the ugly side of this business?"

She purses her lips in thought. "Sometimes, what little I know of it, to be honest. Bratva life is all this family knows, it's what they do best. I've had to accept who my husband is, even if I don't like or agree with every choice he makes."

"Thank you," I say.

"For what?" She grins at me like I've lost my mind.

"For your honesty. There aren't many people willing to speak the truth about this world we live in. It's refreshing when someone tells it like it is."

"Always. I'm here for you, Bianca. Things will get better, you'll see."

I nod and release a small sigh. That's a beautiful thought, but it's simply not true.

# CHAPTER TWENTY-FIVE

## DANIIL

THE CRINKLING of a candy bar wrapper seems to fill up the space of the entire car. My eyes cut to Leo, who pauses with a half-unwrapped Snickers bar partway to his face. He takes a big-ass bite, still holding eye contact, and then thrusts the bar towards me. With a full mouth he asks, "Want some?"

"Is that really necessary?" I ask, sinking lower into the driver's seat. We've been sitting in the parking lot of this pathetic excuse for a strip club for three fucking hours, waiting for Jorge and his entourage to exit.

"What? I'm hungry," Leo grumbles, taking another big bite before crumpling up the wrapper. Having no better place for it, he shoves it in his coat pocket before slinking down in the leather seat. Like me, he's had enough of sitting here waiting for the light show to start.

Our guys have been trailing Jorge for days, barely letting him out of their sight. It's what I should have done from the moment he moved to New York. Kept my eyes on him. Tracked his every move. But hindsight is twenty-twenty, and now I'm learning more than I ever wanted to know about him and the Zegas.

Case in point, this piece of shit strip joint on the outskirts of Jersey is how they spend their nights when not at the Bellair or following Bianca into one of our clubs. They've also set up their base of unofficial operations here, meeting with local dealers to get Zega products out on the street.

Andrei gave his blessing for the Zegas to deal in Jersey, especially since their supply is limited. But that will change if we help them ship their blow. And while it'd be a major cash infusion for us, there's no way I'm going to allow that to happen.

And that's what we're doing here.

My leg bounces up and down, impatience gnawing at my insides. "You say your guy's the best at wiring up cars, huh?"

Beside me, Leo huffs out a little laugh. "Getting cold feet, are you? This was your genius idea."

Yeah, it most definitely was. Provoking Jorge to come at me took some planning. He needs to know we mean business. This message will be clear—enough fucking around, if he plans on making a move, make it already. I'm ready for him.

Leo releases a little hiss and sits up straighter in his seat. "They're exiting the building."

I pick up the set of binoculars nestled in the center console and aim them towards the window, watching from across the street as a group of drunken Zega idiots pour out the back exit of the Zanzibar club.

Lucky for us, the back parking lot here is a virtual ghost town at three in the morning. I really didn't want to have to kill an innocent bystander. Although anyone hitting up this joint at this time of night is guilty of something.

With Días flanked by his men, the group of Zegas pass a beat-up Volkswagen Bug spray-painted red and black, Kozlov colors. The significance of the car's colors hasn't set in yet. But it will when they think back to this moment in time.

We wait till they are ensconced in their bullet-proof SUVs with strengthened and ballistic composite door panels. The idea isn't to kill them, just to send a message, one that they are about to get loud and clear.

"Do it." I give the command, and less than a second later, Leo's thumb connects with the detonator.

The explosion is deafening. Glass and metal combust, scattering debris everywhere in a bright orange ball of flame. Safely ensconced on the other side of the road, the ground shakes beneath us, toppling a garbage can twenty feet away onto the hard pavement. A car alarm goes off. Shouts ring out as Zanzibar patrons and staff scatter in all directions. Some hightail it out the front entrance, others pour out of the back door in a panic. And just like that, the Zegas squeal out of the parking lot, not waiting around to ask or answer questions.

"Shit." Leo whistles under his breath, turning away from the blazing car and fixing his potent gaze on me. "I'd say our work here is done."

With police sirens blaring in the distance, I couldn't agree more. But I need a second to revel in this moment: the Zegas running scared; fucking shit up with my brother like we did when we were coming up, not yet so burdened with responsibility; and a woman I'm addicted to waiting for me in my bed.

Throwing the car into drive, I slam my foot on the accelerator and peel out of the parking lot, heading straight for home.

THE NEXT NIGHT, shouts echo from the other side of my office door. A quick glimpse at the camera feed monitoring the hallway reveals exactly what I expected, even hoped for. Jorge is standing in front of my office, facing off with Yuri. Guess it didn't take him long to figure out who was behind yesterday's fiery message.

"Let him in, Yuri," I call out as my hand seeks the pistol I always keep under my desk. I even have a special compartment for it. I give it one last check—six rounds of ammunition in the magazine and one round in the chamber, enough to do some serious damage if that's what it comes to.

A moment later, the door to my office flies open, and Días stomps in. The thunderous look on his face tells me all I need to know.

"And to what do I owe the pleasure of this visit?" I work to tamp down the smile that threatens to form on my lips.

"Just what the fuck are you playing at, Kozlov?" His hands slam down on my desk.

"Sit down." My tone brooks no room for argument. We are on my turf, and I hold the power here. I gesture to the seat across from the desk. Standing gives him too much leverage if he's going to attack. Not that he has a weapon on him, my men would have made sure of that. "Now tell me, what's got your panties in a knot?"

With his back pin straight, Días lowers himself into the office chair opposite me. His eyes are dark and hooded, a sneer forming on his lips. "I think you know, Kozlov. Message received, loud and clear. And I'll be sure to return the favor."

I lean forward, my forearms on my desk. "Enough of this bullshit. Tell me what you're really after. Why are you slinking around my nightclubs, having one of your men harass Bianca? Make your move already, I'm sick of fucking around."

His eyes flicker with barely leashed violence, and I wonder how many men have been subject to The Madman's evil eye and lived to tell the tale. But the fucker doesn't intimidate me in the least.

"I told you, *parce*, I don't give a fuck about her." He leans back in his chair, his eyes zero in on the picture of Bianca and me on my desk. Kira took it on our wedding day and had it framed as a gift. "She's your problem now."

That's right. Bianca is mine.

Mine to worship and torture as I see fit.

Mine to protect, especially from the scum rotting a hole in the seat across the desk from me.

"You're a liar. And I'm watching you. Every move you make, I'm watching and waiting, and when you fuck up—and you will —everything you've worked so hard for is going to explode in your face like that unfortunate Volkswagen Bug."

His humorless laugh skitters down my spine. "But you forget, our family's partnership is more important than any pussy. We have an empire to grow, and I won't be distracted by a nice pair of tits and a fat ass."

"Get the fuck out of my office. You're not part of this empire, *parce*," I shoot back. I'm sick of him calling me dude, like we're friends or some shit. "You're just a jackal that feeds upon the carcasses of what we leave behind."

He holds up his hands in mock deference. Like a volcano, his exterior is hard rock, but inside, he's pure molten lava. "You're turning soft, Daniil Kozlov. The stories I've heard about you are legendary. Fucking and sucking your way around New York. You'd never let a woman lead you around by the balls. What happened?" He tsks loudly.

My hand dips below the desk and without hesitation, my pistol is aimed at his head.

"She happened, you motherfucker."

Our gazes hold and clash as seconds tick by. He's daring me to shoot him but knows I won't. Not here, anyway. Eventually, he tears his eyes from mine, his expression bored except for the tick of a muscle in his cheek. Slowly, he rises from his seat, his hand on the doorknob. At the last second, he turns and delivers his parting shot.

"Bianca was always so willing to get down on her knees. I hope she affords you the same consideration."

A sharp blast explodes through the air, my finger pressed tightly on the trigger. It's a warning shot. Next time, Días's brains will be splattered all over the wall. With a mad laugh, he slips out of the room, and all I have to show for my outburst is anger twisting in my gut and an empty casing on the floor.

# CHAPTER TWENTY-SIX

## BIANCA

IT'S A THURSDAY AFTERNOON, and the house is quiet. Well, it's always quiet since this place is so spread out, but Andrei and Georgia are out of town, and Kira, who visits often, is spending the night in her funky Brooklyn loft.

Having nothing else to do, I spend part of my day using Georgia's painting studio. I'm a crap artist, but I'm also going a little stir-crazy, so I've learned to branch out and try new things. Georgia's been kind enough to give me a few basic watercolor lessons, and even if my work isn't half as nice as hers, sitting in her gorgeous studio on the third floor of the house, overlooking the sea with Eris by my side is the best way I can think of to relax.

Choosing a cerulean blue for the sky of my landscape, I brush it over the canvas and attempt to layer the colors as Georgia instructed. Another week has passed, and I still have no new information to offer Deidre. She knows I haven't put the bugs in play here at the estate, and the pressure is weighing on me. I need to, I know I need to, but the perfect moment always seems out of reach.

Time slips through my fingers, and before I know it, the sun is so low it's but a vague glimmer in the sky. My masterpiece is hardly that, but it's not terrible. I abandon the painting on the easel—I'll figure out what to do with it tomorrow.

As I stand, Eris stirs from her doggy bed and shakes off the last vestiges of sleep. When she's not stirring up shit, she's a pretty great dog, content to hang by my side for most of the day. Having her with me makes me feel less lonely, ironic considering that was the reason I told Daniil I bought her, though it was nowhere near the truth at the time.

The dog has served both of her purposes well.

I lead Eris—on leash as I've quickly learned—through the grand halls of the mansion back to our suite. Georgia pointed out all the amazing original art in the house, but I have to admit the big names are lost on me. Still, I appreciate the beauty of the home. I wonder if it's Georgia's touch, because it's not just tastefully decorated, but there is a sense of hominess, like people actually live and love here. That certainly wasn't the case with any of my uncle's homes.

Arriving back in our suite, I find Natalia Kashin laying out a tea service for me. The Kozlovs' former nanny turned mother hen handles most of the household business. She's more like a member of the family than an employee, but I think she likes to keep busy overseeing the Kozlovs' domestic needs. And Georgia adores her as much as I've come to.

"Well, well, what is this?" I say, coming further into the room as Natalia pours the steaming liquid into a little china teacup for me. She's a petite woman with silver hair always neatly pulled back from her face, and a warm air about her.

"I thought you and Daniil might want a little afternoon pick-me-up," she responds kindly, bending down to pet Eris. Unlike Nadia, Natalia has much more patience for my unruly dog.

"Daniil?" I say, looking around the room. "I'm sure he's still at the casino."

"He was," she confirms, "but he's home early. Maybe he wanted to surprise you."

Excitement surges. Even though Daniil goes out of his way to make time for me, it's rare that I see him this early in the day. "Where is he?" I look around the room, but there's no sign of him.

"Just in his office finishing up some business. I'm sure he won't be long. I can let him know—"

"No need." I soften my interruption with a little smile. The back of my neck prickles with awareness. If there ever was a reason to visit his office, this would be it.

The excitement I felt a moment ago coils to a dull ache in my belly. Because what I have to do next brings me no joy. Quite the opposite.

"Thank you, Natalia, this is wonderful. I think I'll run a bath and relax until Daniil comes up."

"Of course, my dear." She gives my shoulder an affectionate pat before seeing herself out of our suite.

As soon as she's gone, I move towards our walk-in closet with intent. Slipping to the back of the small space, I stand on a dressing chair to reach the highest shelf. My hand curls around my old childhood music box. I lift it from the shelf, and bring it down, marveling at how solid the carved wood feels in my hand.

Gingerly lifting the top flap of the box, I spend a moment admiring the little spinning ballerina, closing my eyes as the haunting melody spills from the box, transporting me back to another time. When I was ten years old, Papa gifted this to me after my first ballet recital.

"This is for you, sweetheart. A dancing queen. Watch her spin to the music. She looks happy just like you do when you are on stage." He'd hugged me, and then my mom hugged me and brought baby Celeste into the embrace.

A moment etched in my brain forever. I can still remember how warm I felt wrapped in their arms, the smell of Dad's woodsy aftershave, how Celeste would always grab my hair or my cheek, anything she could get her chubby fingers on. The happy memory still has the power to take my breath away. It's been so long, and so much has happened since, and yet I can always conjure up that perfect moment in time, when life was still good, and I still had a family that loved me.

My fingers dig under the surface of the music box for the phone Deidre provided. It's ironic really, that the box my parents gifted to me all those years ago will have a hand in exacting revenge for their deaths.

Heart pounding, I take out one of the bugs and discreetly tuck it under the timepiece of my Bulgari wristwatch. It's the only accessory that I can guarantee will stay on after Daniil's finished with me. My skin is cold and clammy. Nerves, most likely. There is no coming back from this. On some level, I knew that Daniil didn't conduct mafia business from the penthouse. But here at the Kozlov estate, where the brothers often gather with Yulian, I've got a hunch they talk openly.

Once this bug is in play, I've officially sold out my husband to the FBI.

I don't question why the back of my eyelids burn or the pang of hollowness in my chest aches. If I start asking questions now or allowing myself to feel the twist of pain when I think of Daniil behind bars, I'll lose focus on my endgame. One last glance at the music box as I shove it back in its place hardens my resolve. This is the only thing that matters.

I emerge from the closet wearing a little off-the-shoulder red dress, one that broadcasts my intent quite clearly. Releasing my hair from its messy topknot, I allow it to fall over my shoulders in natural waves, better for Daniil to have something to grip onto.

I wander down the east wing where the offices are located. As expected, Timofey steps out of the shadows as I approach Daniil's office and asks if I'm lost. Unless I'm chasing a dog, there's no reason for me to be here. But of course, there is.

"No," I reply, offering him a cheeky grin, "just visiting my husband."

His chagrined expression is exactly the response I was looking for. When he hesitates for a moment, I loosen the belt of the trench coat I threw on before leaving our suite. One glimpse at the skimpy dress visible beneath the coat, and Timofey reddens, stepping back from the door.

Smart man.

I softly knock and Daniil responds with a rough, "Enter."

My foot connects with the wood, pushing it open while I stay planted in place. His eyes soften when he sees me darkening his doorway. Without a word, I release the belt, allowing the coat to swing open, showcasing the goods beneath. I cock one hip to the side, resting my hand on my waist.

It's at the moment I realize he's on the phone, some kind of conference call in Russian, but that doesn't stop him from smiling wolfishly at me and beckoning me forward with a crook of his finger.

Dropping the coat to the floor, I hitch my dress just high enough to make it clear I'm not wearing anything underneath. Air hisses through his teeth, and he hits a button on his speakerphone. The mute button, I hope. "Come here, printsessa."

I sashay towards his desk, stopping directly beside his chair which is pushed back against the wall, giving me ample room to settle between his thighs. He doesn't make a move, merely watches to see what I'll do next.

"I've missed you," I pout while rapid-fire Russian fills the room from the speaker. "Is this an important call?"

"Yes, very." He reaches up to cup my breast lewdly, then trails his hand down over my waist only to land on my ass, giving it a firm squeeze. A fire lights between my thighs, boiling to a rapid heat. I need this as much as he does, but he doesn't seem willing —or able—to end his call.

"Should I come back?" I ask reluctantly.

"Not at all."

*Alrighty then.*

Wrapping my arms around his neck, I lift one leg, slowly bringing it across his lap while his hot stare drags over my body. Straddling him, my dress gathers around my hips.

My fingers trail over his jaw. Strong, with the bloom of a five-o'clock shadow. He is sexy as hell. I think about it all the time when I prop myself on our bathroom sink and watch him shave in the morning. He devastates me. And that's why I need to fuck this feeling away right here, right now.

My lips crash down on his, and I push my tongue into his mouth, undulating my hips over his swollen dick still trapped in Armani. His strained grunt sends an electric shock straight to my clit. Daniil's hands travel from the backs of my thighs all the way up to my ass.

He roughly pulls down the top of my dress to expose my breasts to his heavy stare before his mouth clamps around a nipple. Sucking me. Devouring my tits as he would my lips with hot open-mouth kisses. His other hand moves to my ass, pulling me down roughly over his hard cock. It's so commanding, so predatory, and it makes me desperate to feel his thickness drilling inside of me.

"Be a good little whore and come on me," he commands. Somewhere in the background, I'm vaguely aware of men's voices still coming from the speakerphone, but it only seems to make the moment hotter.

My pussy throbbing, I swing my hips forward, every nerve ending in my body comes alive as my clit grinds against the fabric covering my husband's cock. The friction ignites a path of pleasure inside of me, and I'm high thinking about how dirty this is. Me using his fully clothed body to get off. I'm flushed, and wanting with every glide over his bulge.

And then he pulls away, leaving me breathless and needy. As if nothing out of the ordinary is going on, Daniil leans forward, just past me, hits a button on his phone, and speaks. I can't understand his words, but fuck, his voice is calm and steady. He doesn't sound at all like his wife is grinding on him, about to come on his fully clothed form.

Just the thought of my impending release seems to push me closer to the edge. I can't help it. A breathless moan escapes my lips.

A low chuckle rumbles from Daniil's chest. He must hear the desperation in my moan and register the way my fingers grip his shoulders tight while I rock on him like it's my salvation.

"Better keep it down, printsessa, they don't get to hear my wife come," he whispers against my ear. "But if they do"—he delivers a sharp smack to my ass. A crack rings out through the room and there is a momentary pause in the phone conversation —"there will be consequences."

Motherfucker. He hadn't put the phone back on mute. He's toying with me. Like a cat toys with their prey. But I can't say I mind the idea of his consequences.

"Come on me. I want you to get this ten-thousand-dollar suit messy with your pussy juice."

He keeps his fingers intertwined behind his head, but he looks at me with such a heated stare, I'm surprised I haven't erupted in flames. Biting my lower lip to keep from crying out, I squirm against him, my clit begging for any type of action. And when I find it, a breathy moan slips from between my lips, which Daniil catches, sealing his lips over my own.

Russian male voices continue to drone on in the background, and maybe that's why I'm caught unaware when Daniil grabs my hips forcing them down just as he flexes his hips upwards, my clit colliding with his hardness. That crash is all it takes for me to explode all over him. The orgasm lights my body like an inferno, making my movements jerky, my breaths ragged ... and loud.

Oh, shit.

It's then that Daniil moves. It takes only one second, but he barks something into the phone and then slams a button. This time it's not the mute button, he's hung up the men, and all his focus is on me.

"What did I tell you about keeping quiet?"

"I-I tried, but—"

"You didn't try hard enough, baby." A dangerous thrill jolts through me so intently I can practically taste it.

Burying his hand in my hair, he gathers a handful and tugs back to expose my neck before licking up the tendons. I need to catch my breath. I need to stay sharp, but as it is, I'm floating somewhere in space.

Amusement glints in his eyes. "You made a mess all over me." I glance down to see a wet spot on his crotch, exactly where I just rode out my orgasm. "And now I'm going to make a mess all over you."

In one fell swoop, his arm reaches around me and brushes everything off his desk. Holy mother of Christ. That was not necessary, but it sure was hot. I just pray his laptop is in one piece or this is going to be a very expensive lay.

"Up"—he coaxes me onto his desk—"and spread those pretty thighs wide."

I do as he says. He doesn't bother to strip me, but my dress has been reduced to a band of fabric around my waist. Rough hands brush up the backs of my legs and palm my ass. And then, without warning, he slaps my pussy, hard. I expect pain, but it's nothing like that. The sharp bite quickly gives way to a scorching wave of ecstasy. My eyes close and my head drops back an inch.

"Is this my punishment?" I ask, goading him.

An unholy sound rings out through the room as he delivers another sharp smack to my clit with his fingers. Daniil's gaze flashes black, his eyes glued to my exposed pussy. Arousal hits me like a lightning strike. Blazing, dirty, dangerous.

I grab his collar and pull him towards me with one very clear command. "I need you inside of me."

He slaps my inner thigh. "What have I told you, printsessa? Who gives the orders when we're naked?" His finger slides across my cheek, tracing over my Cupid's bow. "And your face is much too pretty for my head not to be buried between your legs."

"Wha—" But the words die on my lips as he pushes his middle finger deep inside of me, pumping a few times while his expert tongue lands on my bundle of nerves. He keeps it there, lapping at me until I whimper like an animal in need. My hips are grinding on his face, pulling him towards me with a hand in his hair, and in mere seconds, I'm close to hitting my peak.

"Not yet, baby. You'll come with my cock buried deep inside of you." He pulls away from my sex, his mouth still gleaming with my juices he leans in to kiss me. And, my god, the taste of me on his tongue is nearly my undoing.

Holding my thighs open, he pulls me to the edge of the desk, my feet planted wide so that I'm spread out for him. Vulnerable and bare. So obscene. He could do whatever he wants with me right now, and I'd let him.

Without another word, he pushes his pants down past his hips, and frees his cock. With one hand supporting me, I reach towards him, brushing my fingers down his velvety length. He releases a stifled moan and then wraps his thick fingers around my neck. His grasp is not tight, just enough pressure that his act of dominance makes my toes curl.

"I've been thinking about this pussy all day," he grunts. Lined up with my entrance, he pushes inside of me until he's fully rooted. His eyes close in a moment of ecstasy, and when they open, his gaze collides with mine. "You. Are. Mine." He thrusts into me hard with every word before he completely unleashes the beast inside. He's slamming into me. Fucking me hard, using me to get off, like I'm his doll.

What's wrong with me that I crave his brutality? That it makes me come so hard I see stars. Or is it my way of accepting punishment for my betrayal? As if sensing my thoughts, he pulls out of me and replaces his cock with two of his fingers. They dip into my pussy, and, coated with my slickness, he raises them up under his nose, taking one deep inhale before bringing his hand down to trail over my back entrance. A frisson of alarm has me jolting upright, but Daniil doesn't allow me to move, and holds me firmly in place.

"Relax. I'll make this feel good."

"But I've never—"

"Just my finger," he promises. And then he pushes a digit inside, up to the knuckle, before slamming his cock back into my pussy. I've never felt anything like this, so full and dirty, and —oh god, it's intense. My eyes roll up in my head, and he stops moving, demanding my attention.

"Look at me when I fuck you." My throat bobs with a slight tremble, a movement he doesn't miss. "I want all of you, printsessa. All your secrets, all your fears. Everything you've been holding back."

Fuck. What does he know?

My gaze tracks to the wall behind him, unable to maintain the fierce eye contact he demands. He'll see right through me if I do.

He laughs low in my ear and starts to gently move inside of me again. "Don't look so scared," he whispers before kissing my neck, running one hand through my hair. "It's just a reminder that you're mine."

"I am yours," I affirm, pressing my face into his neck. It scares me and thrills me because I like how it sounds so much, even if it can never be true.

"Come for me, like the beautiful slut you are." He twists his finger in my ass, and it sends shivers through my body, burning right through my skin. The brutality of his grip, the way he kisses my neck is all I need to let go.

He follows with one final deep thrust and an agonized groan in my ear before emptying his load inside of me, and whispers in my ear, "You were perfect."

Without another word, he helps me up off his desk and fixes his clothes while I fix mine. I'm shaking, but it's not because of the sex we just had. It's because of what I must do next. It's now or never.

"That was exactly what I needed." He pulls me to him, his lips brushing against mine.

"Why? What's going on?" I press, knowing that the bug is activated, picking up everything we're saying, and everything that just happened. It's humiliating to think about, so I'm not going to.

He shakes his head. "It's stuff you don't need to worry about." He buries his face in my neck, but I push him away.

"No, you don't. Don't pull that 'you're too precious, little lady' shit on me. We're past that. I'm your wife." The word nearly catches in my throat, and I take a moment to clear it. "I'm your partner. That's what couples do, they talk and tell each other things to help ease the burden."

He smiles at me. An unguarded, warm smile that makes me want to claw my eyes out. "Is that so?" he asks, tracing my jaw with his fingers. "I'll keep that in mind, but right now, I don't want to think about all this shit. Let's go upstairs, get some food, take a bath, do it all over again." He waggles his eyebrows at me. This man is insatiable.

"Uh-huh," I say, my heart pounding in my throat as I bend down to start collecting the strewn items from his desk off the floor. This is my moment. My eyes dart around the room, seeking the best place to plant the bug.

A large framed abstract painting hangs behind his desk. It looks like the kind of thing one might see in a museum, a collector piece, the kind of thing that may get lent out to a museum. So forget that. None of the lamps in this room have shades, they're all industrial-design chic with exposed bulb and curved metal stands. But then my eyes fall on a large potted fern in the corner, and I know I've found my spot.

"What are you doing?" His voice is dark and menacing, or maybe it only seems that way.

"Cleaning up," I squeak, not making eye contact with him, continuing to straighten up his office.

"You don't have to. I pay people to do that."

For a moment I think my treacherous heart will pound straight out of my chest. Does he know? Did my shaking hands and averted eyes give me away? I breathe deeply and give him a big smile over my shoulder.

"That's not how I was raised, cowboy. You make a mess, you clean it up." For one tense moment, the air is sucked out of the room. With my back facing him, I shut my eyes and wait for what's coming. But he just chuckles and bends down to join me in collecting the items tossed about the room.

"I like that you care. I can see you'll raise our kids well."

What the fuck. Of all the times to bring up us having kids ... Why now?! My skin is on fire, burning everywhere, but I fight to stay calm and focused. Drawing in a slow deep breath, I force a small smile. "That's right," I agree. "These are important skills."

He takes the other side of the room while my focus remains on the fern by his desk. I busy myself retrieving things off the floor, straightening up knickknacks, and finally, when there is one last item by the plant, I reach down and, with a furtive glance towards Daniil, slip the bug underneath the base of the potted plant.

"Are you fixing my plant?" Daniil's voice booms behind me and I nearly jump out of my skin. "You are one of a kind, printsessa."

My pulse is thudding in my ears, but I force the fear down, and gaze up at him. Sucking in a lungful of air, I stand and brush the hair out of my face, bracing myself for the best acting job of my life.

*I can't forget why I'm here.*

"Plants are important," I mumble. "They clean the air."

If only they cleaned my fetid, rotting soul, because I know there's a special place in hell for me.

# CHAPTER TWENTY-SEVEN

## BIANCA

As WE PULL up to the Bellair, a line of valets are busy opening the back doors of the stretch limos and Bentleys that idle in front of the casino. A light show worthy of a Lady Gaga concert casts the front of the building in swirling shades of red, blue, and yellow—a special touch for a special night.

Tonight is the fundraiser for the arts school Georgia supports. It'll be a who's who of New York society mixed with the underworld's biggest names—much like the opening night of the casino when Daniil and I first met.

We step out of the limo, and with a possessive hand wrapped around my hip, Daniil leads me through the grand lobby with its gilded frescoed ceilings. "This feels strange," he murmurs. "I never come in through the front entrance."

With that comment, we're stopped by a photographer who asks us to pose together in front of a large fountain, the center-piece of the elegant lobby. We pose together, one of Daniil's hands is on my lower back as we're instructed to smile, and the photographer gets off a bunch of shots. My smile is stiff, too formal ... too forced. I hope to hell I never see these pictures in print. I don't want to remember this evening.

Daniil leans forward and whispers into my neck, "Have I mentioned how fucking gorgeous you look tonight?"

I flash him a smile in return, all the while praying he can't feel my thumping heart or sense the nerves fluttering about in my stomach. Because burning a hole in my crystal-flecked clutch is the final listening device that I need to plant in Daniil's casino office.

It's been two weeks since I stowed the last one under the plant, and in that time, Daniil has barely worked out of his office at the Kozlov estate. It's not that he hasn't been home, he has, but when he is, he's spending time with me. It would be appreciated if I didn't have ulterior motives.

The thing is, I feel strangely relieved knowing that the FBI is probably learning nothing from the other three bugs—two of which are at Daniil's penthouse that we've since abandoned. It doesn't make sense that I feel relief. Because if the feds aren't getting the intel they want, they'll only keep on pushing.

And every day that passes, my uncle remains a free man. Worse, with every day that passes, my feelings for Daniil grow. And that's why, no matter what, I have to plant the last bug in the casino office and be done with it. It's the one place I believe Daniil still conducts brotherhood business from.

We enter the main gaming room, which looks majestic as usual. The fundraiser is well underway with New York's glitterati floating from table to table, air kissing and sampling fancy hors d'oeuvres off the trays of passing waiters. Just before we step further into the room, I turn to Daniil, straightening his already immaculate tux. I just need a moment alone with him before we descend into the mayhem.

"Looks like quite an event," I acknowledge, my eyes sweeping the room. "Will I see much of you tonight? Or are you going to be wheeling and dealing all evening?"

He smiles, pulling me against him and kisses my forehead.

"I'll come find you when I have a minute. Promise me you won't wander far."

I nod but can't look him in the eye. "Sure. But don't blame me if I lose all your money. I'm a horrible gambler."

His hand lands on my ass and gives it a quick squeeze. "Spend it like you stole it, printsessa."

"Are you two at it again?" Kira approaches, beaming at the sight of us. "You look amazing," she gushes, capturing me in an embrace.

"So do you!" Kira looks stunning with her cat eyes and blond bob styled into a relaxed retro wave like an old-Hollywood movie star.

"Why thank you," she drawls, fluttering her eyelashes. "Tonight is a good excuse to get stupid drunk and find a willing man to—"

"I think that's my cue to leave," Daniil interrupts, planting a final kiss on my temple before heading towards Andrei, who's already in deep conversation with a group of men.

Kira leads me to the blackjack tables and hands me a stack of her chips to get started. "I really don't know how to play," I argue. "You'd be wasting your money on me."

"Who cares?" She shrugs breezily. "It's for a good cause."

My legs bounces against the table, nerves alighting my veins. After tonight, nothing will ever be the same. "I'll watch you first and learn, okay?"

"Great. You'll learn exactly what not to do," she snorts, joining the game.

Turns out, Kira is as lousy of a player as she claims. She loses all her chips in about twenty minutes but doesn't seem bothered. "Gonna try poker next," she says, reaching for a flute of champagne from a passing waiter's tray.

Shoulders tight, I consider my next move. It's eleven, the room is full, and the guests are drunk enough that the party is really in full swing. It's the perfect time to fade into the background and avoid scrutiny, even from the guards who are on the lookout for bigger threats. No one is paying attention to me, and I need to take full advantage of that.

"I'm going to check out the silent auction," I say to Kira, gesturing to the far wall of the casino. "Catch up with you in a bit?"

She blows me an air kiss and heads off. I make my way along the periphery of the room, and before long, I spy Daniil and his brothers out on the terrace, huddled in a semicircle with a few other men. All men. As it always is in this world. Their conversation looks serious, intense even. Like they'll be at it for a while.

I thank my lucky stars.

Daniil's office won't be locked, but it's usually guarded by one of his men. I'll feign a headache or illness. What guard in their right mind would turn away the boss's wife who needs a place to lie down?

Mikhail's eyes find mine from across the room. He waves. I wave back and point towards the ladies' room. He nods in understanding. Usually, he's stuck to my side like a thorn, but tonight all the Kozlov's men are needed to monitor the casino floor, so I have a little more breathing room. Daniil assured me it's an invitation-only affair, with the guest list tightly monitored.

With Mikhail's eyes tracking me, I head towards the washroom, but the moment I am out of his sight line, I take a sharp left, moving through the kitchen and staff lounge area. It earns me more than a few surprised looks, but I walk with purpose, head held high, knowing that no one will question me. At the very end of the kitchen, I push through a set of double doors and end up exactly where I want to be. The back stairwell.

The one and only time Daniil brought me to the casino, we entered through the back of the building and used these stairs to get to his office because he didn't want to walk through the casino floor. And here I am again. A sickly feeling settles on my skin. I am about to set the match that will incinerate the Kozlovs and crush my heart. All for revenge.

I've ascended only a few steps when I'm yanked back by a

hand clamped around my arm. I stumble and fall back into a hard male chest.

"Bianca." The voice of my worst nightmare hisses in my ear. "Where are you running off to?"

A shiver runs down my spine as bile rises in my throat. His grip is tight, and he swings me back so I'm facing him head-on. His eyes are cold and dark, unfeeling. My stomach roils at his presence, but I won't give him the pleasure of my fear. Instead, I straighten my spine and feign confidence I don't feel.

"What are you doing here, Jorge?" I spit, my gaze searching the desolate hallway, hoping that someone, anyone, blasts through the service doors so I'm not alone with Jorge.

"The Zegas are close associates of the Kozlov Bratva now, thanks to you." His smile is tight; different from what I've seen before. Dressed immaculately, he looks no different from any of the other guests, but Daniil would have warned me if Jorge was invited, wouldn't he?

"Fine," I say, shaking off his grasp, and crossing my arms in front of my chest. "Why are you here ... in this hallway? Have you been following me?"

"I need to talk to you, Bianca, but Daniil hides you away like the crown jewels. You don't belong here, in this world with a bunch of Russian gangsters."

"What are you talking about?" I shiver, hating how uncomfortable he makes me feel.

Jorge steps closer, too close for comfort, but unless I start climbing the stairs backwards, I'm stuck in place. "Emilio regrets marrying you off, losing his only living family member, just like I regret losing you. I think about you all the time, *mi alma*."

Liar.

An eerie sensation crawls over my skin. I don't believe a word out of his mouth. He's never cared for me, and neither has my uncle. I want to know what he's really after, but I also don't want to spend another minute in his presence.

Schooling my expression, I straighten my shoulders and

channel the confidence my mother always possessed. She would have shut down this conversation before it even began. "I'm sorry that's how you feel, but it's too late. You gambled me away, and my uncle forced me into this marriage. What's done is done, Jorge. There's no going back."

He smirks, sending ice through my veins. And then he leans down, so his face is inches from my own. "Do you think your uncle would just give you away so easily? Do you really believe the Kozlovs are smarter than Emilio Morales?"

What is he talking about? But I don't have the time or mental energy to try to untangle his words. I have a job to do, and if I do it well, Jorge and my uncle will be behind bars before I find out what's really behind his declaration of love.

"I don't have time for this, Jorge. Daniil is my husband now, and my husband is waiting for me upstairs," I lie, turning towards the stairs.

I don't get very far before he tugs me back against him. I try to jerk myself free, but his grip is like a vice. Holding me against his chest, he whispers softly in my ear, "Husband. Such a deceiving word. Your place is back in Colombia with your family. With me."

Blood roars in my ears as venom clouds my vision. If he thinks for one second I'll ever be with him again, he's delusional. "Let me go, right now," I demand, and he does, but not before spinning me around to face him.

"You're mad, *cariña*. I understand," he says in a conciliatory tone. "I regret my actions, not only the night of the poker game, but before that. I didn't fully appreciate what I had."

My arms wrap around my body, hugging myself in a protective gesture. "Why are you telling me this now, Jorge? It's too late for us."

"That's where you're wrong. I've quit drinking, I'm a better man. Come back to Colombia with me. Come home to your uncle, your birthright. Say the word, and I'll make it happen." When he looks down at me, his expression is somber, earnest even. And that's the scariest thing of all, because this is not the real Jorge, not The Madman I know who's lurking beneath the surface.

His scarred hands flex, reaching out for me to take his palm. Slowly, I shake my head. "I can't" is all I say, taking a step back and glancing up the stairs. "I have to go."

"Promise me you'll think about it. Call anytime, and I'll come for you, bring you back to your uncle's compound in Colombia. You'll be safe there. I'll make sure of it."

My stomach is in knots, but my desperate need to escape his presence has me nodding. "I'll think about it," I mutter, and then turn for the stairs.

"I still love you" is the last thing he says.

*Fuck me, what was that about?*

His retreating footsteps echo off the cement walls as he takes his exit. I take a moment to catch my breath and pull myself together, but I can't let anyone catch me like this. How would I explain what I'm doing in the back stairwell alone with no guard?

There is no plausible explanation. No one can ever know about this. Even Daniil.

Especially Daniil.

No matter what Jorge's true intention is, it doesn't matter. If I'm successful tonight, Jorge will be in federal custody before he can do more damage. And that's why I must pull myself together and see my plan through.

I take a deep breath and continue up the stairs. When I get to the third floor, I move through the hallways on autopilot, a left and then a right, until I get to Daniil's office. Yuri is standing sentry outside the door. He takes one look at me, and his features fall.

"Are you okay, Mrs. Kozlov?" he asks, his gaze full of concern.

"I had a dizzy spell," I croak. "I just feel a little sick and I need to lie down. Is my husband here?"

"He's not, but I'll call him. You go in and lie down." He opens the door for me, and I enter the room. Without thought, I head towards the leather couch I fell asleep on my first time here.

Yuri is distracted; this is my chance. I reach into my purse, removing the bug covered in a tissue.

Yuri looks up from his phone, frowning. "Everything okay?" he asks.

"Just grabbing a tissue." I dab at my nose and lie back down, rolling the hard nub between my fingers.

My brain screams at me to open my hand and slip the device between the couch cushions, but my hand has other ideas. As if it's incapable of letting go. I'm gripping the bug so tightly I think I may break it. Every fiber of my being tells me to shove it between the cushions and be done with it. Be done with all this shit.

*For Mama, Daddy, and Celeste.*

*That's all that matters.*

Even if it destroys me to betray the one person in the world who cares for me.

So I do it. I release the bug between the couch cushion, snaking it down with my fingers and then I curl into a ball and cry my eyes out.

There's nothing I can do to stop the tears. They fall freely, of their own accord; rage mixing with sadness mixing with regret and all the feelings that have been brewing inside me for years. Being betrayed by a family member is awful but betraying someone you don't want to hurt ... well, it turns out, that's torture.

What feels like an eternity—but in reality is only seconds later—the door bursts open, and Daniil races towards me. His face is a mask of worry as he kneels over me, grabbing my chin in his hand. "What's wrong?" His hands track over my body, touching everywhere, looking for signs of injury.

"It's not like that," I sob. "I just don't feel well. I feel light-headed."

"What can I do, baby?" He picks me up in his arms, cradling

me like a child. "I'll do anything for you. You know that, Bianca," he whispers, kissing my forehead.

His words destroy me. They kick-start a fresh round of tears. It would have been preferable if he ripped out my heart from my chest and stomped on it until it was flat.

"I just want to go home," I say, my face pressed tight into his neck.

"I'll take you home." His voice is an anguished whisper. He kisses my head and gently carries me down the stairs and into a waiting car where I pretend to be asleep because I can't bear his tenderness for one more minute.

# CHAPTER TWENTY-EIGHT

**BIANCA**

THE NIGHT of the casino fundraiser is my undoing.

I spend the next week feigning illness, an excuse to curl into the fetal position with Eris and not leave our bed. Because lying in the dark, questioning my every choice, my every decision that brought me to this very moment, is the only thing I am capable of currently.

Nothing makes sense. Not Jorge accosting me on the stairs. Not Daniil, supposedly a dangerous and lethal bratva boss who treats me like a true printsessa and protects me like I'm the most precious thing on the planet. *He would do anything for me.*

My final act of betrayal cost me dearly. It cost me my sanity.

It's late afternoon by the time I drag my sorry ass into the bathroom. I shower because after days in bed, I can't stand how I smell. Afterwards, I wrap myself in a towel, and brush my teeth, even though it feels like a lot more work than I'm capable of right now. I'm thankful for the fogged-up mirror so I don't have to look at my treacherous face.

Finishing up, I turn off the tap, and make a move to flip off the light, but something stops me. The knowledge that I haven't checked the phone I use to communicate with Deidre since I planted the final bug in Daniil's office a week ago.

Hands shaking, I bend down to open the cupboard door, then reach for the box of tampons. My hand hovers above the cardboard for one long moment. Is this what I want? Deidre will have undoubtedly sent me a message. And once I see it, I can't unsee it.

But what's the alternative? How long can I ignore her for? Because if she doesn't hear from me, it's not like she'll back off the Kozlovs. The feds got what they wanted—four high-tech listening devices planted in the homes and offices of one of the most powerful crime families on the East Coast.

I log into our messaging platform to find that Deidre has left me only one message, sent earlier today.

```
USER3498: We need to meet ASAP.
I'll be waiting for you tomorrow
@ 1500. Same place as last time.
```

Do they have something on my uncle and the Zegas? Hope flares for one brief moment before another thought takes over, a much darker one. *She might have something on the Kozlovs.*

Bile rises in my throat, but I swallow it back down. I need to keep my shit together long enough to find out what Deidre knows. I can't hide from my actions any longer. But I also know I can't face Deidre in person, not when I trust her even less than I trust myself.

```
USER9684: I have the flu, can't
leave the house. Call me at 1500.
I'll make sure I'm alone.
```

I put the phone back into hiding and crawl back into bed to block out the real world for as long as I can.

SOMETIME IN THE middle of the night, Daniil joins me under the covers. This is usually when things take an X-rated turn between us, but he's been hands-off all week since he thinks I'm sick. Which I am. In the head. Instead, he just spoons me, breathing in my scent.

"How are you feeling, printsessa?" he asks, stroking my hair back from my face, dropping a sweet kiss on my cheek.

"Better," I whisper. Although that's not entirely true. Anticipating Deidre's call tomorrow has brought on a fresh wave of anxiety. "How was your day?"

He stills for a second but then melts into me. "Bloody. Card counters, repeat offenders. They had already been warned and told to stay away from the blackjack table. I had to teach them a lesson."

My body stiffens. "At the casino?" I ask, hysteria tinging my voice. Because if so, who knows what the feds picked up on.

He sighs as he brings me against his chest. His hand snaking around me to cup my breast, holding me against him.

"No, we keep bratva business far away from the casino. We own a garment factory in Brooklyn, that's where we handle our shit. It's one of the few places we can talk freely."

Lead drops in my chest, hot and heavy, and the pressure knocks the breath from my lungs. Why did he have to go and tell me that now? I want to curl up into a ball and scrub that piece of information from my brain, but I can't erase what I've learned.

Daniil nips at my neck and grinds me against his hard dick. "I'm glad you're better, printsessa." He flips me on my back. "'Cause I desperately need to fuck you."

I open my mouth to protest because I don't deserve him. I don't deserve his tenderness or his heart, but he swallows my words with his lips and tongue, devouring me like a starving man. One hand wanders down my body, snaking under my nightgown to land between my legs.

Pulsating arousal and a blinding rush of ecstasy fill me, as happens every time his hands are on me. Lighting me up from the inside out, as if we're connected by electrical currents that flow between us. With each touch, each drugging kiss, all those wretched feelings bouncing around inside me melt away. He consumes me with such intensity that all I can do is take shelter in his arms, in our physical connection, and not think about the road to hell I'm leading us both down.

# CHAPTER TWENTY-NINE

## BIANCA

I DREAM of my parents and sister that night. A vivid dream, not a nightmare like I used to have when I was younger. This dream is different.

I am in a beautiful meadow on a sunny day, wandering alone and enjoying the peace and stillness. I bend down to pick a wildflower, and when I stand back up, my parents and sister are there, holding hands, so happy to see me. I run to them, hug them, relish the feeling of them in my arms.

I cry, but they are tears of joy because we are reunited. They are alive and well and so happy to see me. The love between us is still so real, palpable—the familiar way Dad envelopes me in his arms with Celeste pressed between us, my mother's perfume, floral and light, the warmth from her body.

"I'm so happy to see you," I cry. "I miss you so much."

"I know, *mi amor*, I know." My mother kisses my forehead. "But I am still with you. Every day."

"How is that possible?" I sob.

"Can't you feel us with you?" She smiles. "We are still here. And we want the best for you." She strokes my cheek, love shining in her eyes. And then she points to a lone figure walking towards us through the tall grass.

It takes a moment for my eyes to adapt to the bright sunshine, but once they adjust, I see who is approaching. Daniil. Looking as handsome as ever, as devastating as always. I want to run to him, but I don't want to leave my parents.

"Mama," I say, my heart suddenly heavy. "I've ruined everything. He's going to find out what I did soon, and he'll hate me."

"No, sweetheart." She takes both of my hands and stares into my eyes as she so often did in life. "It will be all okay. You're going to make it okay."

As Daniil gets closer, I turn to my mother. "But he's mafia. Is this the man you want for me? Really?"

"It's not about what I want, it's about what you want." Her hand lands on my heart. "And only you can answer that."

As quickly as my family appeared, they disappeared like mist off a lake, and I find myself wrapped in Daniil's arms, enveloped in his heat, consumed by his smell.

When I open my eyes, sunlight floods in through the windows, and like in my dream, Daniil is cradling me into his chest, the safest place in the world.

And just like that, what I need to do next is clear as day.

I'm no longer going to be a pawn. Somehow, I am going to make this right.

At three o'clock sharp my phone rings. I stare at the screen for a moment, hands shaking, because I know whatever news Deidre has for me will change everything. I close my eyes, back pressed into the bathroom wall, and with one final deep breath, answer the phone.

"Deidre. What's going on?"

"Nothing." Her cold voice huffs down the line. "That's the problem. We have nothing. The Kozlovs talk about the weather, they talk about their fitness routines, they talk about restaurants, but what they don't discuss *at all* is business," she huffs. "They know, somehow they know."

I shake my head furiously even though she can't see me. "They don't," I insist. "If they found anything, I'd know about it."

"Would you?" Her voice drips with doubt.

"Certainly, if they suspected me."

Restless energy zips across the line between us. "They must have another office, another place where they actually conduct their mafia business. At the casino and home, they keep it all above board."

This moment was inevitable from the very start. The moment where I choose to either twist the knife or simply step away. I've betrayed Daniil a thousand times over, but miraculously the feds still have nothing. This is my only chance at redemption.

"If they do, I don't know about it." The lie slips as smoothly through my lips as butter.

I'm done being a lapdog for the feds. I am done being strung along by their empty promises. From here on out, I'm firmly Team Kozlov. As difficult as it's going to be, I'm going to come clean to Daniil tonight. He deserves to know everything, the full truth. And although my stomach is a riot of nerves when I consider how he will react, I owe him transparency.

And maybe in time, he'll help me exact the revenge I've been seeking for most of my adult life.

"My bosses are out of patience," she sniffs. "Soon they'll find another way to get to the Kozlovs, and if that happens, the case against your uncle disappears."

"They're not the only ones out of patience. How long have you had to prove my uncle was behind my family's car accident? I handed you the evidence, everything you need—"

"Everything we have is circumstantial," she interrupts harshly. "We've been through this."

The familiar burn of anguish climbs up my throat, and I have to swallow the emotions down. Five years has done nothing to ease my pain. It may as well have happened yesterday.

"I can't work with you anymore," I say, fighting to steady my voice. "I'm done."

There's a tense silence on the line, followed by a defeated sigh. "I want to help you, Bianca. You know I do."

"We must have different definitions of *help* in that case."

"There's something you should know," she responds, a hint of desperation in her tone. "We intercepted a call Jorge made to your uncle a day ago. They mostly spoke in code, but Jorge said that they'd—and I quote—'be able to take over the Kozlovs' shipping routes soon.' What do you know about that?"

It takes me a long moment before I remember to breathe, because if she's saying what I think she's saying, this could be detrimental for the Kozlovs. "Why are you telling me this?" I ask.

"To remind you to be patient. We can still get your uncle. If they start shipping cocaine, working together, we'll have something solid—something that will hold up in court."

A full-body shiver racks my body. Fuck Deidre and her empty promises. "Too little too late."

She sucks in a sharp intake of breath. "You're not done until we say you're done. We make the rules. That's how it works."

With my hands shaking, and my heart in my throat, I stand my ground. "Do your best," I threaten, because tonight I'm setting the world to rights. I'm choosing Daniil.

# CHAPTER THIRTY

## DANIIL

"LOOK OVER HERE," Yulian says. His fingers fly over the keyboard of his laptop, clicking and hitting keys until he finally zooms in on a frozen image on the screen. It takes me a minute to understand what I'm seeing, but my blood runs cold when I realize what I'm looking at.

Jorge and Bianca. Together.

It's from the night of the art school fundraiser at the casino, over a week ago. The image was taken from the back stairwell of the casino that leads to our offices. What either of them are doing there is unclear.

Jorge wasn't invited; I banned all Zega members from attending.

And Bianca, why would she be in the back stairway?

Separately, either of these things doesn't make sense. But together, it raises a serious fucking red flag. Yulian is watching me, gauging my reaction to the freeze-frame.

"What is this?" I rasp, feeling unsteady.

"I had a few motion-activated cameras installed in the less-used stairwells and back rooms. These cameras aren't monitored, but I'm alerted to unusual activity. This stairwell should have been quiet during the party."

"Blyad," I say, an agitated hand running through my hair. I know I will not like whatever comes next.

Yulian presses play on his keyboard and sits back in his seat. The video is grainy because of the low light, but it shows Bianca in the service stairwell, about to make her way upstairs, before a lone male intercepts her with a hand on her arm. She turns, startled. He pulls her off the first step, where they engage in an intense conversation.

"What the fuck was he doing there? He wasn't invited." My mind reels trying to make sense of what I'm seeing. But that's the problem, there's little to see. Jorge's back is to the camera and while Bianca is facing the camera, she is bathed in a deep shadow.

"Did she tell you about this?" Yulian grunts.

My jaw tightens. "No."

Their exchange lasts for only a few minutes before Bianca continues up the stairs, and Jorge exits the camera's view.

"Jesus fucking Christ," I rail, anger blazing down my spine like a bolt of lightning. "How did he make it past security?"

Yulian shakes his head. "Let me worry about that. You need to worry about what's going on with your wife."

"You think they're working together?" A battle plays out inside me. On one hand, I don't believe it, don't *want* to believe it. But on the other hand, there is no reasonable explanation for their secret stairwell meeting. Or for Bianca to not tell me about it.

Yulian's mouth is set in a hard line. "It doesn't look good."

"Have you shown this to anyone else yet?"

"It was just brought to my attention. I thought you should be the first to see it." He runs his thumb across his upper lip. "I'd say this is the proof you need to convince Andrei that Jorge can't be trusted. Because whatever is happening here is not good."

"What am I supposed to do with this?" I yell, anger swallowing me whole. I curl my hand around our wedding picture propped on my desk and hurl it at the wall. Fuck. Violence is the only way to calm my raging nerves right now. My next victim is the decanter on the bar cart.

Yulian leaves the room and lets me rage. I'll smash, burn, and destroy everything in my sight until I'm too broken, too numb to feel anything at all.

I'M BARELY able to form a coherent sentence by the time we pull up to the estate. I'd forced Yuri to stop at every watering hole between Brooklyn and East Hampton, and like a good *soldat*, he'd done his job and kept his mouth shut, accompanying me into every seedy dive bar I demanded we visit. He supported my weight once I got too sloshed to walk in a straight line as we left the final bar on my route to hell.

After we pull up to the estate, I have a vague notion of Yuri trying to help me from the back seat, but I shove him off, and when he doesn't get the message, I pull a gun on him.

"Crazy motherfucker," he mutters, slamming the door and stomping off. It's true. I am a crazy motherfucker. A heartbroken one, too, and I need to be left alone in an alcohol-fueled abyss. So I curl up in the back seat and allow sleep to be my savior.

IT FEELS like I've been dead to the world for days, but in reality, I wake up only hours later, curled on the hard leather seat. I have a throbbing headache, a mouth full of cotton, and a cramp in my neck. In short, I'm a fucking mess. But worse, I'm no longer drunk. I'm no longer a mindless pool of incoherence. I'm way too sober for my liking, and there's no more running from the truth: Bianca used me like a pawn for her own advantage. Why, and how deep her betrayal goes is what I need to figure out.

Stumbling from the SUV, I enter the mansion quietly and get a drink of water from the kitchen. After chugging it down, I chase it with an espresso and two aspirin. I have to be sober for what I'm about to do. Well, get mostly sober. Bianca deserves that much—for her final judgment to be from a sober man.

I'll catch a few more hours of sleep on my office couch before I confront her. The hallway is dark and empty. Not a surprise, considering it's three in the morning, and the guards don't roam the halls unless movement is picked up on the cameras.

I fling the door to my office open and then pause. It takes my brain a moment to register what I am seeing.

Bianca.

On her hands and knees.

Groping the underside of a potted plant. What in the fuck?

She jumps up, her face pale, frozen in a mask of surprise. "Daniil." She reaches out to me, but then drops her hand, seeming to think better of it.

"What are you doing?" I know what she's doing, but I need her to say it.

"I was—" She's breathing hard, her body trembling. "I can explain. We need to talk, you need to—"

I'm on her too fast for her to get the rest of her words out. In a blink, I have her arms restrained behind her back as I push her upper body onto the desk, holding her there, but at a loss what to do with her.

"I know this looks bad. I know you're angry," she sobs. "You have every right to be, but you need to hear me out."

Icy rage works its way through me, a pit in my stomach threatening to explode. My heart jackhammers in my chest as I pull a knife from my ankle strap and hold it flush to her throat. Wrenching her up by her hair, I whisper in her ear, "We'll talk downstairs. Where I question traitors. Now move."

Pushing her along, she walks in front of me, my fingers still curled against her scalp. She silently weeps, her delicate shoulders shaking as she steals a glance at me. I enjoy her pain, her panic—she needs to know how we deal with traitors in the bratva.

But it's not rage filling my chest, though, it's deep sadness. The kind that could suck me under and hold me down like some possessed sea creature, never to rise again.

We are in the dungeon before I realize it. It's not really a dungeon, but it has all the charm of one. It's more like a holding cell. A small bare room, the only light coming from a single naked bulb hanging from the ceiling. Other than the chair I've deposited Bianca on, there's a rickety table, a stripped mattress in the corner, a sink, a toilet, and four blank walls.

In other words, this place looks medieval, and purposefully so. We don't actually torture anyone down here, that happens at the factory, but we keep people here to scare the wits out of them before we're ready to bring them in for questioning.

"Why?" My anguished voice echoes off the barren walls. "I gave you everything. Why would you side with that monster, with Días?"

"I didn't—"

"Don't fucking lie to me," I roar, causing a fresh round of tears to fall down her beautiful face, onto to her thin white nightgown. I can practically see her naked curves, but it only serves to remind me how she manipulated me with sex, with my incredible need for her.

My breath comes fast and hard, I must look as unhinged as I feel because terror flashes in Bianca's eyes. I've never seen her look so wrecked. Devastation written all over her face, but it's nothing compared to the storm brewing inside me. *Nothing*.

I hold her jaw tightly and stuff my thumb into her mouth, wondering if she's going to bite or play nice. I can't stand to see her all misty-eyed and broken. She has no right. I'm the one who is hurting. She inflicted the pain.

But she takes it. She closes her eyes and sucks on my thumb so tenderly. It's fucking confusing. Her warm mouth, the softness of her tongue, and I don't know what she is doing to me, other than rubbing salt in the wound.

I wrench my hand back and bring out the knife instead, but I don't have the heart to press it to her throat. It hangs limply by my side, as I stand in front of her, waiting for answers I don't want to hear.

"It wasn't Jorge and my uncle I was working for, it was the FBI." Her words hit me in the gut. Before I know it, I fist her hair in my hand, and I press the knife into her flesh, hard enough to sting. Bianca's not crying anymore; she's not hysterical. She seems to understand and accept that I must kill her. Even if it destroys me.

Which it will.

"It was never about you. I never wanted to hurt you or your family. I've been working with the feds to sink my uncle. He killed my family, and he will pay for that. I've made it my life's mission."

I pause, her words throwing me. But then I remember she's a master liar. "I don't fucking believe you. I don't believe a word you say."

"It's the truth, Daniil. I swear. I'm not lying. I can prove it."

"Except you're a liar," I bellow, ragged emotion clear in my voice. "We caught you on camera conspiring with Días in the fucking back stairwell at the casino, a place neither of you should have been. Just like now. What were you doing in my office, Bianca? Planting a fucking bug."

"I wasn't planting it, I was retrieving it. Listen to me, Daniil. You can kill me after you hear me out." The tears that spill down her face now are tears of frustration. But I can't look into her beautiful brown eyes anymore, so I throw the knife aside and pace around the room like a tiger stalking restlessly in its cage.

"A year after my family's death, just after my seventeenth birthday, I found a flash drive in the pocket of one of my mother's old cardigans. It was the only piece of clothing I kept because it reminded me of her. She used to wrap it around her

shoulders when she worked late into the night." A silent sob
escapes her mouth before she continues. "In the weeks after my
family died, my uncle dealt with everything—purged their existence. If I was more with it, I would have stopped him. But by
the time I came out of that deep dark hole, he'd erased them.
Clothes, journals, personal items, all of it gone. He acted like he
did me a favor."

"What was on the flash drive?" I question, my voice
unflinching.

She releases a hard breath through her nose. "It was ... everything." She shakes her head as if language is beyond her right
now. Maybe it is. "I told you my parents were journalists, but
they didn't cover the local beat. Maybe that's how things started,
but they'd both moved into investigative journalism. As far as I
know, they focused on the assholes in Washington, preferring to
take down crooked politicians and public figures. But it seems
my mother took on a secret project collaborating with an anti-
corruption organization in Colombia. Nothing had been
reported yet, they'd only been gathering data ... but you can
imagine how it ends."

"Let me guess. They were investigating your uncle."

"Yes," she rasps. "They were building a case against him with
the organization's lawyers. I don't know how my uncle found out,
it was supposed to be top secret, but ..." Bianca's delicate shoulders shrug as emotion swirls in her eyes. "I was young when I
learned all that. I was living with the monster that killed my
family. I didn't have hard proof, but there were enough clues in
my mother's work to suggest my uncle was onto them. What was
I supposed to do? I knew no one, I was surrounded by Zegas.
The FBI was literally my only option for help. And they
agreed ... but with strings. They wanted me to help expose him,
take him down for everything. And I wanted that, too. I want to
see him rot in jail."

"Did I ruin all of your well-laid plans with that poker game?"
I snarl, understanding where this is all going.

"That was the only reason I was with Jorge." She stands and grabs my wrists. For some reason I let her. "He's despicable, and I hate him. But unlike my uncle, after a few drinks, he'd let little details slip. Cartel business I wasn't supposed to know. But then you came along ..." She squeezes her eyes shut and opens them again. "When I was forced to marry you, the FBI insisted that the Kozlovs become part of the deal."

"So you sold me down the fucking river without a second thought." I push her away, but she comes at me again, standing too close. Her scent fills my nostrils, confusing my body. Because when she's near all I can think about is having her. Fucking her mercilessly, like she's my only salvation.

"Yes. I hated you at first, I had no loyalty to the man who called me a 'convenient wet hole.' Taking my uncle down is all I've lived for," she continues, sobbing. "All I've cared about for years, and then you came along and ruined everything."

She slaps me across the face. Hard. As if all of this is my fault. And maybe it is. But I refuse to apologize for any of it. Even if it brought me to this moment, where nothing makes sense and it hurts, everything fucking hurts.

A cocktail of emotions churns in my stomach, but I know without a doubt this is our last time together, and I need to have her right fucking now. There's no logic to it, I'm a man possessed, but I'm not the only one feeling this magnetic pull. Bianca's eyes are dark pools of desire.

Without further thought, I have her lifted and in my arms as my teeth sink into her swollen bottom lip. "I want you to bleed for me," I tell her, "and I'm going to lap up every drop."

She hisses as my tongue sweeps across her bleeding lip. I should slit her throat right now and be done with it, but my dick has other ideas. He always has other ideas when it comes to her.

I drag her to the small table in the center of the room and, with a hand shoved between her shoulder blades, push her down until she's flattened across its surface. I'm so hard for her, and her little moans tell me how much she wants this, too. Pinning her in place with one hand, I lift her nightgown, exposing her ass to me.

"You're wet for me, Bianca," I gasp, running a finger up and down her slit. "Is that a lie, too?"

The moment my cock is released from its confinement, I seek her warm cunt, and white-hot need electrifies every nerve ending as I bury myself deep inside her.

"That was never a lie," she gasps, peeking up at me through her veil of hair. But I can't stand to look at her, so I pummel her without mercy, satisfied when her eyes squeeze shut and she cries out every time my pelvis crashes into her ass.

The way her hot pussy clamps down on my cock is enough to make me explode inside of her, but I will myself to hold off. I'm not ready to let her off the hook yet.

"I'll never forgive you." I pull her head around, and spit into her open mouth. "Never."

"Fine," she gasps. "Just help me. Help me get revenge against my uncle. Help me destroy him, burn his cartel to the ground. Then you can kill me." My hips snap harder into her as she talks about her own demise. I'm the only one allowed to conjure her death. Not her.

"Why?" I roar. "Why should I do anything for you?"

"Because I fucking love you, can't you see that? I couldn't go through with it. I was going to tell you everything."

I stop thrusting and pull her up by her hair while I remain jammed to the hilt inside of her. *Fucking love.* As if I'd fall for the oldest trick in the book.

A response is beyond me right now. I'm lost in the heat of her tight pussy and her perfect flesh, but I can't give in to her. Not yet. I come at her like a wolf unleashed on its prey, using her for my own twisted needs, a slut just for me.

She takes it. Because I have the power here and she knows it, but that doesn't help make any of this better.

No, it makes it so much worse.

# CHAPTER THIRTY-ONE

## BIANCA

*"BECAUSE I FUCKING LOVE YOU, can't you see that?"*

My confession echoes through my mind. Daniil might not believe me, but it's the truth. It might be the most real thing I've ever said to him.

I love him, but he's going to kill me.

Daniil's large hand presses down on my back, rendering me immobile, while his other hand squeezes my hip. His grip verges on pain, but I crave the hurt, welcome it as a distraction from the storm raging on the inside.

"I trusted you," he spits. "You've ruined me. You've ruined everything." His chest slams into my back, and he snakes an arm around my waist, pounding into me with a relentless pace. He wants my misery, he wants to see me suffer, because that's all the punishment he's capable of doling out. But this is far from torture. This is everything I didn't know I needed. Because it's keeping me from thinking about the gaping hole in my chest where my heart once was.

Without warning, he pulls out of me and turns me so I'm facing him. With two hands, he lifts me onto the laminate surface. My ass nearly hangs off the very edge as my legs wrap around his waist. My only support comes from my two hands propped behind me.

And then he reaches out and rips the necklace with his initials from my neck, throwing it onto the floor. Devastation lances up my spine, clamping around my throat. The message is clear. I'm no longer his.

He slams into me again and again, thrusting so hard I'm sure the folding table we're fucking on is going to break with the force of his emotion. But it doesn't scare me. Pleasure blazes a path throughout my body, and I hate myself for responding to him so easily. Even after he punished me—humiliated me—I still crave everything he has to give me.

His eyes grow molten, and even before the words are out of his mouth, I know what he's about to say is going to rip me apart and leave me in tatters. "I would have done anything for you," he rasps.

His words push me towards my breaking point. Like the table groaning beneath us, I feel like I'm going to snap in half. Emotion spills out of me in a harsh sob. All I can do is bury my face against his neck and lose myself in the familiar beat of his body claiming mine.

His thrusts are slower now, less punishing. He's wrapped one protective arm around me, and his other hand is buried in my hair. Our heavy breathing fills the air, but the energy between us has changed. It's no longer strictly a punishment fuck, it's bitter-sweet. There's a sadness for what could have been, but now never will.

He reaches down, swiping a tear from my face with his thumb, then applies the wetness between my legs. Working my clit in circles, taking me right over the edge. My pussy contracts, and I cry out my release against his neck. Daniil is soon to follow, coming with an agonized sigh.

As he pulls out, he instructs me not to move. He pushes my legs wide, watching as his cum slowly leaks out of me, and then he does something unexpected. He drops to his haunches and laps at my pussy like it's his last meal. He's brutal about it. Sucking and flicking at my clit, his fingers scissor inside of me before he pulls them out, covered in his seed.

"Now lick." With his cheek pressed against one thigh, he gives me his fingers and I lap our juices up hungrily as he watches, his eyes glued to where my tongue is wrapped around his smooth skin. Our intermingled taste is so fucking perfect and dirty that it drags me to the edge. When he finally grants me one more hard flick of his tongue on my clit, I come undone with his fingers in my mouth and my heart in my throat.

# CHAPTER THIRTY-TWO

### DANIIL

MY BROTHERS' faces are stoic. Along with Kira and Yulian, we've gathered in our offices, on the top floor of our garment factory in Brooklyn so I could tell them everything. Everything about Bianca's betrayal—well, everything that I'm aware of at least.

Getting the words out nearly destroys me. Splays me open, makes me vulnerable in a way that I hate. I'd become so good at not feeling over the years, and now I remember why. Emotions are a fucking bitch. And the worst part? I still crave her touch, her smiles, her pussy ... like I crave my next breath. It's a real headfuck.

"Shit," Andrei finally mutters, his hands clenched into fists on the desk. "So, let me get this straight. She's been working with the feds for the last two years to take down Emilio—who she says had her parents killed—and when you married her, the feds insisted she spy on us as well. Like a two-for-one deal?"

I nod. It sounds ridiculous when he puts it that way. "Not that we can believe anything she says, but she showed me her messages with her FBI handler. They've learned nothing useful about our family, that's why they were losing patience with

Bianca. There is one more thing," I add, my back molars grinding together. "She asked me to kill her uncle."

"And why would you do that?" Yulian braces his palms on the desk in front of him.

"Because Emilio's preparing to fuck us over, too. The feds intercepted a conversation Días had about taking over our shipping routes."

Andrei's eyes flash. "What does that fucking mean?"

"It means he's a slippery fucker, and you should have listened to me from the start."

Instead of the outburst of anger I expect for Andrei, a wry smile touches his lips. "I suppose I should have." His expression flattens and the next words out of his mouth really take me by surprise. "I'm sorry this happened to you."

"What! No accusations, no anger? Who is this man?" I say to the others at the table.

Kira scoffs and hits Andrei in the shoulder. "A man changed by love."

"Now you've officially gone too far," he mutters.

"Where is Bianca now?" Leo interrupts.

"The basement."

Kira looks shocked at my response but holds her tongue, although I have no doubt she'll take it up with me in private. Leo and I spent all morning hunting down and smashing the bugs she planted. We also did a thorough sweep of our properties for any more listening or tracking devices. We found none, but still, venom courses under my skin like she poisoned me.

Andrei sits back in his seat, darkness crossing his features. "We'll need to sort the feds ourselves. Find out what they know and shut down any further investigation into us."

I have to look away for a moment, rage brewing in my gut again. "We'll need Bianca for that."

"Agreed." Andrei points a pen at me. "Take care of it."

I dip my head in agreement. "She betrayed all of us, and I'll never forgive her for that. After I clean up this big fucking mess, you can deal with her how you see fit."

Beside me, Kira stiffens. "What are you getting at? You can't kill her!" she cries, her blue eyes wide with alarm.

"She's a loose end," Yulian points out with a shrug. "That makes her a liability."

My heart curdles in my chest, and I stare at my hands because I can't bear to look anywhere else.

"She did what she had to do," Kira says, her voice raising an octave. "Like I did when I was desperate to find you, my brothers. Like we would all do to avenge our family. But she redeemed herself by coming clean. You said so yourself, Daniil."

"She came clean," I grumble. "I didn't say she redeemed herself."

Bianca wrecked me in ways I can't yet fathom. There's no coming back from that.

When I raise my head, Andrei is looking at me funny, like he can read my thoughts. My brother and I have had our fair share of differences over the years, but he and Yulian are perhaps the only two people in the room that can understand how vulnerable a woman can make you.

"She's your wife," Andrei intones, "you get to decide how we deal with her."

I flash my brother a fuck-you scowl, but he simply raises an eyebrow in response. "I can't think about that right now. But ..." I pause, reach for my glass of Macallan, and down a shot even though it's far too early to drink. "I am going to kill Emilio. He deserves to suffer."

Yulian's lips twist in distaste. "Killing the head of a cartel isn't child's play. There will be repercussions," he says, always the cautious one. "And with the feds up our ass, seems like a bad time to start a war."

"It's not a war if we wipe them from the face of the earth," I bark. Bianca may have gutted me, but what her uncle did to her family is unforgivable.

Once upon a time, my family was also betrayed by a monster in the worst possible way—I understand how the need for revenge hums under your skin until it's sated. And I have plenty of reasons to gut Emilio and Jorge myself beside the fact that they are traitorous pigs. "Emilio hasn't set foot in the US since the wedding. We could go after him in Colombia where the feds don't have any jurisdiction."

Andrei's jaw ticks in thought; a moment later he clamps a hand on my tense shoulder. "If you want to go after Emilio, then we will. We'll burn the Zegas to the ground when the time is right," he adds. "Right now, we need to wait until the heat settles."

I nod, sitting back in my seat. I'm not sure if the time will ever be right, but it's the one mercy I can offer Bianca before she must meet her fate, whatever that fate may be.

# CHAPTER THIRTY-THREE

## BIANCA

WHEN I WAKE UP, the space beside me is empty. Again. I roll over and bury my face in the pillow beside me and inhale. It still smells like Daniil, but just barely.

It's been two days since Daniil discovered I was an FBI informant. Two long days locked in the basement and most recently our bedroom, while Daniil figures out what to do with me. I'd like to say I get it, but I'm mad as hell. He knows why I did what I did. He saw my mother's letters to the NGO where she talked about the increasing danger to herself and her family. She told them she believed her brother was onto her and the repercussion would be severe.

When my family was killed, they were on the way to pick up our updated passports before we left for what I thought would be a family vacation. I was supposed to be with them, but I had a cold and decided to stay home. That's the only reason I'm alive today. Turns out, our flights were booked for the very next day, and the trip I thought we were taking was actually going to be permanent. We were relocating to Canada to escape danger—one day too late.

My uncle's men got to us first.

I am curled on the ledge of the bay window with Eris in my lap, overlooking the ocean in the distance, when the click of a lock fills the room. I expect it to be a member of staff with a meal for me, but I turn my head to find Kira standing in the doorway.

"Hey," she says softly.

"Hey," I echo, standing to meet her.

I brace myself for her wrath, because I didn't just betray Daniil, I betrayed his whole family. But that doesn't happen. She strides into the room, bends to pat Eris going berserk at her feet, and then motions to the bed.

"Can we talk?" I nod, sinking onto the bed beside her. "Daniil told us."

I swallow the lump in my throat. "I'm sorry. I know that's not enough. If there were another way, I wouldn't have involved you or your family. If things had been different—"

"I get it," she interrupts, dragging a hand down her face. "I'm not going to pretend that everything is going to be alright—my brothers are livid—but nothing is more important to them than family. Maybe in time, they'll understand why you made the choice you did."

I give a small shake of my head, throat thick with emotion. "I don't think Daniil will ever understand."

She lets out a soft laugh, tucking a strand of her blonde hair behind her ear. "He's hurt. He's hurt because you didn't go to him to get revenge. He would have done anything for you."

My heart sinks deeper in my chest. The only good thing in my life, and it's lost forever. I couldn't believe that Daniil loved me enough to go to war with my uncle. So many years spent fighting my own battles with no one on my side, I forgot how to share my burdens and lean on the comfort and stability of someone who loves you.

*Loves.*

I do love him, even if I realized it much too late.

I started falling the moment he let me keep Eris even though he is allergic to this ridiculous fluff ball of destruction. When I planted the final bug in his casino office, my devastation was so heavy, I didn't realize the dark tunnel I was plummeting down was more than guilt.

So much more.

He's never told me he loves me, but I know he feels the same way I do. Despite my betrayal, feelings can't be wiped out in a day, which makes this all so much worse.

"I fucked up." I let out a choked sob and bury my head in my hands. "And I don't think I can fix it."

The tears flow, and there is nothing I can do to stop them. I'm an idiot, breaking down beside a woman whose family hates me, might even kill me, but instead, Kira pulls me into her arms and lets me cry for as long as I need. Which turns out to be a very long time. Eris tries to get in on the action, licking my face, and swallowing my tears. It makes both of us laugh.

When I've calmed down enough, I tell her, "Thank you. I don't know how I got so lucky to have you on my side, but it means everything."

She squeezes my hand, then leans back and gazes out the window towards the endless sea. "Before I found my brothers, the only person in the world who loved me was my aunt Masha, and she was taken from me. Killed by my father." She smiles sadly. "I wish things had turned out differently, but I understand why you would need to avenge your family. How it can make you blind to everything else."

"I'm sorry about your aunt. And ..." I swallow hard. "I'm just really sorry about everything."

Kira stands and regards me thoughtfully. "I don't want to see you killed, but Andrei has left it in Daniil's hands." She shrugs helplessly, like there's nothing more he can offer me. "Georgia took her dad to Greece to visit family, but when she's back, she'll give Andrei hell. She'll be on your side, too, I know it."

With that, she takes her exit, and I'm left to wonder how I

can fix this. If I can fix it. Can betrayal this deep be forgiven? There's also the matter of bratva pride. Daniil may act the gentleman, but underneath the ten thousand-dollar suits and bespoke leather shoes, he's as vicious as any other man raised in the brotherhood.

Pulling Eris into my lap, I drop back onto the pillows. The most loving thing I can do now is to take the decision away from Daniil. Sending me to my death or keeping me around to ... well, to do what? Either way, the choice will eat him up inside. If there's one kindness I can pay him, it's to direct my fate.

Curled up on the covers, I let sleep pull me from this nightmare I'm living, into a place of numbness where nothing hurts, there are no feelings, no terror, no mistakes. Just numb.

A WARM HAND brushes over my face, rousing me from sleep. I keep my eyes shut tight for a moment, basking in his smell, in the heat of his hand. For one moment I pretend everything is okay, that it's a normal morning and he's waking me up to make love.

But the illusion is ruined the moment I open my eyes and see his stony stare boring into me.

"Get up," he barks, voice flat, devoid of emotion. I'll no longer get sweet whispered words pressed against my skin.

I sit up slowly, taking a minute to get my bearings. The sun has migrated west, meaning it's sometime in the late afternoon. Eris is still snoring at the end of the bed.

Throwing the covers off, Daniil's eyes sweep over me. For just one moment, his gaze warms my body, and I'm consumed by the heat in his stare watching the rise and fall of my breasts through my flimsy camisole. He reaches out and, for a brief second, runs a finger between them. My nipples tighten in anticipation of his touch, and feverish need flares between my thighs.

Just as quickly as the heat sparked, he lets it die with a mumbled curse and eyes that turn to cold steel.

"What's going on?" I ask, mildly.

"Get up and get dressed." His back is to me now, and he's staring out the big bay window. "I'll explain on the way."

An hour later, we're stepping off the Kozlovs' helicopter at a private heliport just south of FDR Drive in Manhattan. Daniil ushers me into a waiting car, settling in beside me in the back seat.

It was too loud to talk in the helicopter, or at least that's what I assume, but now that we are alone together, the silence is near deafening, I wonder if this is how he'll kill me. Bring me to an abandoned warehouse on the docks and end it all. My body will be found floating in the Hudson days or weeks later.

"Where are we going?" I ask, sounding as unsteady as I feel. It's then that I notice he looks feral. Unshaven, hair mussed, tension pulling the corners of his mouth tight.

"To see your FBI handler, prin—" He grunts, his eyes finding mine. He nearly called me *printsessa* but stopped himself. The hard frown that settles on his lips is proof enough that I'll never be printsessa again.

"What!? How did you—?" And then I recall he has my cell phone, and I showed him exactly how I communicate with Deidre. He set up a meeting pretending to be me. "I left things on bad terms with her when I refused to give up any more information about you. She'll think something is up."

He snorts in derision. "How very honorable of you," he spits. "But you've seen the error of your ways, and you're willing to give up information about the Kozlovs to further your cause. Shouldn't require much acting from you."

"I don't understand." He presses a piece of paper into my hand. "Why would you want me to tattle on you? To expose your family like this?"

"You didn't give me much choice," he growls. "Read this script. Memorize it. Tell her exactly this and nothing more."

I stare at the words in my hands, trying to make sense of why he'd want me to reveal any of this. "I don't get it," I say, pushing a thumb into my temple.

"Because, my sweet Bianca, you need to become valuable to her again. You need to gain her trust, and that won't happen until you give her something solid."

He glances at the watch on his wrist, then back out the tinted window. "We're going to be there in ten minutes. I suggest you study up."

I swallow thickly. My fate is still very precarious, and the man who holds my future in his hands has hardened his heart to me more than I ever thought possible.

DEIDRE DOESN'T OFFER me her usual warm greeting when I step into the back room. The scowl on her face confirms I'm going to have to work to win her trust back.

She waits till I'm sitting down, fidgeting with the hem of my skirt before she speaks. "You called this meeting. What do you have to say for yourself?"

"I made a mistake," I say, hanging my head in an attempt at acting contrite. "Now that I've had time to think, it's stupid to protect those bratva monsters. I still need your help, Deidre, and I'm willing to work with you in any way I can."

Waves of doubt emanate off her. Deidre is no fool, and I honestly hope Daniil didn't set me up to get arrested. "Why the change of heart?" It takes every ounce of strength to keep my expression neutral while she stares me down.

"It was my little sister's birthday two nights ago. Anniversaries are still the hardest days to get through," I say, biting my cheek to keep the emotion from overflowing. That part is at least true. Birthdays and anniversaries always send me on a downward spiral.

Deidre nods. A little humanity shines through in her expression. She's seen me at my worst, and for that I'll always be grateful. "Your husband couldn't console you?"

"It was just an act," I say, fighting to get the words out over the lump in my throat because it wasn't an act, nothing was an act. "You told me to develop a relationship with him, and I did. He's an asshole, like all the other mobsters." I take a stick of gum out of my purse and pop it in my mouth. A stalling technique. "Listen, Diedre, I was frustrated with you, with the feds. I've had to wait a long time to see my uncle punished, but I've come too far to give up now."

Deidre lets out a long slow breath, her head tilting to the side. "Did you watch the show *Homeland?*" she asks casually. I shake my head not sure where she is going with this line of questioning. "Well, it's about a Marine Corps scout sniper that was held captive by al-Qaeda as a prisoner of war. When the sniper returns to the US, a CIA agent is convinced that he was 'turned' by the enemy and poses a threat to the United States."

I swallow hard. "What does that have to do with me?" I ask, barely able to breathe.

She shakes her head. "I think the Kozlovs turned you."

"My loyalty remains with my dead family," I spit. "But you want to test me, fine. Test me."

"Give me something to work with. Something real. No bullshit leads. Break into your husband's office and give me something that we can chase or prosecute."

"I have something," I grit out, my mouth as dry as toast. I honestly don't know what shit Daniil is setting me up for, but here goes. Deidre raises an eyebrow in interest.

"The Kozlovs own a building and real estate corporation called ADL Holdings. Look into it. This is the company they use to clean dirty money. They mostly pay for the properties in cash. Other times, loans or mortgages are used, and repayments are made with a mix of dirty and clean money. They also take loans from foreign companies they control and use it to buy real estate all over the US. Then they resell these properties, so the money from the sale looks legit."

Deidre's eyes spark with interest. "How did you learn this?"

"Daniil is beginning to trust me. We were at a dinner with some associates, and they talked business. After I fucked his brains out that night, I asked questions and he answered."

She nods. "If this is true, it's a good start. We'll look into it and get back to you."

"And my uncle?" I ask, because I genuinely want to know.

"He's still in Colombia, we can't monitor him there. But if Jorge slips up on American soil, we'll be all over him." My face falls at her news, always the same old story. When she sees my devastation, she squeezes my arm. "Get us the Kozlovs, and I'll find a way to bring your uncle down as well. It's a matter of time."

"Sure." I force a smile, but I know better than to believe her promises. The only person I can trust from here on out is myself.

WHEN I GET BACK into the car, Daniil is waiting, his shoulders pulled taut, his face a stony mask. His stare is menacing, lacking any of the sparkle or lightness I crave. He drags his teeth over his bottom lip, waiting for me to make the first move.

"How do you think it went?" I ask him since I'm wearing a wire and he heard the entire exchange.

Tension rips through the air like static. It's so heavy, it feels like I can reach out and touch it. "Fine," he says, mouth pinched, his attention soon drops to the phone in his hands. He's dismissed me already, his attention elsewhere. Anywhere but on me. And I can't take it anymore. I can handle his hate, but not this weird in-between where he freezes me out in the cruelest way possible.

Before I can consider the consequences, I rip the phone

from his hand, demanding his attention. "Enough of this bullshit silent treatment," I whisper, gripping his phone. "Kill me or forgive me. I can't stand you freezing me out."

His laugh is deep and cruel. It rings out right before he strikes, quick as a panther. I barely have time to breathe, never mind move. One large hand encircles my neck, pushing me into the seat back. His eyes are wild, unhinged to match his appearance. The phone slips from my hand onto the floor but he barely seems to notice. "I'd like to kill you. Nothing would give me greater pleasure than snuffing the life out of you with my bare hands." A whimper escapes from between my lips. "But as much as I want to, I can't. I can't bring myself to do it. So guess what, printsessa—I'm in hell, too. Purgatory actually. Wanting you erased from this earth, and unable to do it."

His words are spoken with such devastation it takes my breath away. His eyes are on me, glinting near black in the fading light. My pulse jackhammers in my throat, the whoosh of blood through my ears sounds like a freight train. I feel too much; overwhelmed, drunk in his presence, spiraling out of control, and powerless to stop it.

He's broken, and I did this to him.

"Tell me how to fix it." Tears flow down my face, desperate and silent. "I'll do whatever I have to do to make things right with you, Daniil. I love you. I *do*. Please ... tell me," I plead, needing him to take me in his arms and make everything better. Because without Daniil, I have nothing to live for.

He releases a low groan, and I don't like the way it coats my skin. He won't look at me, instead he pinches the bridge of his nose, a hiss slipping between his teeth. Like being caught out in an electrical storm, the air feels fraught, like all hell is about to break loose and I should run for cover.

"Do you know what we've been through, my family? A man raised alongside my father betrayed us in the worst possible way. My mother took her own life because of him. He stole our sister from us, and had our father killed. Trust doesn't come easy to me, but I trusted you, I really fucking did, and you shit all over it."

I sigh, closing my eyes and leaning back into my seat. I can't convince Daniil that I fell in love with him when I never thought it was possible to let anyone in. Somehow, he's changed me. Changed everything.

The car comes to a stop, I open my eyes to find we've pulled up in front of our Brooklyn penthouse. "What's going on?" I ask.

"You'll stay here until I figure out what comes next."

I want to ask what the fuck he means by that, but before I can respond, my door is yanked open. Mikhail stands there, looking as somber as I've ever seen him. I turn to Daniil one final time, sadness biting at my edges. He won't look at me, but I look at him, memorizing every hard line and stubborn set of his jaw.

Because if this is the last time I see the man I love, I want to make it count.

# CHAPTER THIRTY-FOUR

## DANIIL

ANDREI IS A HELL OF A BOXER. I don't know why I insisted he spar with me other than the fact I need to rid myself of this manic energy before I self-destruct. Maybe he knows that, because without hesitation, he comes for me, light on his feet, throwing a series of lightning-fast jabs followed by a mean right hook. But I know how he fights, and I anticipate his moves, blocking the jabs and ducking the right hook, which makes him bare his teeth. A feral smile.

"Look at you, *brat*. It's as if you've learned to actually fight."

"Better believe it," I snarl, which makes him laugh until I come back at him with a vicious uppercut that catches Andrei right under the ribs. He lets out a low hiss, but it doesn't stop him from advancing on me, his chin tucked low and eyes dancing with challenge. I want nothing more than to pound him into the ground, simply because all this pent-up energy is going to be the death of me.

It's been two days since I dropped Bianca off at the penthouse, leaving her locked up high in the tower like Rapunzel, but not for one minute have I forgotten about her. Night and day, she's the only thing on my mind. Eris and I are like two lovesick fools wandering the halls of the Kozlov estate at all hours, pining for a five-foot-nothing bombshell that crashed into my life and changed me forever.

The only thing that's helped is planning Emilio's downfall. We haven't made a move yet, but we're putting our assets in play, gathering intelligence, waiting for the right moment to strike. For now, we've continued on with the Zegas as if all is normal. We don't want them to see us coming.

I haven't told Bianca our plans to destroy her uncle. Not yet, anyhow. I can't face her, because I know if I do, I'll crumble at her feet, forgive her every sin. My will to punish her is waning; more and more, staying away from her feels like I'm punishing myself.

I'm a goddamn mess.

The momentary distraction costs me. Andrei's fist connects with my jaw, snapping my head back before I right myself, anger boiling to the surface. Faster than I can retaliate, he advances on me again with a cross punch that I bob in time to avoid.

"Fuck this," I announce, ripping the boxing gloves off my hands and throwing them to the floor. "I can't do it."

Andrei holds up his hands in surrender, slowly unlacing his gloves. "If you don't feel like boxing, just say so."

"I can't kill her." I don't know why I ever thought I could. Days earlier it seemed like the only way forward. Her betrayal cut me like a knife, and I was under the false impression that feelings can be controlled, like water from a tap. But with Bianca, I can't turn it off.

"I know." He leans against the ropes, looking a bit too pleased with himself. "I never thought you would."

I rake my hands through my hair, looking around the boxing gym as if I can find my salvation within these four walls. "I'm fucked." I sit down heavily on the side of the ring, and long for a cigarette I haven't smoked since my teen years. Just something to release the pressure.

A moment later, Andrei sits beside me, releasing a heavy sigh. "Welcome to the club. It doesn't get better. You're a ruined man now."

I don't know whether to laugh or sob at his admission. Andrei, the toughest motherfucker I know, is admitting that Georgia has him wrapped around her finger, baby toe, thigh ... all of it, really. And I'm no better.

"What am I going to fucking do?" I ask, throwing my empty water bottle in defeat. "She's a liability, you said so yourself."

A caustic smile graces his lips, and he reaches for a towel to mop up the sweat on his brow. "Maybe we see things too cut-and-dried. Kira has argued her case, and Georgia gave me a fucking earful about it when I spoke to her last night." He frowns, as if he doesn't like what he's about to admit. "The pakhan in me wouldn't hesitate to slit her throat, but as a family man, I understand why she did what she did. I would have done the same, and you would have, too."

"She could have come to me. She knew how I felt ... that I would have done anything for her."

"She did come to you, Daniil. Maybe not on your timeline, but she did." Andrei rises, slinging his towel around his neck just as Yulian comes careening into the room. The intensity in his eyes sets off waves of anxiety.

"What is it?" I demand.

Andrei's expression is thunderous. "Georgia?" It's one word but it holds all the meaning in the world.

"Georgia is fine, it's Bianca." Yulian's dark eyes meet my own. "She's gone."

Panic shoots through me like a superhit of drugs in my veins.

"What do you mean gone?" Andrei growls. "The penthouse has security, there are guards everywhere."

"She had help escaping."

"Escaping?" Frustration claws up my throat—I feel as if I've wandered into a funhouse where reality is stretched and distorted, and I'm not sure how I will find my way back to normal.

A muscle ticks in Yulian's jaw as he pulls a piece of paper from the inside pocket of his jacket. He hands it to me. "From Bianca. She left it for you."

Daniil,

I'm sorry for the pain I've caused you. I've never been in love before you, maybe that's why it took me so long to notice how madly and deeply I'd fallen. If I could go back and do things differently, I would.

Know that.

The one mercy I can offer you is that I've taken my fate into my own hands. The terrible decision to let me live or die is no longer yours. I'm going to get my revenge. I'll be the one to steal the last breath from my uncle's body, to watch the life bleed out of him. I probably won't live long after that, but it will be worth it.

I've told Jorge to come and get me, to take me back to my uncle's compound in Colombia. He thinks I want him back—but I want to see him dead, too. Jorge and my uncle.

My only regret is that I didn't listen to my heart sooner. If I had, I would have realized that you were my greatest ally, that you would have helped me get revenge more swiftly and brutally

*than the FBI ever would have. Which is what I*
*want. Hindsight is a bitch.*
*   I love you,*
*   B*

I jolt to my feet, turmoil consuming me from the inside out. A sickening crack fills the air as I take a swing at the wall closest to me, but I need to feel the pain. It's the only thing that can ground me right now.

I'm responsible for this.

I'm the reason Bianca has sacrificed herself. Because of me, because I'm a hardheaded asshole who refused to give her an ounce of softness. Even worse, I never told her the one thing that would probably make a difference. That I am going to give her uncle exactly what that motherfucker deserves—a slow, painful death where I make him recite his every wrongdoing and sin before I spill his guts at my feet.

But my stupid stubborn pride got in the way, and now I've lost her forever.

# CHAPTER THIRTY-FIVE

## BIANCA

THE SMELL of tropical plants and musky air invades my nostrils. My body is sticky with the humidity that hangs heavy in this part of the world. It's familiar to me, having partly grown up here, but it's not comforting.

I open my eyes and it all comes back to me. The phone call, the Zegas breaking into the penthouse, Jorge's wandering hands as he escorted me onto my uncle's private plane back to Colombia. What have I done? Bile rises in my throat, but I force it down, ripping off the mosquito net that covers my bed. An unfamiliar bed.

We'd arrived in the dead of night, but it hadn't taken me long to realize that we were not at my uncle's compound in Urabá. We're somewhere unfamiliar. Another remote palace in the jungle. Caution wormed through me at this development, but Jorge assured me the estate is more like a resort. It's smaller, more remote, he said, a chance for us to relax after the craziness of the last few months.

I don't believe him for one hot second, but for what I am

here to do, I don't need to. By the end of the day, the gleaming marble floors will shine with my uncle's blood.

I've rehearsed what I am going to do a million times in my head. I'm ready for this. Tonight at dinner, steak knife in my hand, my uncle Emilio will die. If I live long enough to stab Jorge, all the better. But I may not. The guards will probably kill me the moment I plunge the steel blade into my uncle's neck. I have one chance to get it right, and I intend to.

I've resigned myself to my death.

But there is one casualty I care about in all of this. Daniil.

My heart slams against my ribs as it always does when I think of him. He's likely found the note I left him by now. He knows what I've done. And he knows that my fate is out of his hands. I hope that brings him peace.

I wash and dress, preparing to meet my uncle for breakfast. Wearing a simple white linen dress, I head downstairs to a lavishly appointed table on the terrace. I greet him as I normally would, leaning down and giving him a peck on his cheek as my nails dig into the flesh of my palm. Any kindness towards him costs me.

"Tío," I say politely. "Thank you for bringing me here." I take a seat beside him and smooth my dress over my legs. "I hope this won't cause problems with you and the Kozlovs."

"I'll smooth it over." He waves his hand dismissively. "Your happiness is more important."

Prickles of unease dance down my spine. That's something he's never said before. I don't know what my uncle and Jorge are really after, but something is going on.

"I'm thankful to hear you say that," I reply, false cheerfulness in my tone. My fingers clutch my coffee cup so tightly I'm afraid the porcelain might shatter. "Where is Jorge this morning?"

"Attending to a few important matters. Don't worry, he's not running off back to America. He's eager to spend time with you again."

I swallow. "Wonderful."

"Tell me, Bianca, what happened with your husband? I was under the impression that you were happy being married to Daniil Kozlov. Was I mistaken?" My uncle studies me with an intensity that makes me want to jump out of my skin.

*Hold it together. Just for a little while longer.*

"Not exactly," I say, careful to keep my expression blank. "It was fine at first, but then his true colors came out. It was clear he had no interest in being a married man. So when Jorge reached out to me at the charity event and told me you wanted me home, here with you, I knew it was time to leave."

"I did not know you were so loyal to the Morales family." A chill descends on the table and when I look up, the glint in his eyes is pure ice.

"Of-of course I am," I stammer. A server brings us a platter of fresh-baked goods, and my uncle offers me a croissant. I hesitate, but he continues to hold it out for me. I swallow and moisten my lips. This is what a mouse feels like when it spots a cat about to pounce. Finally, I take the pastry from his hand, my stomach in knots.

The smile my uncle offers me is predatory.

"Jorge made new friends in America. Learned such interesting things. Do you want to know what he discovered?" I shake my head, but he continues anyway. "That you are an FBI informant. That couldn't be true, could it, my dear?"

I drop my hands into my lap, steadying myself with a deep breath. He knows. My uncle knows. A riot of emotions erupts inside of me: pain, betrayal, confusion. Had the Kozlovs set me up? As angry as Daniil is, I can't believe he'd ever do something so ruthless.

Whatever the case, the only thing to do now is play the game and hope my uncle doesn't gut me right here over breakfast. I've certainly seen him do worse.

I release a haughty laugh. "That's ridiculous. Why would the niece of a major cartel player and the wife of a vor squeal to the FBI? What reason would I—"

He puts up his hand to stop me. "I can think of many reasons. But I think the most likely one is that you made a very tragic discovery about your past."

My teeth gnash together. "What would that be?" I ask, my voice strained.

"You found out I killed Mommy and Daddy? And let's not forget baby Celeste. That must have hurt." I lunge for him then, fury hijacking any good sense or self-preservation. But I'm no match for my uncle. He has me restrained in a blink, his hand wrapped around my throat. "Ah, that's what I thought. You do know. I suppose you've been biding your time, planning your revenge." His face is red, spittle flying from his mouth. "But that won't happen."

I struggle against him, but he squeezes my trachea and blackness dances around the edge of my vision. It's only when I'm close to losing consciousness that he relaxes his grip.

I gulp in a full breath of air. "Why?" I choke out. "Why not kill me, too? What kind of monster raises the child of the family he murdered in cold blood."

"Why do you think, you dumb bitch? The only reason to keep you alive is because you were useful. As my only living relation, I could marry you off to create a powerful alliance, and I did exactly that."

"That doesn't make sense," I gasp. "Before Daniil, I was promised to Jorge."

His expression turns gleeful. "And you still are."

"What!?" My adrenaline surges hard as my eyes dart around the property, looking for an escape, anywhere to run. But of course, guards patrol every square inch of the property.

*I'm fucked.*

"You and Daniil aren't legally married. I made sure of that. The paperwork was a forgery. In the eyes of the law, you are not married to Daniil Kozlov, and in the eyes of God ... well I don't fucking care."

On instinct, I break free from my uncle's grasp and take off running toward the edge of the property. For one sweet second, I taste freedom before I am brutally tackled to the ground by a strong male body. I thrash in the arms of my captor, legs flailing as he rolls on top of me, pinning my hands to my body. The cloying smell of Jorge's cologne invades my nostrils, the familiarity making me wretch.

It's then that I feel two competing sensations. He grows hard against my leg, grinding against me. And then the unmistakable snap of cold metal against my temple.

"Stop fighting, *hermosa*. It's pointless." I ignore him and continue to thrash until he releases the safety on the gun, a resounding *thunk* against my temple. That stops me cold. "There you go, now you know we're not playing."

My uncle stands above us, a snarl parting his lips. "Did you think you outsmarted us, Bianca, finding a man to take you away from me? If you weren't such a worthless bitch, I'd commend you for leading us right into the pocket of those two-cent Russian gangsters. It's been a fruitful working relationship wouldn't you say?"

Jorge laughs. "I'd say it was nice while it lasted. But we have what we want now. You see, the Kozlovs have the best shipping routes locked down, and thanks to everything we learned working closely with the bratva, we plan to take over those routes very shortly."

Dread snakes its way through me as everything comes into sharp focus. My uncle's insistence on the wedding and having Daniil work closely with Jorge. They were playing the Kozlovs the entire time, and it was me who gave them access. I opened the door to Daniil's ruin.

My heart snaps in my chest. That's all the more reason to keep on fighting. If I can somehow find a way to take my uncle down now, he can't go after the Kozlovs ever again. So I play the same twisted game Jorge is playing.

"Fine," I gasp, pressing on Jorge's shoulders, and wrapping a leg around his waist. "Daniil wasn't half the lover I imagine you are," I whisper into his ear. "You made me feel things he never did."

Jorge pulls away from me, eyes alight with something like excitement. He's smart enough to know I'm trying to butter him up, but dumb enough to want the sex anyhow. At least to hurt me.

He pulls my hair hard and bites my neck as my uncle watches. "I'm going to whip you for every time you let him put his hands on you. And then I'm going to make you my wife."

What the fuck? This man is so deeply deranged there's no sense in responding. But what he wants is my fear, he's always thrived on other people's pain. So I roll myself into a ball on the ground, and sob into my hands.

"Don't worry, my sweet, I'll make it good for you, too." He laughs cruelly now.

And my uncle laughs right along with him before adding, "No one can find you here. Not your beloved Kozlovs, not your new friends at the FBI, no one. Daniil underestimated me. Your mother made the same mistake and look how it turned out for her."

With that, he spits in my face and snaps at Jorge to lock me up. I can't imagine what they have in store for me, but even as dread bleeds through my system, I know there is no margin of error. Every move I make from here on out has to be as cunning and calculated as my uncle's. Even more so.

# CHAPTER THIRTY-SIX

## DANIIL

YULIAN HANGS UP the phone and hits me with a grim look. "Do you want the good news or the bad news first?"

I rake a hand through my already mussed hair. "Fuck, I don't know. Just spit it out," I demand. We've been holed up in Andrei's office since discovering Bianca is missing. Leo and Yulian have been working their intelligence contacts to find out where she is and to try to make sense of everything that's happened in the last twenty-four hours. At Andrei's insistence, Georgia flew back from Greece in case this is part of something bigger.

"Good news," Kira chimes in, giving me a sympathetic smile. "Always start with the good."

Leo pulls up a satellite image on a big screen on the far wall. "We have confirmation that Jorge, Bianca, and senior Zega members arrived in Antioquia, a province in northwestern Colombia, via Morales's private jet yesterday evening. It's a relatively rural area, close to the border of Panama. Bianca appears to be unharmed. She wasn't wearing any shackles upon arrival."

My fingers drum on the desk in front of me, not feeling any

relief that Bianca is alive. The truth is anything could have happened between then and now. Time is not on our side.

"The bad news is that they are not at the Morales estate. A team of three Land Rovers picked them up after landing and swept Bianca, Jorge, and his guards away, we just don't know where yet."

Kira sits beside me, a hand landing on my back. "I'm sorry, Daniil," she says. "We'll find her."

I nod absently, filling up my whisky glass with another two fingers of the amber liquid. Something big is going on, I can feel it.

"Are the feds looking for her as well?" Georgia asks from where she is curled into Andrei on the settee.

I shake my head bitterly. "The feds aren't doing shit. If they were better at their jobs, they would have protected their informant in the first place." Andrei shoots me a sour look for snapping at his wife, but I'm not angry with her. I'm angry at the world. "Sorry, Georgia. I'm just frustrated. I failed her. I fucking failed her," I say, the familiar bloom of self-hatred hitting me square in the chest.

Kira throws her arm around me. "We all failed her. We should have trusted her when she came clean, but what's done is done so forgive yourself. And let's figure shit out."

Leo, who's had his head down, typing away on his laptop for the last few hours, suddenly looks up. "I have something," he announces. "My hackers pulled up satellite footage of the Land Rover caravan moving through the jungle towards a five-acre spread in the mountain village of Jardín, about three hours south of Medellín."

"What's there?" I ask, immediately sobering.

"Looks like a compound of some sort." Leo hands me his phone, and I manipulate the satellite images he shows me to focus on an estate nestled in a mountainous region. There is no electrical fence, or guard towers like his main compound, but the remote location ensures its security. None of this bodes well for us.

"Why there?" Kira asks, peeking at the image over my shoulder.

"To throw us off their scent. Going to Emilio's estate would be too obvious," I say somberly. Then to my brother I say, "You promised your support in taking down Emilio. Well, the time has come. We need to go to Colombia. We need to handle this."

The air in the room goes still. We're used to fighting on our home turf, but to bring the fight to the mountains of Colombia, a place we're not accustomed to or familiar with is dangerous. I know that, but it's the only way. I also know my brothers would walk through fire for me. As I would for them.

Andrei's fiery eyes take me in, I'm asking him to risk his life and the lives of our friends and family. He asks a silent question, communicating in a way only brothers can. *Do you love her?*

Yes. The answer is obvious. Yes, I fucking love her. If by some goddamn miracle we survive this hell on earth, I am going to try so much harder. I am going to be a proper husband.

Whatever he sees in my eyes is enough for him. His nod is nearly imperceptible.

Andrei stands. "We need a day to prepare. Yulian, you collect our team and resources. Leo, gather any relevant intel and make sure your hackers are on standby from the moment we land in Colombia. We'll need live communication with them for every moment of this mission." My brother's eagle eyes land on me. "And Daniil. I suggest you shave, shower, and try to appear human." His lips quirk up at the corner. "You're going to need to have your shit locked down for this."

I nod at him from across the room. My way of saying thank you, because we're about to engage in the fight of our lives to save the woman I love.

# CHAPTER THIRTY-SEVEN

## BIANCA

THE FANCY BEDROOM from my first night here is long forgotten. I've been on the floor of this dank basement cell for what must be two full days, but I have no way to keep track of time. There have been no visitors other than whoever passes a tray of food under the door twice a day. It's not enough. I'm hungry and thirsty, and perhaps the worst, my sanity is starting to go.

I see things. I hear things. Rats in the walls, cockroaches skittering across the floor, or worse.

People survive months in solitary confinement—but surviving, staying alive, is different from staying sane. I spend too much time thinking about Daniil. What he's doing, what he thinks, if he hates me. And I suppose I did betray him in a way. There's nothing I wouldn't do for him, but this was about showing him one last time how much I love him and taking care of myself. Seeing through the promise I made to myself when I was a scared teenage girl who lost her family much too early.

I adjust myself on the thin mattress splayed out on the floor and pull the thin blanket tighter around me. There were so many years where I could have just murdered the man in his sleep, but

I was a good girl then. Playing by the rules of society. And I didn't want to sink as low as him. But now it's too late. My uncle knows I detest him, that I've hated him for a long time for killing my parents. He also knows my involvement with the feds, which doesn't bode well for me.

I'm down but not out. I refuse to be. Whatever it takes to kill my uncle, I'll do, or die trying.

The lock jangles in the door, and for the first time in too many days, the door opens, and Jorge stands at the thresholds. "Ah, it's my soon-to-be bride."

I blanch at his words. I assumed he'd said that to scare me, because both he and my uncle must know nothing is more frightening than the thought of marrying this monster. But I don't give him the dignity of responding. Instead, I turn away from him, flopping on the mattress towards the wall.

"I don't think so." His mirthless laugh rings out, and he steps into the room. A hard kick to my legs causes me to grunt and curl into a ball to protect myself. "Get up," he demands.

As bile rises in my throat, I turn to face him, his handsome face always seemed like a mask obscuring the demon inside. It's then that I notice a white dress clutched in one of his hands.

"What is that?" I intone, panic invading my voice.

"Your wedding dress. Although I don't think white is the appropriate color now that we know you've fucked Daniil Kozlov ten ways to next Sunday," he sneers. "But don't worry, beauty, I'm going to fuck you so long and hard you'll forget that man ever existed."

He grabs me by the hair and pulls me up from the mattress. Already, tears are falling down my face, my revulsion clear. I tried and failed to make him believe I could want him. I don't know if I have it in me to try anymore. He wouldn't believe it anyhow.

He pulls me viciously towards him, taking a deep breath of my neck. Like a vampire seeking his prey. "We are going to get married today, and then I am going to fuck a baby into you. A proper Morales heir, even if your whore of a mother was a traitor. And after you give me what I want, I am going to gut you from end to end because you are a lying, cheating bitch."

My body is shaking uncontrollably all over. The contents of my stomach come up, and I'm retching all over his shoes before I can stop myself.

"You idiot, look what you did!" He drags me from the room, his hands still clasped tightly in my hair. After traveling through a dank hallway, he drags me up a flight of stairs and then another flight of stairs until we're somewhere on the second floor of the grand estate. Opening a tall oak-paneled door, he pulls me into a neatly appointed bedroom where a small army of women stand at attention. They nod at Jorge but don't make eye contact with me.

"She needs to be cleaned up, then have this dress fitted properly." He throws the silk gown at them. "You have two hours."

He shoves me at a tall woman with stern lines on her face who looks at me suspiciously. She sniffs haughtily and directs me to a shower with shampoo, conditioner, and a bar of soap. No razor in sight. My new jailer stands outside of the shower, clearly watching me for any wrong move.

Once I am clean and dry, I'm led out of the bedroom to a tall woman with glasses perched on the edge of her nose. She introduces herself as Lyla and takes me by the hand. At least she seems kind.

"My dear, we need to get you fitted for a new dress right away. We don't have long," she says, her English gently accented.

She leads me to a riser in the corner of the room with a full-length mirror resting against the wall. The dress that Jorge had in his hands is lowered over my head as I slip on a pair of silk high-heeled shoes. A team of Lyla's workers gather around and get to work, letting out the hem and taking in the bust area.

I don't even know why Jorge cares how I look. This marriage is a pure sham, he said so himself. He only wants to breed me before killing me. Had that always been his end goal?

"I'm from France," Lyla says, pinning the hem of my dress. "Do you speak French, my dear?"

I nod at her. I attended an international French school for most of my education. "That's so nice, I rarely get the chance to speak French anymore," she adds. Lyla's eyes sweep the room, taking in the other women working close by. No one looks up in recognition. My guess is these local women only speak Spanish and a limited amount of English.

"Have they hurt you?" she asks in French, as she continues to work away. Her tone is light, but her question holds meaning.

"I'm fine," I respond, unsure of where she is going with this line of questioning.

She smiles again giving the impression that we're simply making small talk. "Don't worry, I'm here to help. Just stay calm, we are going to get you out of here."

*We* are? Who could *we* be? Daniil wouldn't come after me, would he? Not after the letter I left him. The other option is the FBI. I'm not sure how they would know my whereabouts, but they are a huge federal agency. If they wanted to find me, they have the means.

Either way, hope soars.

I keep my eyes glued to the mirror in front of me as if I am admiring myself. "Who sent you?" I murmur.

"Friends," she replies cautiously.

"What should I do?"

"Do nothing. Go along with whatever they have planned. Act as you normally would. We'll extract you when the time is right."

I nod and swallow heavily, my nerves getting the best of me.

"Perfect," she says, switching to English. "Don't you look wonderful. We need an hour with the dress, and we will make sure it fits you like a glove. Now if you don't mind, go into the other room and the nice ladies there will do your hair and makeup. You'll look *magnifique* on your wedding day, *oui?*"

"Of course." I give her one more meaningful look that I hope communicates my thanks as her team removes my dress, replacing it with a big comfy robe.

I turn towards the door but stop when my fingers are resting on the door handle. A small pair of four-inch detail scissors lay on a small desk by the wall. Before I can think better of it, I've slipped the scissors into the big folds of the robe. I may have help, but I believe in helping myself first and foremost. Because the FBI won't kill my uncle, they'll only arrest him. And I want to see his blood stain the ground beneath my feet.

# CHAPTER THIRTY-EIGHT

## DANIIL

I SPEND the entire six-hour flight to Colombia pacing the aisles of our Boeing, wondering if they've hurt Bianca, if she's all right, if she hates me for how I treated her. I don't typically go around quoting hymns, but the lyrics from "Amazing Grace" play in my head, specifically the line about being blind, but now I see. Well, now I see what a fucking idiot I was.

I've never prayed a day in my life, but at one point—somewhere over the Caribbean Sea—I locked myself in the bathroom and prayed to the patron saints of fallen angels and Russian gangsters that I'm not too late. That I'll get another chance to prove to Bianca that I'm worthy of her.

My brothers and Yulian have worked around the clock since we found out she was in Colombia. They've commissioned a private security team to help us with the extraction, because apparently this shit ain't easy, and it certainly is not in the area of our expertise. We know how to take someone out in broad daylight on the sidewalks of NYC, but the jungle of South America is not our territory—that's where Mercy Kate comes in.

One of Leo's underground contacts suggested the private

security team that she runs, SPK Security. They know this territory well, employing the best mercenaries in the business. Now we're huddled in a one-room hut Mercy secured, located fifteen miles outside of the compound that Emilio is based in. Mercy has a team of half a dozen ex-Special Forces men and women, to support Yulian, Leo, Andrei, and I. The first thing Mercy told me when I arrived was that Bianca is still alive, and for that, I'll forever be grateful to her.

In the bare-bones village hut, Mercy leans over the blueprint she's acquired on the wooden table. She spreads out the large sheet and glances up at me, as if she knows I'm the most invested. Her long dark braid swings over one of her shoulders, her brown skin already perspiring in the gentle humidity. But she's used to this. Word is she spent twelve years undercover with US Army Special Forces, working deep in the jungles of South America. So if anyone can handle this world, it's her.

Gesturing for everyone to look carefully, Mercy says, "Alright, this is the main house." She moves her finger. "The east wing is the living quarters, the west wing is where they conduct business. I have an agent infiltrating their ranks right now. Last she confirmed, Bianca was being held in some sort of prison." My sharp intake of breath doesn't go unnoticed. Mercy frowns at me. "She won't be there long. Jorge plans to marry her."

What in the fuck? My head shoots back at this nugget of information. "How does he plan to do that? She's already a married woman."

"Are you sure about that?" The look on Mercy's face tells me everything I need to know.

Andrei swears under his breath. "She's right, *brat*, Emilio's people took care of the wedding, including the paperwork."

I pinch the bridge of my nose. Why in the hell would he want to marry Bianca? He has to know that's a death wish. But the one positive twist—it means they have reason to keep Bianca alive. For now.

"My agent infiltrated Emilio's property as a staff member. She'll be able to help us gain access inside the compound."

"If you have an agent in there already, why not have her kill Emilio and save us a lot of trouble?"

She shoots a withering look my way. "Emilio is protected at all times. He's never alone and armed to the teeth. The moment she took him down, she'd be dead. We need to attack strategically, as a team."

A volcano threatens to erupt in my chest. "Fine. But the goal of this mission is to extract Bianca, and then eliminate Emilio, Jorge, and any other fucker remotely connected with their cartel. We're going scorched earth."

"Well, shit," she breathed. "I like your style, boy."

Leo sinks back onto a bench in the corner of the hut. "I suggest we use a distraction method. Something that will cause chaos all around. Either a fuse bomb or a power outage if we can swing it."

"I like that, but it means we need to go in at night to create the most confusion," Mercy says shrewdly. Then to one of her men she says, "See if you can hack into the power grid."

"How are we going to get near this place?" Andrei asks, looking at the satellite image on his phone. "It's like a fort in the mountains."

"We can take the Humvees to the foot of the hills. Then we hike. It's the best way to get in undetected. The compound is remote enough that there is no fence, just eagle-eyed guards with AR-15s itching their hot little hands. Especially with the wedding taking place today. Once we've handled our business, choppers will extract us."

My chest burns, and a vein throbs in my forehead. The thought of another man's ring on Bianca's finger, especially that evil fuckwad's, makes my blood boil. His death will be long and slow, and as painful as possible. Doubly so if she's hurt.

Activity buzzes to life around me. Mercy's team is well-trained, understanding exactly what needs to be done, and how to move forward undetected. Yulian, Leo, and Andrei join the fray. This might not be our usual line of operation, but bratva business is not so different. We're used to leading a team and taking down any enemy that needs to be eliminated.

Yet here I am. Glued to the spot. Clenching and unclenching my fists that hang at my sides.

Mercy eyes me carefully. "Gonna be honest with you here. This mission is gonna be tense. We can't afford to have emotions running high. If you want to wait here—"

"Fuck no." I scowl. "I have no intention of sitting this one out. I'll be the one to gut the motherfuckers who did this to her. Who hurt her." But even as the words roll off my tongue, I know that I'm no better. I'm the reason she's here.

And if that's not fucked-up, I don't know what is.

She may want nothing to do with me ever again, and frankly, I'd understand. But I'm going to make sure she gets her revenge, and I'm going to make sure it's ugly. "This is my mess, and I'm going to clean it up."

"Giddyap, cowboy. We leave at seventeen hundred hours," Mercy says before punching my shoulder with more force than seems entirely necessary and stalking off.

# CHAPTER THIRTY-NINE

## BIANCA

I NEVER IMAGINED I would die on the same day as my wedding, but hell, life is full of surprises.

The idea of death coming for me today should terrify me, but it doesn't. It's comforting. It means I'll get my revenge, and Daniil won't be collateral damage.

Small mercies.

Daylight had faded behind the majestic mountains, the sky transformed into dusk. With the sun's disappearance, the humidity has eased up, and it's a pleasant enough evening for a wedding. And a funeral.

As I take a final look in the mirror, minutes from walking down the aisle, I think that in another world, with another man, this would be a perfect day. If I were marrying Daniil—like *really* marrying him, not like before—we'd pledge our life together, in sickness and in health, and in every way that matters. If it were Daniil, today might be the best day of my life. But as it stands, today's probably going to be the last day of my life.

I'm escorted to the threshold of the mansion by a half dozen guards. Music floats in from the courtyard, even though there

are no guests, just a bunch of bored looking Zega soldiers who
were ordered to standby.

I don't know why we're going through this farce of a cere-
mony other than it appeals to Jorge's giant ego. What a joke. But
I'll get the last laugh. A quick glimpse into the plush bouquet of
white roses I am holding confirms that the sewing scissors I
took earlier are well hidden within the full blooms. Hidden in
plain sight. It's great that the feds are here, but revenge is mine.

The "Wedding March" begins to play, my cue to get on with
it. Anxious eyes of the domestic staff drink me in, perhaps
wondering if I am going to bolt. They have no idea. Even if I was
inclined to do so, the submachine-gun-toting guards would definitely be a deterrent. Luckily, I have other plans.

Jorge waits for me on a pedestal below a white gauzy canopy
with my uncle standing impatiently beside him. Emilio is not
usually a presence I welcome, but today is different. I want him
close to me for one reason, and that reason will come soon.

As I make my way down the aisle—which is a simple white
liner spread over the hard ground—I keep my gaze focused on
the horizon, past the men gathered around the canopy, past
Jorge, whose eyes track me like a hunter stalks its prey. The look
he gives me causes my insides to clench. It's not quite desire, but
something more like triumph gleams in his eyes.

With each step towards the altar, my ears buzz and I fight a
wave of nausea. Can I really do this? Can I go through with it?
I've never hurt anyone in my life, but rage compels me forward.
I draw in a breath, hoping the oxygen might focus me. Might
give me strength.

The men I can't call guests all look bored, sweating in the
humid evening air, sitting down to take in this farce of a wedding
at my uncle's bidding. Although there's no doubt everyone here
is packing heat, only one man is obviously armed as he stands
holding a submachine gun. I do a double take as I pass him, not
because of the weapon, but because he's familiar. I take a
moment to place him, but when I finally do, my insides twist.

He's the man from Stereo, the one who accosted me when I was on the way to the VIP room.

He's part of Jorge's crew. I should have known.

He smirks at me, but I ignore him. I can't allow distractions right now.

As I approach the pedestal, I allow myself to look behind me at the domestic staff standing with their backs to the house, watching from afar. I gave them clear instructions that no one is to come close under any circumstances. They don't deserve to be caught up in the carnage. Whatever comes next, it will be vicious and ugly.

A sweaty priest with beady eyes and a shifty gaze nods at me as the music fades. Jorge leans in close, his cologne assaulting my senses, and whispers, "I can't wait until I own you. Think of my ring as a shackle. A smaller version of what I'll use to chain you to my bed."

A slow, wicked smile curves his mouth as his gaze travels the length of my body. Not that he can see it through the veil, but I give him my best *fuck you* glare while holding my tongue. This is my only chance, and I will use it wisely.

I've played this moment in my head a million times. I need to wait until they are distracted, even for a fraction of a second before I go in for the kill. And if that moment never comes, I'll create a distraction. Whatever that may be.

Behind Jorge, my uncle releases an aggravated huff. "Just get on with it," he growls, but the priest sticks to the script. Droning on about the meaning and importance of marriage, how as a couple we can grow closer to God through our sacred union.

He's wasting his breath, but at least it buys me time. My eyes sweep the courtyard looking for any sign that the feds are nearby, perhaps in hiding. If they are, I certainly hope my would-be saviors hold off long enough for me to do the job I came here to do. I don't care what happens after that.

That's not entirely true. I hope they burn this place to the ground.

The sun has sunk below the horizon, and fairy lights strung along the side of the house flicker to life, creating a magical glow. A laugh of disbelief catches in my throat at how romantic this all appears. What a fucking joke. Jorge's eyes gleam, but I don't allow my focus to leave his neck. The carotid artery. Aim there, if somehow I get the chance to take down Jorge after my uncle.

"And now the couple will make their vows in the presence of God and with the understanding that God is part of the union." The priest's monotonous voice steals my attention as he looks at Jorge and asks him if he takes me as his wife.

He responds with a smirk before muttering, "I do."

It's my turn to say the words, but they seem to stick in my throat. My lips part, but the only thing that comes out is an aggrieved sob. My uncle gives me a glacial glare, while Jorge grabs my chin brutally.

"Say the word, traitor, or you won't like what happens next," he hisses, his fingers digging into my skin.

I know I should, but I can't. My body simply won't cooperate. I struggle to suck in a breath, as his eyes darken from gray to the blackest of black. He's close enough that I could sink the scissors into his neck, but I won't have time to kill my uncle as well, not with all eyes on me. And Emilio is the target.

Jorge squeezes my neck. A warning that it's time to play his game. Fighting every instinct to back away from his touch, I blink rapidly and suck in a breath in through my nose.

Steadying my nerves, I nod, and then in the barest whisper, force out the words. "Yes, I do."

I remind myself that those words mean nothing. I'm a dead woman walking, anyhow.

Before the priest can declare us man and wife, the lights go out, drowning the yard in a pitch-black wave.

Relief fills my chest, as a low murmur of confusion sweeps through the small crowd. Turning to the guard closest to him, my uncle barks, "Go see what the issue is. And if it can't be fixed immediately, switch to generator power."

The guard nods and runs off to do my uncle's bidding just as an explosion from the west side of the property lights the night sky. Holy shit, the feds are moving in. Jorge and my uncle exchange a cursory look before they start shouting instructions at their men. Chaos ensues, scared staff take off in all directions, and I know this is my time.

Before I can make a move, my uncle storms off, well past my reach, but Jorge remains in my crosshairs. Here goes nothing.

In one fluid motion, I grab the handle of the scissors from my bouquet and lodge the pointy blades deep in Jorge's neck. His horrified shriek pierces the air, but the sound gets lost in the melee. His eyes fly open in shock, and I enjoy a moment of satisfaction knowing the stainless-steel landed exactly where intended. Blood drips from his wound but he shows no signs of slowing down, one hand reaching for me as he hisses, "You fucking bitch."

I have just enough time to yank the scissors from his artery, then stab him again through his corded flesh, his eyes bulging with my repeated assault. I'm pure rage and scorn, my fury unleashed as I thirst over the sight of his blood spilling down his neck.

Gunshots echo in the distance, shaking me from my bloodlust. There is no time to think. No time to panic. Jorge has dropped to the ground, curled up on his side when he makes a move for his holstered gun.

"I don't think so." I laugh callously as the spiked heel from one of my bridal shoes, now soaked crimson, lands on his arm, stopping further movement. I grind my heel into the soft flesh of his forearm, pulling expletives and a tortured groan from his throat.

Reaching down, I relieve him of his gun. Luckily, I had the foresight to learn how to use a pistol years ago. That training is about to pay off. I watch with glee as Jorge's life force seeps from him. Who knew sewing scissors could do such damage? But I won't be satisfied until the man that took everything from me is dead.

Screams echo in the distance, along with another wave of gunfire. Most of the guards have scattered, attempting to figure out what in the hell is going on, while the priest cowers below a bench. Only one person remains standing in the middle of the courtyard.

My uncle.

He watches me callously, enjoying every minute of my discomfort.

He hasn't missed a thing. He's been biding his time, waiting for me to come at him. But now he comes after me instead. Full force. His face contorted in an angry mask. I raise the gun, releasing the safety but I'm a moment too late. My uncle has me pinned to the ground before I can defend myself.

"You made a big mistake," my uncle spits while raising his fist. Less than a second later, it comes crashing down on the side of my face.

I bite my lip, tasting blood.

Then the world goes black.

# CHAPTER FORTY

**DANIIL**

EITHER EMILIO HAS HUGELY UNDERESTIMATED us or we're being set up, because none of this makes sense. Leo and I are lying belly down on the edge of the property, obscured by the shadows as a small group of Zegas gathers only thirty yards away. Even in the fading sunlight, I know what I'm looking at.

A fucking wedding.

The Madman is marrying my woman like it's a grand fucking event, and everyone is invited.

The sight sets my blood on fire. Rage, regret, guilt—all of it —comes roaring to the surface, but I use it as fuel. It sharpens my focus, drives my revenge. Because only one thing matters right now, and that's getting Bianca out of this alive.

Mercy has two sharpshooters perched in the hills above us, but I don't know what their vantage point is, and they're too far out of range to communicate. The rest of the team has the perimeter covered, spread out in pairs over a two-mile radius.

Leo and I are on the south end of the property, facing the courtyard where I have a front-row seat to the action. The Zega guards are few and far between. There's no way Emilio could bring his whole crew here. He was probably relying on its remoteness to pull off whatever this is about.

He can't imagine that what I feel for Bianca is real. That I would travel to the ends of the earth for her.

Beside me, Leo counts down to the action. "Three, two, one ... cut power."

Mercy's group of hackers use their techno magic to kill the power, plunging the world into darkness and shutting down all the lights and any alarm systems on the property.

An eerie hush falls over the yard. There's no sound save for the soft hiss of the wind through the tall palm trees. The silence does not last long. It's quickly replaced by men shouting in a mix of Spanish and English, unmistakable words of panic.

And then an explosion. One that we orchestrated on the north side of the property. A distraction technique. A warning, meant to intimidate and cause chaos, giving them the impression that we are a bigger group than we really are. I'm dying to move forward and fuck these guys up, but Mercy was clear. We are only to move forward on her word. Before her call, we're putting Bianca's life in danger.

From all around, gunfire erupts, mingling with the frightened yelps of the staff. Pleas and screams reverberate through the open yard like a gruesome symphony. Mercy said her men will engage the guards on the far side of the property, leaving us clear to swoop in and extract Bianca. But that's not what is happening right now.

I tighten my hold on the trigger and double-check the night vision goggles hanging from my helmet. Thank the mafia gods for these suckers. They're the only reason I can see shit right now. And what I see makes my blood run cold.

Bianca lifts her hand, and when it comes down, something is plunged into Jorge's neck. I blink twice to make sure what I'm seeing is actually happening. Is Bianca stabbing Días? A primal cry releases from between his lips, and at that moment I know she's taking her revenge on him. But the one thing that doesn't add up—Emilio stands by, watching. Not helping. Not interfering. It's as if he's taking an objective interest in watching Bianca kill his right-hand man in front of him.

Unable to standby any longer, I make a move, but Leo clasps his hands around my wrist.

"Don't," he whispers. "We haven't gotten word yet."

"Are you seeing this?" I hiss back. "I need to go in and help."

"She seems to be managing just fine without you."

I glimpse back to the action just as Bianca is pulling a gun from Días's holster as he lays curled up on the ground, hopefully bleeding out. I'm not sure how my girl did it, but she managed to pull off a kick-ass feat. But her victory is short-lived. My heart thuds against my rib cage as Emilio makes a move towards Bianca.

As I stand by helplessly, he swiftly pulls his fist back and punches Bianca in the face. She falls like a sack of potatoes, down for the count as my heart nearly jumps out of my chest. Without another thought, I charge forward, gun raised, uncaring that we haven't gotten the signal yet. My only thought centers on killing Emilio with my bare hands.

Before I can get a shot off, he heaves Bianca over his shoulder, then turns around, eyes burning into my own as he raises his gun and aims in my direction. Time stands still, the only thing I'm conscious of is the near-deafening pop of a bullet, then my torso goes numb momentarily before erupting in fiery heat.

He shot me. The fucker shot me. Even though I'm kitted out in a vest, the force is like being hit full force with a baseball bat. The impact is jarring down to my bones. I'm stunned, doubled over in pain as my groan slices through the orchestra of gunfire blasting around me. All I can do is focus on getting air into my lungs and staying conscious as a figure drops beside me.

Leo's voice is a panicked snarl. "Fuck, Daniil. Are you hit?" He rips off his goggles and checks for blood, injuries, anything.

"I'm fine," I gasp. "The fucker got me right in the chest."

"Jesus. We need to get you out of here and to the team medic. You could have a ruptured organ, internal bleeding—"

"Fuck that," I say, heaving my body upright. "I don't fucking care, I'm going after her. He took her into the house."

"Do you have a death wish?" Leo's back molars grind together. "We need to wait for the team before we infiltrate the house." He looks up, taking in the war zone the compound has turned into. Skirmishes in the pitch-black. The one advantage we seem to have.

I push Leo away from me, struggling to my feet. "We don't have time," I argue to my brother, fighting to catch my breath. "You don't have to come, but I'm going in."

"I*diyot*," he mutters, fitting his goggles back over his face. "Don't ever accuse me of not being supportive of your crazy-ass."

# CHAPTER FORTY-ONE

## BIANCA

I GASP FOR AIR, rousing as a rough hand slaps my face. I open my eyes to find my uncle's harsh nose mere inches from my own.

"Wake up. The fun is about to start," he growls.

*What?*

Wiping something warm and sticky from the side of my face, I force myself to calm down and breathe, but my chest burns with each desperate gulp of air. My hand comes up covered in blood, *my* blood judging by the coppery taste in my mouth and headache pounding my skull.

And then it all comes back to me. I killed Jorge, then my uncle knocked me out cold. I spit blood and struggle to sit up, but Emilio pushes me back down onto the floor. My back is slumped against the wall of what appears to be a little sitting area tucked away beyond the main foyer. He towers over me, a smarmy expression on his face. He's gloating because he thinks he's won. But this battle is far from over.

I cast a glance around the dark room, looking for anything to use as a weapon. A lamp, a statue, a spoon to gouge his eyes out.

Because I have no doubt this is our last standoff. One of us isn't walking out of here alive.

He bends, grabbing my chin roughly so I'm forced to look him in the eye. "You can thank your friends for the power outage. It ended up being quite convenient for my purposes."

It comes back to me now. The power outage followed by the explosion. The feds are making their move. I jerk my chin out of his grasp. "Good luck taking down the FBI. The only way you're getting off this property is in cuffs or a casket. And I truly hope it's the latter."

His delighted laugh reverberates through the small room. "Oh no, *puta*, it's not the FBI. It's your beloved Kozlovs. Can you believe they came all this way to get you back after you betrayed them so ruthlessly? They are stupider than I ever imagined."

Heat shoots up the back of my neck.

He came for me. Daniil is here!

My happiness is short-lived; if Daniil is here, he's in danger. My uncle is planning something.

In the shadows, I recognize two of Emilio's most loyal guards, the ones who are always by his side. They are using me as bait, dragging me into a tucked-away corner in order to ambush Daniil and his team. The fine hairs on my neck stand up in alarm. I can only pray Daniil has the sense not to come in here, that he recognizes it for what it is. A trap.

My uncle's lips curl back in an approximation of a smile as he watches me piece it all together. His loafers make a shuffling sound as he paces the natural stone floor, gun in hand. "The Kozlovs can't blame you entirely. Betrayal is in your blood, isn't it? Your whore of a mother betrayed her whole family. I suppose the apple doesn't fall far from the tree."

My chest hollows at the mention of my family. A reminder that I've failed them, again. Jorge may be dead, but my uncle has the upper hand.

"Either let me go or kill me," I demand. "I'm not here to chitchat, especially with a man so fucking twisted he killed his own flesh and blood and then raised her orphan. You make me sick," I scream, spitting in his direction.

His upper lip pulls back into a sneer, and he delivers a hard kick to my legs. "Don't make demands of me, stupid girl. And I *will* kill you once you serve your purpose."

I refuse to cry out in pain and give him the satisfaction. Instead, I hug my arms around my legs and make myself as small as possible. It occurs to me that I'm not restrained in any way. Yes, there are two lunatics sporting AR-15s on either side of me, but if I'm going to die anyhow, I'm going to drag my uncle down to the depths of hell with me.

"And what exactly is my purpose?" I ask to keep him talking. Outside, I'm vaguely aware that the gunfire has died down, replaced by an eerie quiet.

"You haven't figured it out yet? I'm after Kozlov territory. Prime shipping routes. An open door to the New York market. It's quite remarkable how your little stunt worked out in my favor."

My stunt? As if I orchestrated being traded like cattle at an illegal poker game. But it's a useless point to make now. "You think you can best the Kozlovs? They're better than you. They've always been. You may inhabit the same underworld, but they're nothing like you. Daniil is a better man than you could ever dream of being."

Every cell in my body is ready to spring into action, primed with the crackling tension in the room. I expect my uncle's fury, but instead he grabs me by the hair, the cold glint in his eyes shining bright. "*Was*, my dear. He *was* a better man."

The ache in my gut blooms, a sick feeling crawling up my spine like ants. "What ... What do you mean?"

His face falls in mock sadness. "Poor Daniil, still in love with the traitorous women that double-crossed him. He just couldn't resist coming to your rescue. At least he died a hero."

I explode from the floor. Despite the pain and my injuries, I charge my uncle, spurred on by the ghosts of my family. The pain of the past mingles with the horror of the present, and I slam into him, both of us tumbling onto the hard stone floor. Landing flush on my side, the wind is knocked out of me.

The guards raise their weapons, but my uncle stops them with harsh words. "No, she's mine," he spits. "Get your asses out there and kill anyone who makes it in the house." He points towards the door, and then he's on top of me, pinning me down, his hands around my throat.

I fight for air, swinging at him as best I can, but he only squeezes tighter, and a shiver of excitement runs through him. "It's like I'm punishing your mother all over again. Your father, your sister. She thought she was better than all of us setting up her life in America, fighting the cartels when we put food on her table, clothes on her back. She was the worst kind of traitor."

His eyes lance through me, piercing me with blame as his grip tightens. My vision swims, goes in and out of focus. My lungs are on fire, but all I can think about is that I did this. I led Daniil to his death, led the Kozlovs to their graves.

My uncle squeezes tighter, his face inches from my own, taut with concentration, watching as life slips from my body.

This is it. This is how I die.

I close my eyes, giving in to the dark pull that promises to set me free. Grateful for the peace that I'm slowly sinking into.

And then a howl from the depths of hell rings out, and I know my time has come.

# CHAPTER FORTY-TWO

## DANIIL

It's too late.

A scream rips from my throat, grief shredding my insides.

I don't think I've ever seen something so horrifying in my life, and that says a lot. Emilio has his hands wrapped around Bianca's neck, her lifeless body in his merciless grasp. I fall to my knees, my heart splintering as the world around me turns black.

And then I catch it. The faint movement of her hand, clenching and unclenching.

Holy fuck—she's still alive!

Adrenaline floods my veins as I slam into Emilio with the force of a thousand armies. We roll together, but I end up the victor. Straddling him, I swing for his jaw and observe with glee as his head snaps to the side, blood spraying from his nose like a broken fire hydrant.

I refuse to use my gun on him. It's too easy. I want to leech the life out of him slowly and painfully with my bare hands, in the same way he almost took Bianca from me. I want him to suffer like she's suffered.

Out of my field of vision, Bianca's coughs and sputters assure me she's alive. Relief floods my system, but I can't give her my attention yet because Emilio is thrashing wildly. He's not going to go down without the fight of his life. And neither am I.

The motherfucker thought he was so clever drawing us into the house with the intention of ambushing us. As if it's our first rodeo; we don't rule the East Coast for nothing. Leo and I were stealth, entering from a secret side entrance, the night-vision goggles made it child's play to take out Emilio's dumb-ass guards with a silenced pistol. We dropped them one by one before anyone realized we had even breached the house.

Leo is hunting down any final Zegas roaming the halls.

Emilio thinks his men will save him, that he still has a chance.

He's wrong.

"See how it feels?" I spit in his face. "Not so good."

Emilio's bloody face tenses as I pin him down with an elbow against his throat.

In the background, I'm vaguely aware of Bianca whispering my name. That's the only reason I haven't poked out Emilio's eyes. I want her lucid, to enjoy watching his death as much as I will enjoy orchestrating it.

He grunts as I get my arms around him in a choke hold that has him thrashing for air. I smile watching his panic mount as I restrict his airflow. "I underestimated the joy it would bring me to kill you like an animal. My only regret is that I can't bring you back to life and then kill you again."

His eyes glaze over, sweat drips down his neck as I increase the pressure against his carotid artery.

"Daniil!" This time Bianca's voice is stronger, insistent, she warns me but it's too late. Something sharp and deadly sinks into my thigh, just above my hip. White-hot agony shoots through me, and I momentarily lose my grip.

Emilio pounces as soon as his knife does its damage. His

fingers dig into my injured thigh and with a triumphant growl, he twists so hard my vision dims. It's all I can do to stay conscious as fire shoots through my body, the pain causing me to seize up. In that moment, Emilio gains the upper hand, flipping me over and pinning me down, the blade tip digging into my neck.

"Not so fucking tough after all." Emilio smiles down at me like a deranged Joker coated in his own blood. I struggle against him, attempting to reach my holstered gun, but every movement causes the blade to notch deeper. "You're not walking out of here alive," he hisses. "You or that bitch niece of mine."

"I don't think so, tío," Bianca's voice rings out clear across the room. From the corner of my eye, I register a blur of motion, and then a sickening crash as something heavy breaks over Emilio's head, splintering in hundreds of pieces and raining down on me. A vase of some kind. I take advantage of the chaos to sucker punch Emilio in the face. His head snaps back once again. He loses his hold on the knife pressed to my neck, and in that one moment, the world turns upside down.

From above, Bianca's face comes into view, brandishing the knife that Emilio just lost his grip on. Without hesitation, she reaches down and slits her uncle's throat from ear to ear. A red arc spurts from his throat, covering my face with the coppery, warm liquid. As much as I'm rejoicing in Emilio's spilled blood, this is Bianca's moment. I roll out of the way and allow her to finish him off.

"This is for underestimating me," she seethes, and kicks him in the stomach, a gruesome gagging noise echoes in the room. He's flipped onto his back, gripping his neck as he takes his final breath. "And this is for killing my family." A stab to the heart. "And this, this ..." she growls, "is for trying to kill the man I love." This time she delivers a swift kick to the balls, but he doesn't react. He's gone. His lifeless body splayed on the floor between us.

Damn. I don't know if I'm more bowled over by her words or

by the savage way she sent her uncle into the bowels of hell. Either way, I'm fucking impressed, turned-on, and more in love than I ever thought possible.

Standing, I grab Bianca and bring her mouth against mine. She tastes like heaven and victory—and blood if I'm going to be honest. But I will never get enough of this. Of her.

"Are you hurt?" I whisper into her hair.

"Yes, but I don't care. You came for me." Tears shine in her eyes. "I thought you hated me."

"Fuck, no. I was an idiot, a stubborn idiot. And I nearly lost you." Shame coats my words. "I'd never forgive myself if something had happened to you. I've been a goddamn mess since I found out you offered yourself up to your uncle like some sacrificial lamb. All because of me." My throat is tight, regret turning sour in my mouth. "I fucked up, printsessa, real bad."

She leans into me, a smile on her face, and captures my lips with her own. "I guess we both learn the hard way. But I'm done with the lessons, Daniil. I only want you. No more lies or deceit between us."

"Never," I vow, and take her in my arms, relief running through me. "God, you were a total rock star." I cradle her head and make sure she's looking into my eyes for what I'm about to tell her. "I fucking love you, and I'm going to marry you. For real this time. What do you say?"

I'm stunned by the intensity of emotion reflected back at me. "I say it's about time. There is no one else for me, Daniil. You are it—my everything."

I'm back to devouring her face when Andrei, followed by Leo, Mercy, and a host of her men come charging into the room, guns at the ready.

"What the fuck happened here? Are you okay?" Andrei's eyes are frantic as he takes in the bloodshed and general chaos of the room. His gaze finally lands on us, still wrapped in each other.

"We're more than okay." A deep possessive rumble breaks free from my chest. "We're getting married."

Cheers erupt, as Bianca wraps her arms around me and buries her head against my chest. We're both messy as hell and looking worse for wear, but nothing in the world would make me as happy as making Bianca my wife. For real.

## EPILOGUE - SIX MONTHS LATER

### BIANCA

"HOLY SHIT, YOU'RE A MARRIED WOMAN!" Kira exclaims, wrapping me up in a big bear hug. "I mean, married *again*. Like for real this time." She laughs, tripping over her words.

"I can't believe it either," I say, looking out over the crowd of people assembled in our penthouse. An hour ago, we'd exchanged vows at St. Patrick's Cathedral, and now it's party time. Eris is even dressed in a little tiara, her tail wagging, as Daniil makes his rounds at the party, dog tucked under his big arm.

Our little fluff ball of chaos is no longer that. After I admitted Eris's original purpose to Daniil, he insisted we hire the best dog trainer in the country to work with her one-on-one. And while she still has a little bit of naughty implanted in her DNA, she's actually quite sweet, and for a man who's allergic to dogs, he's as bonded to her as I am.

As if he can sense my thoughts from across the room, Daniil looks over at me and winks. There is so much promise in that gesture. A promise of what's to come as soon as we have a moment alone, which I'm guessing won't be until we board our plane to Tahiti for our honeymoon.

I can't believe I married my best friend, the person who matters most to me in this world. As he stood across from me on the altar reciting his vows that we wrote together, promising to be my everything, my family, emotion heavy in his voice, the truth of his settled in my bones. There was barely a dry eye in the crowd, perhaps the first time some of these *vory* had ever cried.

And I cried, too. Tears of sadness for the family I lost and tears of joy for everything I've gained. I have a new family now, a real one that loves and cares for me despite everything I did. If they understand one thing, the Kozlovs understand the need for vengeance.

I got mine. We all did.

"Girl, you look amazing," Rowan says, holding my hands out to get a better look at my Vera Wang dress, sweeping me up in her tiny arms. I giggle. The women surrounding me now—Georgia, Kira, Alyona, and Rowan—are not only my family, they've also become close friends.

"I literally couldn't stop crying." Georgia dabs at her eyes. "Oh fuck, here I go again." A fresh wave of tears falls down her face.

"Jeez, you're awfully emotional these days," Alyona notes. "You cried through the entire *Top Gun* reboot. Seriously, what's going on?"

Georgia looks like a deer in headlights, and then smiles softly. Her eyes drift down to her flat belly.

Oh. OH. That's what's going on.

All four of us crowd around her in an enthusiastic group hug. "Congrats, this is incredible news!" I squeal.

"It is," she admits, "but maybe keep it quiet for now. Andrei doesn't know yet. I'm going to tell him tonight."

Kira slashes her hand across her mouth. "Lips sealed." And

then her eyes glaze with emotion. "I am going to be an aunt." She looks at Georgia as if she can hardly believe it. "And you're going to be a mom!"

"Shit." Georgia's face pales. "I have no idea what I'm doing."

"You're going to be great," I say, squeezing Georgia's arm. "You're the most nurturing person I know."

"And you'll have all of us to help," Rowan adds, beaming. "I am going to spoil the shit out of this little one." Rowan elbows her sister-in-law as Alyona looks off into the distance.

My gaze follows hers to find Leo standing in the corner, nursing a drink, returning Alyona's broody gaze.

"Aren't you excited?" Rowan insists. "We get to shop for adorable baby clothes!"

Alyona flashes Georgia a soft smile. "Of course I'm happy," she says, "I can't wait to meet this baby." But a second later, her focus is diverted back to Leo. I haven't seen them exchange a word, just moody glances. Apparently these two have history. Whatever went on between them, they clearly have unfinished business.

I'm about to tell her that when a soft hand on my shoulder has me turning and staring into the eyes of Deidre. What!? A federal agent is at my wedding? A pit forms at the bottom of my stomach as I excuse myself from the group, and pull Deidre aside, frantically scanning the space for SWAT team or something equally messed up.

"Relax," she chides. "I come in peace."

"What does that mean?"

"It means I'm here to offer my congratulations. Nothing more."

At that moment, Daniil's comforting presence settles beside me, his arm moving protectively around my shoulders.

"Deidre." Daniil tips his chin in greeting. He must have invited her or there's no way she would be standing before me right now with the amount of security we have everywhere. I tilt my head at Daniil, silently asking what she's doing here, but he just smiles and kisses my head.

The truth is, the FBI has nothing on the Kozlovs. The information Daniil had me feed Deidre in our final meeting was not incriminating, in fact, it proved that the Kozlovs have solid legal businesses. Not that Daniil made it easy for them—he made sure the FBI chased their tail before realizing they had nothing.

With my uncle out of the way, the Kozlovs delivered proof to the feds that the Zegas were a danger to Americans. The authorities took the peace offering that the Kozlovs gave them and walked away without further questions. They had been bested.

Deidre swallows heavily and takes a sip from the champagne flute in her hand. "I owe you an apology, Bianca. I wish I had pushed harder to get the Bureau to pursue your uncle when he was alive. I always believed you. I know he was a monster and ..." She shakes her head, dismayed. "Well, what's done is done, but I want you to know I'm not with the Bureau anymore. After all of this, I realized it's time for me to move on."

I look away for a moment, needing to process her words. I'm not sure how I feel about Deidre's apology. Triumphant on one hand, but also bitter that I was put through hell and back all in the name of vindicating my family. But Deidre can't wear the blame all on her own. We all serve the people above us, and I understand there were other factors at play. So I offer her a smile, and tell her, "I forgive you."

Daniil looks a little less forgiving, but he's protective of me, and I understand why.

"Well, you certainly make a beautiful couple," Deidre remarks, her eyes crinkling at the corners. "After all you've been through, you two deserve happiness."

"Thank you," Daniil says plainly.

"My door is always open to you." Deidre nods, before turning on her flats and disappearing in the crowd.

"Well, that was unexpected," I say, as Daniil loops his arms around my waist and pulls me in tight to his side.

"Not for me it wasn't. You deserved that apology. It was a long time coming," he murmurs, kissing the side of my neck.

"Thank you," I say, looking up at him. His gaze searches mine, flickering with dry amusement.

"Thank me after I fuck you six ways to Sunday." His voice is black silk, a promise of what's to come. He quickly scans the room, and then smiles down at me. "Speaking of which ..." He practically drags me down the hall to his office. The office I now have free access to. Closing the door behind us, he wastes no time hoisting me onto his desk and settling himself between my legs.

"A quickie," he explains, as if it wasn't clear.

"Luckily, I came prepared," I boast, and gather the hem of my dress, flashing him my bare pussy. I figured panties would only get in the way today.

"Shit." His pants are lowered so quickly, you'd think they were on fire. "I need to be inside you right now."

He holds the nape of my neck as he lines himself up between my legs, and in one wicked thrust, buries himself inside of me. My eyes roll back in my head.

As usual, I am blown away by the intensity of our bond. It must be illegal in some states for sex to be this good, because this connection between us, it's like fire and oil, one only fuels the other. I spread my legs wider and tilt my body back in order to take him deeper. To savor every minute that we have alone together, wrapped up in each other. With a groan, he brings his hand up to cup my cheek, staring intensely into my eyes.

"I love you," he groans, brushing his thumb over my throbbing clit. I can already feel him swelling inside of me, on the verge of release. "And I can't wait to make you swell with my babies." At that, he pounds into me one final time before filling me with his hot cum. My back buckles at the unexpected sensation, and with one more flick of my clit, my orgasm crests, consuming my body like a raging fire.

He collapses forward, holding me against him. "I love you, too," I murmur against his neck, drinking in his scent. I'll never get sick of this—his touch, his smell, his Daniil-ness. "But hold on, partner, I'm not quite ready for those babies."

He laughs and kisses my neck.

We didn't only exchange vows today, we made a pact. No more lies between us, no more secrets moving forward. And that includes freezing me out of bratva business. Daniil admitted that Jorge had been fucking with him from the moment we got married. It's not a surprise to me, but from now on, we've agreed to be truthful with each other, no matter how much it hurts or how much worry it may cause.

We're building a life together—a real one—and for it to work, there's no more room for deception. I've decided to go back to school and study business management. Observing Daniil in his element, crunching numbers and making strategic business decisions, is honestly one of my favorite things. When I graduate, I'll work for the Kozlovs on the legitimate side of the empire.

What feels like forever ago, I tried to convince Daniil to give me a job working for him—of course I had ulterior motives then. Now, I want to do good work that has meaning. And that's why, with the family's blessing and Kira and Georgia's assistance, I will spearhead the creation of the Kozlov Foundation. This fund will help women leaving abusive relationships get back on their feet. Maybe this will balance out some of the brotherhood's sins.

My husband is bratva, and I've learned to make peace with it since he's nothing like my uncle or Jorge. He's a good person who sometimes does bad deeds.

But the world is not black and white. It's gray, and I can live with the in-between if it means I get to sleep next to and wake up beside this man. This man who risked life and limb to rescue me and would do it all over again in a heartbeat.

He is my family now.

My guiding light.
My everything worth living for.

**Thank you so much for reading Cruel Deception!**

Want more of Daniil and Bianca? Download a free **BONUS
EPILOGUE** here:
https://geni.us/CDbonusepilogue

# ALSO BY MONICA KAYNE

## THE KOZLOV EMPIRE SERIES

Merciless Heir

Cruel Deception

Fierce Vow

Shattered Crown

## TARNISHED REIGN SERIES

Ruthless Reign

Savage Reign

## ABOUT THE AUTHOR

Monica Kayne is a TV producer turned proud romance writer. She writes dark and swoony romance novels with a liberal dose of sass and humor. Her favorite characters to write are sweetly possessive bad boys and the feisty, smart mouthed heroines they can't resist. When she's not dreaming up sexy plots, she can be found searching for the perfect negroni and her next K-drama fix. She lives with her family in Toronto, Canada.

### Connect with me!
www.monicakayne.com

### TikTok
@monicakayneauthor

### Instagram
@monicakayneauthor

### Facebook reader group
Monica's Mafia Queens

Made in the USA
Las Vegas, NV
16 October 2024

96945122R00173